Rocco, Christian and Francesco
are about to whirl three beautiful women,
Amber, Meg and Sonia, into a world of desire,
passion and romance—*Latin style!*

Latin Lovers

A collection of three sizzling stories
by bestselling authors
Lynne Graham, Penny Jordan and Lucy Gordon

Praise for these three bestselling authors

About Lynne Graham

"Lynne Graham delivers an engaging, sensual tale."
—*Romantic Times*

"Once again Lynne Graham
delivers another keeper...a mesmerizing blend
of wonderful characters, powerful emotion
and sensational scenes."
—*Romantic Times* on *The Winter Bride*

About Penny Jordan

"Ms. Jordan sprinkles sensual spice..."
—*Romantic Times*

"Women everywhere will find pieces of themselves
in Jordan's characters."
—*Publishers Weekly*

About Lucy Gordon

"Lucy Gordon pens an emotionally gripping tale."
—*Romantic Times*

"Lucy Gordon once again delivers a heart-wrenching
love story with extraordinary characters, a gripping
conflict and wonderful story development."
—*Romantic Times* on *Rico's Secret Child*

PENNY JORDAN
LYNNE GRAHAM
LUCY GORDON

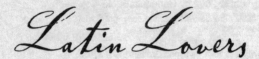

Latin Lovers

HARLEQUIN®

TORONTO • NEW YORK • LONDON
AMSTERDAM • PARIS • SYDNEY • HAMBURG
STOCKHOLM • ATHENS • TOKYO • MILAN • MADRID
PRAGUE • WARSAW • BUDAPEST • AUCKLAND

ISBN 0-373-83532-9

LATIN LOVERS

Copyright © 2002 by Harlequin Books S.A.

The publisher acknowledges the copyright holders of the individual titles as follows:

THE CHRISTMAS EVE BRIDE
Copyright © 2001 by Lynne Graham

A SPANISH CHRISTMAS
Copyright © 2001 by Penny Jordan

CHRISTMAS IN VENICE
Copyright © 2001 by Lucy Gordon

CONTENTS

CONTENTS

THE CHRISTMAS EVE BRIDE

Lynne Graham

Dear Reader,

Christmas has always had a special meaning for me, and I like to keep faith with the old traditions.

In Ireland we like to place a large candle in the window on Christmas Eve night, a symbolic reminder of how Mary and Joseph sought shelter in vain on that very first Christmas. The honor of lighting the candle goes by tradition to the youngest member of the household, and the flame serves as a welcoming beacon to passing strangers and, of course, to Santa Claus. We also like to put a holly wreath on the front door, a custom that originated here in the days when the poor adorned their homes with evergreens that were plentiful and cheap.

In my home I put up several Christmas trees, so that wherever I am in the house, I am never too far from one. I began collecting decorations many years ago, and a gorgeous angel wreath sent to me by one of my readers takes pride of place in my hall. Making the festive season a happy and magical time for my family means always having an advent calendar and sharing out the three traditional Christmas wishes as the Christmas cake mix is stirred in November. Actually, we stretch the custom there, as we have five children.

I hope that you will all find your own happy fulfillment at this special season, as do Rocco, Amber and their child when they discover their love for each other in my story.

Merry Christmas to all.

Yours sincerely

Lynne Graham

CHAPTER ONE

ROCCO VOLPE was bored and, as it was not a sensation he was accustomed to feeling, he was much inclined to blame his hosts for that reality.

When the banker, Harris Winton, had invited him to his country home for the weekend, Rocco had expected stimulating company. People invariably went to a great deal of trouble to entertain Rocco. But then he could hardly have foreseen that Winton would miss his flight home from Brussels, leaving his unfortunate guests at the mercy of his wife, Kaye.

Kaye, the youthful trophy wife, who looked at Rocco with a hunger she couldn't hide. His startlingly handsome features were expressionless as his hostess irritated him with simpering flattery and far too much attention. He had never liked small women with big eyes, he reflected. Memory stirred, reminding him *why* that was so. Swiftly, he crushed that unwelcome recollection out.

'So tell me…what's it like being one of the most eligible single men in the world?' Kaye asked fatuously.

'Pretty boring.' Watching her redden without remorse, Rocco strolled over to the window like a tiger sheathing his claws with extreme reluctance.

'I suppose it must be,' the beautiful brunette then agreed in a cloying tone. 'How many men have your power, looks *and* fabulous wealth?'

Striving not to wince while telling himself that if he ever married *his* wife would have a brain, Rocco surveyed the well-kept gardens. Fading winter sunlight gleamed over the downbent head of a gardener raking up leaves on the extensive front lawn. There was something familiar about that unusual honey shade of blonde that was the colour of toffee in certain lights. He stiffened as the figure turned and he realised it was a woman *and*…?

'Your gardener is a woman?' Not a shade of the outraged incredulity and anger consuming Rocco was audible in his deep, dark drawl. But someone ought to warn Winton that he had a potential tabloid spy working for him, he thought grimly. Harris would never recover from the humiliation of the media exposing one of his wife's affairs.

His keen hostess drew level with him and wrinkled her nose. 'We have trouble getting outside staff. Harris says people don't want that kind of work these days.'

'I imagine he's right. Has she been with you long?'

'Only a few weeks.' The brunette studied him with a perplexed frown.

'Will you excuse me? I have an urgent call to make.'

Amber's back was sore.

It was icy cold but the amount of energy she had expended had heated her up to the extent that she was working in a light T-shirt. She could hardly believe that within ten days it would be Christmas. Her honey-blonde hair caught back in a clip from which strands continually drifted loose, she straightened and stretched to ease her complaining spine. About five feet three in height, she was slim, but at breast and hip she was lush and feminine in shape.

It would be another hour before she finished work and she couldn't *wait*. Only a few months back, she would have said she loved the great outdoors, but working for the Wintons had disenchanted her fast. Nothing but endless back-breaking labour and abysmally low pay. Her rich employers did not believe in spending money on labour-saving devices like leaf blowers. On the other hand, Harris Winton was a perfectionist, who demanded the highest standards against impossible odds.

'Brush up the leaves as they fall,' he had told her with a straight face, seeming not to grasp that, with several acres of wooded and lawned grounds, that was like asking her to daily stem an unstoppable tide.

You're turning into a right self-pitying moan, her conscience warned her as she emptied the wheelbarrow. So once she had had nice clothes, pretty, polished fingernails and a career with a future. She might no longer have any of those things but she *did* have Freddy, she reminded herself in consolation.

Freddy, the pure joy in her life, who could squeeze her heart with one smile. Freddy, who had filled her with so much instant love that she could still barely accept the intensity of her own feelings. Freddy, who might not be the best conversationalist yet and who loved to wake her up to play in the middle of the night, but who still made *any* sacrifice worthwhile.

'*Buon giorno*, Amber…what an unexpected pleasure!'

At the sound of that dark, well-modulated voice coming out of nowhere at her, Amber jerked rigid with fright. Blinking rapidly, disbelief engulfing her, she spun round, refusing to accept her instinctive recognition of that rich-accented drawl.

'Strange but somehow extraordinarily *apt* that you should be grubbing round a compost heap,' Rocco remarked with sardonic amusement.

A wave of stark dizziness assailed Amber. As she focused in paralysed incredulity on the formidably tall, well-built male standing beneath the towering beech trees a few yards away, her heart was beating at such an accelerated rate that she could hardly get breath into her lungs. She turned white as milk, every ounce of natural colour evaporating from her fine features, her clear green eyes huge.

Rocco Volpe, the powerful Italian financier, once christened the Silver Wolf by the gossip columns for his breathtaking good looks and fast reputation with her sex. And there was no denying that he *was* spectacular, with his bronzed skin and dark, dark deepset eyes contrasted with hair so naturally, unexpectedly fair it shone like polished silver. Rocco Volpe, the very worst mistake she had made in her twenty-three years of life. Her tummy felt hollow, her every tiny muscle bracing in self-defence. But her brain just refused to snap back into action. She could only wonder in amazement what on earth Rocco Volpe could possibly be doing wandering round the grounds of the Wintons' country house.

'Where did you come from?' she whispered jaggedly.

'The house. I'm staying there this weekend.'

'Oh…' Amber was silenced and appalled by that admission. Yet it was not a remarkable coincidence that Rocco should be acquainted with her employer, for both men wielded power in the same cut-throat world of international finance.

Tilting his arrogant head back, Rocco treated her

to a leisurely, all-male appraisal that was as bold as he was. 'Not good news for you, I'm afraid.'

Amber was as stung by that insolent visual assessment as if he had slapped her in the face. *Grubbing round the compost heap?* The instant he bent the full effect of those brilliant dark eyes on her, she recalled that sarcastic comment. But a split second later thought was overpowered by the slowburn effect of Rocco skimming his intense gaze over the swell of her full breasts. Within her bra, the tender peaks of her sensitive flesh pinched tight with stark awareness. As his stirring scrutiny slid lazily down to the all-female curve of her hips, an almost forgotten ache clenched her belly.

'And what's that supposed to mean?' Amber folded her arms with a jerk, holding her treacherous body rigid as if by so doing she might drive out those mortifying responses. Only now she was horribly conscious of her wind-tossed hair, her lack of make-up and her workworn T-shirt and jeans. Once, she recalled, she had taken time to groom herself for Rocco's benefit. Suddenly she wanted to dive into the wretched compost heap and *hide*! Rocco, so smooth, sophisticated and exclusive in his superb charcoal-grey business suit and black cashmere coat. He had to be wondering now what he had *ever* seen in her and her already battered pride writhed under that humiliating suspicion.

'Why are you working for Harris Winton as a gardener?' Rocco asked drily.

'That's none of your business.' Pale and fighting a craven desire to cringe, Amber flung her head high, determined not to be intimidated.

'But I am making it my business,' Rocco countered levelly.

Amber could not credit his nerve. Her temper was rising. 'Being one of the Wintons' guests *doesn't* give you the right to give me the third degree. Now, why don't you go away and leave me alone?'

'You really have changed your tune, *cara*,' Rocco murmured in a tone as smooth as black velvet. 'As I recall, I found persuading *you* to leave *me* alone quite a challenge eighteen months ago.'

That cruel reminder stabbed Amber like a knife in the heart. Indeed, she felt quite sick inside. She had not expected that level of retaliation and dully questioned why. Rocco was a ruthless wheeler-dealer in the money markets and as feared as he was famed for his brilliance. In automatic self-protection from that cutting tongue, she began walking away. Eighteen months ago, Rocco had *dumped* her. Indeed, Rocco had dumped her without hesitation. Rocco had then refused her phone calls and when she had persisted in daring to try and speak to him, he had finally called her back and asked her with icy contempt if she was now 'stalking' him!

'Where are you going?' Rocco demanded.

Amber ignored him. She had been working near the house. Obviously he had seen and recognised her and curiosity had got to him. But it struck her as strange that he should have acted on that curiosity and come outside to speak to her. A guy who had suggested that she might have stalking tendencies ought to have looked the other way. But then that had only been Rocco's brutally effective method of finally shaking her off.

'Amber…'

Bitterness surged up inside her, the destructive bitterness she had believed she had put behind her. But, faced with Rocco again, those feelings erupted back out of her subconscious mind like a volcano. She spun back with knotted fists, her small, shapely figure taut, angry colour warming her complexion. 'I hate you…I can't *bear* to be anywhere near you!'

Rocco elevated a cool, slanting dark brow. He looked hugely unimpressed by that outburst.

'And that is not the reaction of the proverbial woman scorned,' Amber asserted between gritted teeth, determined to disabuse him of any such ego-boosting notion. 'That is the reaction of a woman looking at you now and asking herself how the heck she could ever have been so *stupid* as to get involved with a rat like you!'

Alive with sizzling undertones and tension, the

splintering silence almost seemed to shimmer around them. Glittering dark golden eyes flamed into hers in a crash-and-burn collision and she both sensed and saw the fury there that barely showed in that lean, strong face. No, he hadn't liked being called a rat.

'But you'd come back to me like a bullet if I asked you,' Rocco murmured softly.

Amber stared back at him in shock. 'Are you kidding?'

'Only making a statement of fact. But don't get excited,' Rocco advised with silken scorn. 'I'm *not* asking.'

Unfamiliar rage whooshed up inside Amber and she trembled. 'Tell me, are you trying to goad me into physically attacking you?'

'Possibly trying to settle a score or two.' With that unapologetic admission, Rocco studied her with cloaked eyes, his hard bone-structure grim. 'But let's cut to the baseline. You can only be working here to spy on the Wintons for some sleazy tabloid story—'

'I beg…your pardon?' Amber cut in unevenly, her eyes very wide.

Ignoring that interruption, Rocco continued, 'Harris is a friend. I intend to warn him about you—'

'What sleazy tabloid story? Warn him about *me*?' Amber parroted with helpless emphasis. 'Are you out of your mind? I'm not spying on anyone… I'm only the gardener, for goodness' sake!'

'*P-lease,*' Rocco breathed with licking contempt. 'Do I look that stupid?'

Amber was gaping at him while struggling to master her disbelief at his suspicions.

'How much money did you make out of that trashy kiss-and-tell spread on me?' Rocco enquired lazily.

'Nothing…' Amber told him after a sick pause, momentarily drowning in unpleasant recollections of the events which had torn her life apart eighteen months earlier. A couple of hours confiding in an old schoolfriend and the damage had been done. What had seemed like harmless girly gossip had cost her the man she loved, the respect of work colleagues and ultimately her career.

Rocco dealt her a derisive look. 'Do you really think I'm likely to swallow that tale?'

'I don't much care.' And it was true, Amber registered in some surprise. Here she was, finally getting the opportunity to defend herself but no longer that eager to take it. But then the chance had come more than a year too late. A time during which she had been forced to eat more humble pie than was good for her. She had stopped loving him, stopped hoping he would contact her and stopped caring about his opinion of her as well. After he had ditched her, Rocco had delighted the gossip columnists with a series of wild affairs with other women. He had provided her with the most effective cure available for a broken heart. Her pride had kicked in to save her and she had pulled herself together again.

'You already have all the material you need on the Wintons?' Rocco prompted with strong distaste.

The rage sunk beneath the onslaught of sobering memories gripped Amber again. 'Where do you get off, throwing wild accusations like this at me? What gives you the right to ignore what I say and assume that I'm lying? Your *superior* intellect?' Her green eyes flashed bright as emerald jewels in her heart-shaped face, her scorn palpable. 'Well, it's letting you down a bucketful right now, Rocco—'

'My ESP is on overload right now. I don't think so,' Rocco mused, studying her with penetrating cool.

A hollow laugh was wrenched from Amber's dry throat. 'No, you naturally wouldn't think that you could be wrong. After all, you're the guy who's always one hundred per cent right about everything—'

'I wasn't right about you, was I? I got *burned*,' Rocco cut in with harsh clarity, hard facial bones prominent beneath his bronzed skin.

I got burned. Was that how he now viewed their former relationship? Amber was surprised to hear that, but relieved to think that the hurt, the embarrassment and the self-recriminations had not only been hers. But then he was talking about his pride, the no-doubt wounding effect of his conviction that she had somehow contrived to put one over him. He wasn't talking about true emotions, only superficial ones.

'But not enough,' Amber responded tightly, thinking wretchedly of the months of misery she had endured before she'd wised up and got on with her life without looking back to what might have been. 'I don't think you were burned half enough.'

'How the hell could you have expected to hang onto me after what you did?' Rocco demanded with a savage abruptness that disconcerted her. His spectacular eyes rested with keen effect on her surprised face.

'Only two possible explanations, aren't there?' The breeze clawing stray strands of her honey-blonde hair back from her flushed cheekbones, Amber tilted her chin, green eyes sparkling over him where he now stood only feet from her. 'Either I was a dumb little bunny who was indiscreet with an undercover journalist *or*...I was bored out of my tiny mind with you and decided to go out of your life with a big, unforgettable bang!'

'*Dio*...you were *not* bored in my bed,' Rocco growled with raw self-assurance.

Rocco only had to say 'bed' in that dark, accented drawl and heat pulsated through Amber in an alarming wave of reaction and remembrance. Punishing him for her own weakness, she let a stinging smile curve her generous mouth. 'And how would you know, Rocco? Haven't you ever read the statistics on women faking it to keep tender male egos intact?'

The instant those provocative words escaped her, she was shaken by her own unusual venom. But she was even more taken aback by the level to which she had sunk in her instinctive need to deny even the physical hold he had once had on her. Ashamed of herself and furious with him for goading her to that point, she added, 'Look, why don't you just forget you ever saw me out here and we'll call it quits?'

'*Faking* it...' His brilliant dark eyes flared to stormy gold, his Italian accent thick as honey on the vowel sounds of those two words. He had paled noticeably below his bronzed skin and it was that much more noticeable because dark colour now scored his hard masculine cheekbones. 'Were you really?'

Connecting with his glittering look of challenge, Amber felt the primal charge in the atmosphere but she stood her ground, none too proud of her own words but ready to do anything sooner than retract them. He was sexual dynamite and he had to know it. But he need not look to any confirmation of that reality from her. 'All I want to do right now is get on with my work—'

Without the smallest warning, Rocco reached for her arm to prevent her from turning away and flipped her back. 'Was it *work* in my bed too?' he demanded in a savage undertone. 'Did you know right from the start what you were planning to do?'

Backed into the constraining circle of his arms, Amber stared up at him in sensual shock, astonished at the depth of his dark, brooding anger but involuntarily excited by it and by him. Mouth running dry, breath trapped in her throat, she could feel every taut, muscular angle of his big, powerful body against hers. She shivered, conscious of the freezing air on her bare arms but the wanton fire flaming in her pelvis, stroked to the heights by the potent proof of his arousal, recognisable even through the layers of their clothing. The wanting, the helpless, craving hunger that leapt through her in wild response took her by storm.

'I wouldn't touch you again if I was dying...' As swiftly as he had reached for her, Rocco thrust her back from him in contemptuous rejection, strong-boned features hard as iron.

Her fair complexion hotly flushed, Amber turned away in an uncoordinated half-circle, heartbeat racing, legs thoroughly unsteady support. 'Good, so go—'

'I'm not finished with you yet.' Leaving those cold words of threat hanging, Rocco strode off.

In a daze, she watched him walk away from her. He had magnificent carriage and extraordinary grace for a male of his size. He soon disappeared from view, screened by the bulky evergreen shrubs flourishing below the winter-bare trees that edged the lawn surrounding the house. Amber only then realised that she was trembling and frozen to the marrow, finally conscious of the chill wind piercing her thin T-shirt. She grabbed her sweater out of the tumbledown greenhouse where she had left it and fumbled into its comforting warmth with hands that were all fingers and thumbs.

What had Rocco meant by saying he wasn't finished with her yet? She tried to concentrate but it was a challenge because she was so appalled by the way he had made her feel. Suppressing that uneasy awareness, she tensed in even greater dismay. Only minutes ago, he had told her that he intended to warn Harris Winton about the risk that she could be spying on him and his wife in the hope of selling some scandalous story to a newspaper.

Dear heaven, she could not afford to lose her job, for it might not pay well but it *did* include accommodation. Small and basic the cottage might be, but it was the sole reason that Amber had applied to work for the Wintons in the first place. Indeed, the mere thought of being catapulted back into her sister Opal's far more spacious and comfortable home to listen to a chorus of deeply humiliating 'I told you so's' filled Amber with even more horror than the prospect of grovelling to Rocco!

CHAPTER TWO

ROCCO was certain to be lodged in the main suite of the opulent guest wing, Amber reckoned. Just to think that she had probably fixed that huge flower arrangement in there purely for Rocco's benefit made her wince as she headed for the rear entrance to the sprawling country house.

Helping out the Wintons' kindly middle-aged housekeeper, who had been run off her feet preparing for guests the previous month, had resulted in Amber finding herself landed with another duty. The minute that Kaye Winton had realised that their gardener had done the magnificent floral arrangement in the front reception hall, she had demanded that Amber should continue doing creative things with flowers whenever she and her husband entertained.

A time-consuming responsibility that Amber had resented, however, was now welcome as an excuse to enter the house. How on earth could she have let Rocco take off on that chilling threat? His suspicions about her were ridiculous, but she knew *why* he believed the Wintons might be the target for media interest of the most unpleasant kind. Harris Winton was an influential man, who was often in the news.

But, for goodness' sake, the whole neighbourhood, never mind the staff, knew about Kaye Winton's extra-marital forays! Sometimes, men were so naïve, Amber reflected ruefully. A newspaper reporter would only need to stop off in the village post office to hear chapter and verse on the voracious brunette's far-from-discreet affairs!

Catering staff were bustling about the big kitchen. Leaving her muddy work boots in the passage and removing the clip from her hair to finger-comb it into a hopeful state of greater tidiness, Amber hurried up the stone service staircase in her sock soles. With a bit of luck, Rocco would be in his suite. If he was downstairs, what was she going to do? Leave him some stupid note begging him to be reasonable? Grimacing at that idea, Amber wondered angrily why Rocco was allowing his usual cool common sense and intelligence to be overpowered by melodramatic assumptions.

I got burned. Well, if Rocco imagined the slight mortification of that newspaper spread on their affair eighteen months back had been the equivalent of getting burned, she would have liked him to have had a taste of what she had suffered in comparison. Her life, her self-respect and her dreams had gone down the drain faster than floodwater.

In the guest wing, she knocked quietly on the door of the main suite. There was no answer but, as she was aware that several rooms lay beyond and Rocco might be in any one of them, she went in and eased the door closed behind her again. She heard his voice then. It sounded as if he was on the phone and she approached the threshold of the bedroom with hesitant steps.

Rocco's brilliant dark eyes struck her anxious gaze and she froze. Clearly, he had heard both her initial knock and her subsequent entrance uninvited. Her skin heated with discomfiture when, with a fluid gesture of mocking invitation, he indicated the sofa several feet from him. He continued with his call, his rich dark drawl wrapping round mellow Italian syllables with a sexy musicality that sent tiny little shivers of recall down her taut spinal cord. She recognised a couple of words, recalled how she had once planned to learn his language. With a covert rub of her damp palms on her worn jeans, she sat down, stiff with strain. He lounged by the window, talking into his mobile phone, bold, bronzed features in profile, his attention removed from her.

He stood about six feet four and he had the lean muscular build of an athlete. Broad shoulders, narrow hips, long, long powerful legs. His clothes were always beautifully tailored and cut to fit him like a glove. Yet he could look elegant clad only in a towel, she recalled uneasily from the past. Her colour rising afresh at the tone of her thoughts, she looked away, conscious of the tremor in her hands, the tension licking through her smaller, slighter frame.

They had been together for three months when Rocco had ditched her. For her, anyway, it had been love at first sight. He had called her 'tabbycat' because of the way she had used to curl up on the sofa beside him. When he had been out of the country over weekends and holidays, he had flown her out to join him in a variety of exotic places. Her feet hadn't touched the ground once during their magical affair. All her innate caution and sense had fallen by the wayside. Finding herself on a roller coaster of excitement and passion, she had become enslaved. When the roller coaster had come to a sudden halt and thrown her off, she had not been able to credit that he'd been able to just abandon what *she* had believed they had shared.

That was why she had kept on phoning him at first, accepting that he was furious with her about that ghastly newspaper story, accepting that that story had been entirely her fault and that *she* had had to be the one to make amends. Loving Rocco had taught her how to be humble and face her mistakes.

And how had he rewarded her humility? He had kicked her in the teeth! Her delicate bone-structure tightened. She pushed her honey-blonde hair off her brow, raking it back, so that it tumbled in glossy disarray round her slim shoulders. Her hair needed cutting: she was letting it grow because it was cheaper. At the rate that her finances were improving, she thought ruefully, she would have hair down to her feet by the time she could afford a salon appointment again. Loving Rocco had also taught her what it was like to be poor…or, at least, how utterly humiliating it was, after a long period of independence, to be forced to rely once more on family generosity to survive.

Her tummy churning with nerves, she focused on Rocco again, noting the outline of his long, luxuriant black lashes, comparing them to Freddy's… Freddy's hair was as dark as Rocco's was fair, black as a raven's wing. She squeezed her eyes tight shut and prayed for concentration and courage.

'To what do I owe the honour of this second meeting?' Rocco enquired drily. 'I thought we were just about talked out.'

Worrying at her lower lip, Amber tilted her head back. But she could still only see as high as his gold silk tie because he had moved closer. In a harried movement, she stood up again. 'If you tell Harris Winton that there is the slightest possibility that I might be spying on him for some newspaper, I'll get the sack!'

Rocco studied her with inscrutable dark eyes. In the charged silence that he allowed to linger, his lean, powerful face remained impassive.

'I can't understand why you should even *think* such a thing of me…it's nonsensical!'

'Is it? I remember you telling me that you once very much wanted to *be* a journalist…'

Amber stilled in consternation and surprise. *Had* she told Rocco that? During one of those trusting chats when he had seemed to want to know every tiny thing about her? Evidently, she had told him but she hadn't given him the whole picture. During her teens, Amber's parents had put her under constant pressure to produce better exam results and, when they'd finally realised that she was not going to become a doctor, a lawyer or a teacher, she had been instructed to focus on journalism instead. They had signed her up for an extra-curricular media studies course on which she had got very poor grades.

'*And* how desperately disappointed you were when you couldn't get a job on a newspaper,' Rocco finished smoothly.

For the first time it occurred to Amber that, eighteen months back, Rocco had had more reason than she had appreciated to believe that the prospect of media limelight might have tempted her into talking about their relationship. She was furious that one insignificant little piece of information casually given out of context could have helped to support his belief that she was guilty as charged.

'Do you know the only reason I went for that job?

My parents had just died... It was *their* idea that I should try for a career in journalism, not my own. And what I might or might not have wanted at the age of sixteen has very little bearing on the person I am now,' Amber declared in driven dismissal.

Rocco continued to regard her in level challenge. 'I can concede that. But when we met, you were employed in a merchant bank and studying for accountancy exams. Give me one good reason why you should now be pretending to be a gardener?'

'Because, obviously, it's *not* a pretence! It's the only job I could get...at least the only work that it's convenient for me to take right now.' In a nervous gesture as she tacked on that qualification, Amber half opened her hands and then closed them tight again, her green eyes veiling, for the last thing she wanted to touch on was the difficulties of being a single parent on a low wage.

'Convenient?' Rocco queried.

'I live in a cottage in the coachyard here. Accommodation goes with the job. My sister lives nearby and I like being close to her—'

'You never mentioned that you *had* a sister while I was with you.'

Amber flushed a dull guilty red for she had allowed him to assume that she was as alone in the world as he was. Rocco was an only child, born to older parents, who had both passed away by the time he'd emerged from his teens.

'So explain why you kept quiet about having a sister,' Rocco continued levelly.

But there was no way Amber felt she could tell him the honest truth on that score. She had been terrified that Rocco would meet her gorgeous, intellectual big sister and start thinking of Amber herself as very much a poor second best. It had happened before, after all. It didn't matter that Opal was twelve years older and happily married. People were always amazed when they learnt that the highly successful barrister, Opal Carlton, was Amber's sibling. From an early age, Amber had been aware that she was a sad disappointment to her parents, who, being so clever themselves, had expected equally great things from their younger daughter as well. Her best had never, ever been good enough.

'Well, I have a sister and I'm very fond of her,' she mumbled, not meeting his eyes because she was ashamed that she had kept Opal hidden like a nasty secret when indeed she could not have got through the past year without her sister's support.

'Why are you feeding me this bull?' Rocco demanded with sardonic bite. 'Nothing you've said so far comes anywhere near explaining why you should suddenly be clutching a wheelbarrow instead of fingering a keyboard!'

Amber swallowed hard. 'Within a month of that kiss-and-tell story appearing in print, I was at the top of the hit list at Woodlawn Wyatt. They said they were overstaffed and, along with some others, I lost my job.'

'That doesn't surprise me,' Rocco conceded without sympathy. 'Merchant banks are conservative institutions—'

'And the regular banks are still shedding staff practically by the day so I couldn't find another opening,' Amber admitted, tight-mouthed, hating the necessity of letting him know that she had struggled but failed to find similar employment. 'I also suspect that, whenever a reference *was* taken up with my former employers, the knives came out—'

'Possibly,' Rocco mused in the same noncommittal tone. 'But had you stayed in London—'

'Being out of work in a big city is expensive. I hadn't been with Woodlawn Wyatt long enough to qualify for a redundancy payment. I moved in with my sister for a while—'

'This is a rural area but it's also part of the commuter belt. Surely you could have found employment *more*—'

Her patience gave out. 'Look, I'm happy as I am and I only came up here in the first place to ask you to back off and just forget you ever saw me!'

Rocco lounged back against the polished footboard on the elegant sleigh bed, bringing their eyes into sudden direct contact and somehow making her awesomely aware that they were in a bedroom together. 'Do you really mean that?'

Amber blinked but it didn't break the mesmerising hold of his arresting dark golden eyes for long enough to stifle the terrifying tide of sheer physical longing that washed over her. Memory was like a cruel hook dragging her down into a dangerous undertow of intimate images she was already fighting not to recall. Rocco tumbling her down on his bed and kissing her with the explosive force that charged her up with the passion she had never been able to resist; Rocco's expert hands roving over her to waken her in the morning; the sheer joy of being wanted more than she had ever been wanted by anyone in her entire life.

'What are you t-talking about?' Amber stammered, dredging herself out of those destabilising and enervating memories.

'Do you really want me to forget I ever saw you?' Rocco viewed her steadily from beneath inky black lashes longer than her own.

'What else?' Already conscious of her heightened colour and quickened breathing, Amber was very still for every fibre of her being was awake to the smouldering atmosphere that had come up out of nowhere to entrap her.

'Liar…' The effect of the husky reproof Rocco delivered was infinitely less than the sudden sensual smile of amusement that curled his wide, eloquent mouth.

Images from a distant, happier past assailed Amber: the sound of a smile in his deep voice on the phone, the feeling of euphoria, of being appreciated when he looked at her in just that way. What way? As if there were only the two of them in the whole wide world, as if she was someone *special*. Before Rocco came along, nobody had ever made Amber feel special or important or needed.

Her breath catching in her throat, she stared back at him, wholly enchanted by the charisma of that breathtaking smile. 'I'm not lying…' she muttered without even being aware of what she was saying.

Rocco reached out and closed his hands over hers. At first contact, a helpless shiver ran through her. Slowly, he smoothed out her tightly clenched fingers, one by one. Like a rabbit caught in car headlights, she gazed up at him, heart banging against her rib-cage, aware only of him and the seductive weakness induced by the heat blossoming inside her. He eased her inches closer. His warmth, the feel of his skin on hers again, the powerful intoxicant of his familiar scent overpowered her senses.

'I said I wouldn't touch you again if I was dying

but...' The rasp of his voice travelled down her responsive spine like hot, delicious honey.

'But?'

'*Dio...*' Rocco husked, drawing her the last couple of inches. 'I believe I could be persuaded otherwise, tabbycat...'

The sound of that endearment made her melt.

'However, you would have to promise to keep it quiet—'

'Quiet?' All concentration shot, she didn't grasp what he was talking about.

'I don't want to open a newspaper on Monday morning to find out how I scored between the sheets again—'

'Sorry...?'

Without warning, Rocco released her hands and, since he was just about all that was holding her upright on her wobbling lower limbs, she almost fell on top of him. He righted her again with deft cool. 'Think about it,' he advised, stepping away from her.

For an instant, Amber hovered, breathing in deep, striving to get her brain into gear again. She did not have to think very hard. 'Apart from the obvious, what are you trying to imply?'

'I'm bored this weekend and you challenged me.'

In considerable emotional disarray as she appreciated that she had been standing there transfixed and hypnotised, entirely entrapped by the sexual power he had exercised over her, Amber spun round. 'I beg your pardon?'

Rocco sent her a sizzling glance of mockery. 'Maybe I want to see you *faking* it for my benefit.'

Amber reddened to the roots of her hair. 'No chance,' she said curtly and stepped past him to hurry back out to the sitting room.

Without the slightest warning whatsoever, the door she was heading for opened and Kaye Winton walked in. At the sight of Amber, she frowned in astonishment, pale blue eyes rounding. 'What are you doing up here?'

Mind a complete blank, Amber found herself glancing in desperation at Rocco.

Brilliant dark eyes gleaming, Rocco said, 'I asked for someone to remove the flowers.'

'The flowers?' the beautiful brunette questioned.

'I'm allergic to them.' Rocco told the lie with a straight face.

'Oh, no!' Kaye surged over to the centre table as if jet-propelled. Gathering up the giant glass vase, she planted it bodily into Amber's hastily extended arms. 'Take them away immediately. I'm so sorry, Rocco!'

Her sweater soaked by the water that had slopped out of the vase with the other woman's careless handling, Amber headed for the corridor at speed, her shaken expression hidden by the mass of trendy corkscrew twigs and lilies she had arranged earlier that day. It was ironic that she should be grateful for Rocco's quick thinking, even more relieved that her employer's wife had not come in a minute sooner and found her in his bedroom. How on earth would she ever have explained that?

Indeed, how could she even explain to *herself* why she had allowed Rocco to behave as he had? She had acted like a doll without mind or voice and offered no objection to his touching her. Sick with shame at her own weakness, Amber disposed of the floral arrangement and pulled on her work boots again with unsteady hands. Rocco was bored. Rocco was playing manipulative games with her to amuse himself. Dear heaven, that *hurt* her so much. And she knew it shouldn't hurt, knew she should have been fully on her guard and capable of resisting Rocco's smouldering sexuality.

Wasn't she supposed to hate him? Well, hatred had kept her far from cool when he'd turned up the heat. And there she was blaming him when she ought to be blaming herself! Rocco had made her want him again…instantly, easily, reawakening the hunger she had truly believed she had buried for ever. But with every skin-cell alight with anticipation, she had just been desperate for him to kiss her. And he hadn't kissed her either, which told her just how complete his own control had been in comparison to her own.

Well, she was going to spend the rest of the week-end at her sister's house and stay well out of Rocco's way, she told herself impulsively. Then she recalled that she *couldn't* do that. True, she was babysitting at her sister's that evening, but she had to work Saturdays and would have to turn in as usual. Harris Winton was usually home only at weekends and the reason Amber got a day off mid-week instead was that her employer insisted that she be available for his weekly inspection tour of the grounds.

She trudged round to the old coachyard and climbed into the ten-year-old hatchback her brother-in-law, Neville, had given her on loan, saying it had been a trade-in for one of the luxury cars he imported, but not really convincing her with that less-than-likely story. Furthermore, the car was on per-manent loan, Amber reflected heavily, once again reminded of just how dependent she *was* on Neville and Opal's generosity.

The independence she had sought was as far out of her reach as it had ever been, she conceded heavily. Her sole source of pride was that she was no longer living under her sister's roof. But she was only able to work because she shared the services of the expensive but very well-trained nanny her sister employed to look after her own child. Amber's low salary would not stretch to full-time childcare or in-deed towards much of a contribution towards the

nanny's salary. So she kept on saying thank you to
her family and accepting for Freddy's sake, striving
to repay their generosity by making herself useful in
other ways. It occurred to her then that she could
have wiped the sardonic smile from Rocco's darkly
handsome features with just a few words.

As she drove over to the exclusive housing development where her sister lived, she asked herself why
she hadn't spoken those words to Rocco when she
had finally got the opportunity.

'Rocco Volpe is pond scum,' her sister, Opal, had
pronounced on the day of Freddy's birth. 'But I'd
sooner cut my throat than watch you humiliate yourself trailing him through the courts to establish paternity and win a financial settlement. Rich men fight
paternity suits every step of the way. The whole process can drag on for years, particularly when the father is not a British citizen. He could leave the country and stonewall you at every turn. Keep your
pride…that's my advice.'

Her pride? The very thought of telling Rocco that
she had given birth to his child flicked Amber's pride
on the raw. Rocco had pulled no punches when he'd
ended their relationship. Amber's troubled thoughts
took her back in time an entire eighteen months. Had
she had proper pride and sense, she would never have
got as far as a first date with Rocco Volpe…

CHAPTER THREE

WHEN she was seventeen, Amber had started work as clerk in an accountant's office. She had gratefully accepted the offer of day release and evening classes to study for accounting qualifications; it had been four years before she'd moved on. At twenty-one she had applied for and got a job at the merchant bank, Woodlawn Wyatt, where she had become second in command in the accounts department; her salary had doubled overnight.

'You're the token woman,' her section senior had told her patronisingly.

But Amber hadn't cared that she'd had to work with a male dinosaur, angry that his own choice of candidate had been passed over. Finally having got her foot onto a promising career ladder with that timely move and promotion, she had been happy to work long hours. Busy, busy, busy, that was what she had been, little time for friends or a man in her life, falling into bed exhausted night after night, driven by a desperate need to prove herself and terrified of failing.

She had met Rocco when Woodlawn Wyatt had thrown a big party for the outgoing managing director. Sitting with a fixed smile during the speeches, she had surreptitiously been drawing up a study schedule on a napkin in preparation for her next exam. She had not even noticed Rocco at the top table and when the lights had lowered and the dancing had begun, she had been on the brink of going home, having made her duty appearance.

'Would you like to dance?'

Rocco came out of nowhere at her. She looked up with a frown, only to be stunned by the effect of those spectacular tawny eyes of his. 'Sorry...who are you speaking to?' she mumbled, not crediting for one moment that it might be her.

'You...' Rocco told her gently.

'I don't dance...I was about to leave, actually—'

'Just one dance—'

'I've got two left feet,' she muttered, getting all flustered. 'Did one of my colleagues put you up to this for a joke?'

'Why would anyone do that?'

As it was her responsibility to keep a choke hold on business expense claims, Amber knew herself to be disliked by executive personnel, who loathed the way she pursued them for receipts and explanations of extraordinary bills. It was an unpopular job but she told herself that she wouldn't be doing it for ever.

Embarrassed then by the low self-esteem she had betrayed with her foolish question, she found herself grasping Rocco's extended hand and rising. And from that moment, her safe world started tilting and shifting and becoming an unrecognisable place of sudden colour and emotion. Nothing that followed was within her conscious control. After midnight, she left the party with him, aware of the shaken eyes following in their wake, but it had truly been as if Rocco had cast a spell over her. She had *still* been with Rocco at lunchtime the following day.

'What attracted you to me?' she had asked him once, still mystified.

'My ego couldn't take not being noticed by the one woman in the room worth looking at?'

'Seriously…'

'You had your shoes off under the table and you have these dinky little feet and I went weak with lust—'

'Rocco'

'I took one look and I wanted you chained to my bed, day and night.'

Had she initially been a refreshing novelty to a sophisticated male accustomed to much more experienced women? Sinking back to the present, Amber parked at the rear of her sister's big detached house and went inside. As they often did, her sister and brother-in-law were staying on in London to go out for the evening with friends before returning home.

Amber was booked to babysit as it was their nanny Gemma's night off.

The red-headed nanny was sitting in the airy conservatory with the children. Amber's two-year-old niece, Chloe, was bashing the life out of an electronic teaching toy while Freddy sat entranced by both the racket and the flashing lights.

Freddy…with the single exception of hair colour, Freddy was Rocco in miniature, Amber conceded. He had black hair, big dark golden brown eyes and olive skin. She studied her smiling baby son with eyes that were suddenly stinging. She loved Freddy so much and already he was holding his arms up for her to lift him. As Gemma greeted her while attempting to distract Chloe from the ear-splitting noise she was creating, Amber crouched down and scooped Freddy up. In just over a week, when Christmas arrived, Freddy would be a year old. She drank in the warm, familiar scent of his hair, holding his solid little body close to her own, grateful that she didn't need to worry about taking him back to her cottage at the Wintons' for at least another twenty-four hours.

'You're very quiet. Don't tell me you're still worrying about your car not starting,' her brother-in-law, Neville, scolded as he dropped her off in the cobbled coachyard at the Wintons' early the following morning. 'Look, I'll have that old banger of yours back on the road by this lunchtime. One of my delivery drivers will run it over here for you.'

Sheathed in the fancy black designer dress that she had borrowed from her sister's dry-cleaning bag because she had forgotten to pack for her overnight stay the evening before, Amber climbed out of Neville's Mercedes sports car, and gave him a pained smile. 'Yes, as if it's not bad enough that I have to drag you out of bed on a Saturday morning to take me to work, I now wreck the *rest* of your day by sentencing you to play car mechanic—'

The older man gave her a wry grin. 'Give over, Amber. I'm never happier than when I'm under the bonnet of a car!'

Yeah, sure, Amber thought, guiltily unconvinced as he drove off again. Maybe that was true if the car was a luxury model, but she could not credit that a male who owned as successful a business as Neville did could possibly enjoy working on an old banger. Barefoot and bare-legged because she hadn't wanted to risk waking her sleeping sister by going in search of shoes and underwear to borrow, a bulk, heavy carrier bag containing the previous day's clothes weighing down her arm, Amber rummaged for her keys for the cottage.

She got the fright of her life when a slight sound alerted her to the fact that she had company. Head flying up, she focused in astonishment on Rocco as he stepped into view out of the shadowy recesses behind one of the open archways fronting the coach-yard. Casually, if exclusively clad in a husky brown cashmere jacket and tailored beige chinos, luxuriant silver fair hair tousled in the breeze above his de-vastingly attractive dark features, Rocco literally sent her composure into a downward tailspin.

'So it's *true*,' Rocco pronounced with grim em-phasis. 'You've got a middle-aged man in a Merc in tow.'

The hand Amber had extended towards the key-hole on the cottage door fell back limp to her side. 'What are you d-doing out here at this hour?' she stammered, wide-eyed, still to come to grips with his first staggering statement.

Rocco vented a humourless laugh. 'You should know I never lie in bed unless I've got company—'

'But it's barely eight in the morning.' Amber didn't really know why she was going on about the actual time. She only knew that she was so taken aback by Rocco's sudden appearance and her own inability to drag her eyes from that lean, darkly hand-some face that she couldn't think straight.

'I've been waiting for you. I want to know if what Kaye Winton said about you after dinner last night was a wind-up,' Rocco bit out flatly, raking brooding dark eyes over the short fitted dress she wore, lingering in visible disbelief on her incongruously bare legs and feet. '*Dio mio*…he chucks you out of the car half naked in the middle of winter. Where have you been? In a layby somewhere?'

Shivering now in the brisk breeze, Amber was nonetheless welded to the spot, frowning at him in complete incredulity. 'What Kaye Winton *said* about me? What did *she* say about me?'

'She warned me to watch out for you coming onto me as you were the local sex goddess…only she got rather carried away and didn't manage to put it quite that politely.'

Amber's generous lips parted and stayed parted. 'Say that again…' she finally whispered shakily when she was capable of emerging from the severe shock he had dealt her with that bombshell.

'I believe you enjoy a constant procession of different men in flashy expensive cars and regular overnight absences…' Rocco grated in seething disgust, striding forward to snatch her keys from her loosened grasp and open the door. 'Go inside…you're blue with cold!'

'That's an absolute lie!' Amber exclaimed.

Rocco planted a hand to her rigid shoulder and thrust her indoors, following her in to slam the door closed again in his wake. 'I think it's past time you told me what's going *on* with you—'

Amber flung down her carrier bag and rounded on

him. 'Now, let me get this straight…Kaye Winton *told* you—'

'After what I've seen with my own eyes I wouldn't swallow a denial,' Rocco cut in angrily. 'So don't waste your breath. Are you hooking to support some kind of life-threatening habit?'

Amber closed her eyes, outraged and appalled that he should even suggest such a thing. 'Are you insane that you can ask me that?'

Rocco closed his hands over hers and pulled her closer. 'Amber, I want the truth. I was tempted to close my hands round that vicious shrew's throat last night and squeeze hard to silence her! I honestly thought it was sheer bitching I was listening to—'

'I want to hear this again. In front of witnesses, that woman—'

'*No* witnesses…the other guests were at the far end of the room when she chose to get confidential—'

Only a little of Amber's growing rage ebbed at that clarification. 'Right, I'll have it out with her face to face—'

'It would be wiser to keep quiet than encourage her to spread such tales further afield—'

Amber lifted angry hands and tried to break his hold. 'Let me go, Rocco. I'm going to tip that dirty-minded besom out of her bed *and*—'

Rocco held fast to her. 'Looking like you're just

home from a rough night at a truck stop, that will be *so* impressive!'

'How dare you talk to me like that? How dare you suggest that I might be…that I might be a whore?' Tears that were as much the result of distress as fury lashing her eyes, Amber slung those words back at him with the outrage of raw sincerity.

'I'm sorry if I've offended and hurt you, but I need to know.' Releasing her with relief unconcealed in his brilliant dark incisive eyes, Rocco expelled his breath in a stark hiss. 'So when *did* you get into men in the plural just for fun?'

Amber swept up the jampot of dying wild flowers on the small pine table and flung it at him. The glass jar hit the stainless steel sink several feet behind him and smashed, spattering shards all over the work surface.

'That was buck stupid when you have no shoes on,' Rocco pointed out with immense and galling cool.

'I wish it had hit you!' Amber launched wildly, but the truth was that she was already calming down out of shock at what she had done. She breathed in slow and deep. 'I don't have any life-threatening habits to support either…have you got that straight?'

'I'm very pleased to hear it. But I do wish you had retained the same exclusive attitude to sex.'

Ignoring that acid response, Amber fought to get

a grip on her floundering emotions and understand
why Kaye Winton, who had never demonstrated the
slightest interest in her private life but whose husband bought their cars through Neville's business,
should have muddied her reputation in such an in-
excusable way. Had the other woman somehow
sensed in Rocco's suite the day before that more was
going on between Amber and Rocco than she had
seen? Amber had never subscribed to the general local belief that Kaye Winton was an air-head. That
might well be the impression the brunette preferred
to give around men, but Amber was unconvinced
and, recalling the manner in which she herself had
automatically looked at Rocco for an inspiring excuse or being found upstairs with him, she suppressed a groan.

'I bet Kaye Winton noticed the way I glanced at
you for support yesterday. Strangers don't do that.'
Amber sighed. 'But as for the rest of her nonsense…'

It only then occurred to Amber that it was true
that she spent regular nights away from the cottage
and that it was equally true that she might often have
been seen climbing in and out of different cars.
Between them, Neville and Opal owned five luxury
vehicles. Neville often picked her up on his way
home if she was coming over to stay and just as often
dropped her back in the morning. Someone watching
from an upstairs window would not be able to tell

that the driver was always the same man. Even so, she was shattered by the apparent interpretation the brunette had put on what she had seen, yet surprised that the other woman did *not* appear to have mentioned that Amber was also an unmarried mother.

Amber breathed in so deep, her full breasts strained against the fabric of her sister's dress which was too snug a fit under that pressure. She glanced across the room. Rocco had his attention riveted to her chest. She reddened, feeling the sudden heaviness of her own swelling flesh, the tautening of her sensitive nipples. 'Stop it…' she muttered fiercely before she could think better of it.

'Tell me *how*…' Rocco invited in a raw undertone, fabulous cheekbones taut and scoured with colour, eyes like burning golden arrows of challenge on her lovely face.

'I need to get dressed for work—'

'Or you could get *undressed* for me. In fact, you don't need to move a muscle,' Rocco murmured roughly as he closed the distance between them. 'I'll do it for you—'

'But—'

He caught her into the circle of his strong arms and she gazed up at him, heart beating fast and furious in the slight hiatus that followed. She told herself to break away but somehow she did precisely nothing. He lifted her up against him with easy strength. She wrapped her arms round him. He meshed one fierce, controlling hand into the fall of her honey-blonde hair and brought their mouths into hungry devouring collision.

It was like being shot to sudden vibrant life after a long time in suspended animation. With a strangled gasp of shock at the intensity of sensation surging through her quivering frame, she kissed him back with a kind of wild, clumsy, hanging-on-tight desperation. If she stopped to breathe, she might die of deprivation, she might stop *feeling* everything she had thought she would never feel again. A soaring excitement thrummed low in her pelvis, awakening the dulled ache of a physical craving way beyond anything she could control.

But, breathing raggedly, Rocco dragged his expert sensual mouth from hers and stared down into her shaken green eyes with febrile force. 'You're wearing next to *nothing* under that dress—'

Aghast that he had realised that reality, for she had scarcely clothed herself for entertaining, Amber mumbled in severe discomfiture, 'Well…er—'

Rocco dumped her down on a hard chair by the table. 'How many ways did he have you in the Merc? And when the hell did you turn into such a tramp?' he ground out wrathfully.

'For your information, that was my brother-in-law driving that car!' Amber shot at him furiously.

'Tips you out barefoot at dawn on a regular basis, does he?'

'When my car breaks down and I've spent the night at my sister's home...*yes!*' Amber hissed back. 'And I wasn't going to put a pair of dirty workman's boots on with this dress *and* without clean socks, was I?'

'I suppose all these guys in the expensive cars you've been seen in are married to *sisters* of yours?' Shooting her a look of splintering derision, pallor spread round his ferociously compressed mouth, Rocco strode to the door.

'Two minutes ago, you didn't much care!' Amber heard herself throw at his powerful back in retaliation.

Rocco swung back and surveyed her with shimmering golden eyes. '*Per meraviglia*...who was it who called a halt? I didn't come here to get laid—'

Enraged by that assurance, Amber threw herself upright again. 'I'm still waiting to hear why you did come here because I sure as heck didn't want you anywhere near me!'

'Then isn't it strange that you should find it so difficult to say that one little word, ''no''?'

Amber paled and turned away, biting her lip to prevent herself from making some empty response which would only prolong her own agony of mortification.

'After what I heard last night, I was concerned about you—'

Amber whirled back. '*You* concerned about *me*? Give me a break!'

Rocco stared at her with cold, dark eyes of censure. 'I would do as much for any ex if I thought they needed a helping hand. And don't curl your lip like that. I'm serious,' he spelt out with chilling cool. 'If you need financial help to get yourself out of what appears to be a crisis period in your life, I'll give it to you…no questions asked and *nothing* expected in return.'

The silence hung there like a giant sheet of glass waiting to crash and smash when the seething tension broke. She stared back fixedly at him. A shaken and hollow laugh was wrenched from her convulsed throat. 'So where were you, Rocco…when I *really* needed you?'

A tiny muscle pulled tight at the corner of his expressive mouth and he did not pretend not to follow her meaning. 'I was very angry with you eighteen months ago—'

'*So* angry you couldn't even take a phone call?' Amber squeezed out the reminder with burning bitterness.

His lean, powerful face clenched. 'You knew how much I valued my privacy. I won't apologise for that. You destroyed us when you decided to share salacious details of our relationship with a muck-raking journalist. I could never have trusted you again after that.'

'I gave no salacious details whatsoever, but those sort of details are fairly easily guessed when it comes to a guy with your reputation…and I did not *know* I was talking to a journalist—'

'Amber,' Rocco incised flatly, 'I don't know what you're trying to prove but it's way too late to make the attempt.'

But whose fault was it that it was now too late for her to speak in her own defence? Hatred as savage as the hunger he had roused only minutes earlier flamed into being inside her. 'I'll never forget what you did to me back then,' she said without any expression at all, her heart-shaped face pale but composed. 'You're right. It's way too late to discuss any of that now. Go on…take your precious charity and your nauseatingly pious offer of help out of here and don't you dare come back!'

Stubborn as a rock and contrary in the face of an invitation he should have been all too keen to take in the circumstances, Rocco stood his ground. 'I wasn't being pious and I wasn't offering you charity.'

'You're talking down to me, though, and I won't stand anyone doing that to me.'

'Better that than dragging you back into bed,'

Rocco murmured in a savage undertone that shook her as he yanked open the door again.

'I wouldn't *go* to bed with you again!'

His arrogant silvery fair head turned back to her, a searing sexual hunger blatant in the all-encompassing appraisal he gave her. 'If it's any consolation, no woman ever gave me as much pleasure as you—'

'Consolation?' Amber almost choked on that mortifying word and what followed very nearly sent her into orbit with frustrated rage.

'But I need a woman to be exclusively mine—'

'Only you're not so scrupulous yourself,' Amber heard herself remark. 'After you dumped me, according to the gossip columns you were like a sex addict on the loose!'

Taken aback, Rocco froze, and then he sent her a smouldering look of what could only be described as sheer loathing.

Reeling in shock from that revealing appraisal, Amber went white and she could not drag her stricken gaze from his lean, strong face. 'Rocco…?' she whispered unsteadily.

'You did that to me,' he imparted with savage condemnation.

The door thudded shut on his departure, leaving her trembling and in more confusion and turmoil than she had ever thought to experience again.

CHAPTER FOUR

AN HOUR later, just as Amber was ready to go outside and start work, a brisk knock sounded on the
cottage door.

She was stunned to find Kaye Winton waiting outside. The brunette, clad in a skin-tight green leather
skirt suit, her beautiful face stiff, took advantage of
Amber's surprise and strolled in uninvited.

'I'm going to lay this on the line,' Kaye told her
curtly. 'If I catch you coming on to one of our guests
again, I'll inform my husband.'

Amber gave her an incredulous look. 'Coming *on*
to one—?'

'Rocco Volpe. Oh, I don't blame you. In your position I might have done the same. Rocco's a real
babe and some catch,' Kaye cut in with a tight little
smile, green as grass with envy and resentment. 'But
you needn't think I didn't work out that when I in-
terrupted you both yesterday, you were walking out
of his bedroom—'

Amber found herself in the very awkward position
of being guilty as charged on that count of inappro-
priate behaviour. And while she had initially intended to confront the other woman about the hatchet

56

job done on her own reputation, nothing was quite that simple. Admitting that Rocco had repeated the brunette's allegations to her would reveal that Amber was much more intimate with Rocco Volpe than she was prepared to admit. Indeed, so fraught was the entire situation with the risk that she could end up losing her job or, at the very least, be forced into making personal confidences in her own defence, Amber had not yet decided what to do for best.

'Mrs Winton, I—'

'I did my best to limit the damage last night and turn his attention away from you,' Kaye revealed, surprising Amber with that blunt admission. 'When all's said and done, Rocco's just another testosterone-charged bloke on the lookout for sexual variety, but he's *not* going to find it with our gardener. Is that quite clear?'

'I believe you've made yourself very clear,' Amber said grittily, fingernails biting into her palms to restrain her from saying anything she might later come to regret.

The other woman nudged the tiny toy train lying on the tiled floor by the table with the toe of her stiletto-heeled shoe. 'I forgot about your kid…where do you keep him, anyway? Does he only visit you? Now that I think about it, I've never laid eyes on him.'

'I'm sure you're not interested.' Having wondered

why Kaye had neglected to inform Rocco that Amber had a baby, Amber concealed her relief at the casual admission that the other woman had simply forgotten Freddy's existence. It was hardly surprising, though, when at the outset of her employment Harris Winton had warned her that he didn't expect to see her using the grounds of the house outside working hours.

Kaye shrugged her agreement. 'You're taking this well—'

'Maybe…maybe not.'

Opening the door again, the brunette dealt her a wry glance. 'I've done you a favour. My husband would have sacked you yesterday. Harris has Victorian values on staff behaviour.'

Since it was a well-known fact that Kaye Winton had once been a lowly groom working at the riding stables owned by her husband's first wife, Amber could barely swallow that closing comment.

'Men…' Kaye laughed in frank acknowledgement of that hypocrisy. 'Can't live *with* them, can't live without them!'

It was noon when Kaye's husband, Harris, finally came in search of Amber. A small, spare man with a very precise manner, he was much quieter than usual and he cut short his usual lengthy inspection tour by pointing out that he had guests staying. As the rain was coming on heavily by then, Amber was unsurprised at his eagerness to head back indoors again. Resigning herself to a day spent skidding on muddy lawns and getting soaked to the skin, for the rain always found its way through her jacket eventually, Amber got on with her work. Around lunchtime she went back to the cottage and made herself a sandwich before returning outside.

Never had she been more conscious of the vast gulf that had opened up between herself and Rocco. There he was snug indoors on his fancy country-house weekend, being waited on hand and foot, entertained, fed like a king by special caterers and lusted over by his shapely hostess. And here *she* was, in the most subservient of positions with a list of instructions from her employer that she would be lucky to complete in the space of a month, never mind over the next week!

In addition, Rocco *hated* her. So why was that making her feel as if the roof of the world had fallen in around her? She relived that look of his at the outset of the day…violent loathing. She shivered. He went out pulling women as if he had only days left to live and went out hell-raising for an entire six months before sinking into curious obscurity and then he had the neck to say to her, '*You* did that to me!'

Louse! Not the guy she recalled, but then there was no denying that she had had a very rosy and false image of Rocco until reality had smacked her in the teeth. That first night they'd met they had stayed up talking until way past dawn in a variety of public places. Her brain had been in a tailspin. She had let him take her home for breakfast and he had seduced her into bed with him. Well, possibly, she had been fairly willing to be seduced for the first time in her cautious existence. After all, she had only been in love once before Rocco and that had been nothing but a great big let-down.

She grimaced, recalling Russ, whom she had fallen for the year before she'd met Rocco. Meeting Opal over dinner one evening, Russ had taken one stunned look at her beautiful sister and had barely noticed Amber's existence from that point on. Sitting there like a third wheel while the man she'd thought she'd loved had ignored her and flirted like mad with her sister, Amber had stopped thinking he was special. That very night, Amber had been planning to surrender to Russ's persuasions and acquire her first experience of making love. But by the time Russ had finished raving about how gorgeous and how totally fabulous and fascinating Opal was, Amber had known she never, ever wanted to see him again. Opal turned heads in the street with her flawless ice-blonde perfection. As Amber had learned to her cost, a lot of men couldn't handle that.

Rocco had never got the chance to make the same mistake.

Their first day together, Rocco had woken Amber up about lunchtime and told her that he had been looking for someone like her *all* his life. Well, all his life from the night before, she could only assume in retrospect. Rocco, who had stood outside his own locked bathroom door swearing that it was *so* romantic that she had fallen into his bed within hours of meeting him, declaring that he did not have one-night stands, that he would never, ever *think* of her in that light and finally, in desperation, apologising for not having kept his far-too-persuasive hands off her. On the other side of the door, she had been biting back sobs of chagrined self-loathing and struggling into her clothes with frantic hands.

'I'm not letting you go,' Rocco told her when she emerged. 'I'm hanging onto you.'

Three months of excitement and joy, interspersed with occasional violent rows that tore her apart at the seams, followed. No longer did she want to work endless overtime: she wanted to be with Rocco but she valued her career. Rocco offered her a position on his own staff at much more than she was earning. She didn't speak to him for two solid days. Such a casual proposition insulted all that she had achieved on her own merits. Rocco had made the very great error of allowing her to see how unimportant and small that job of hers was on his terms.

Crazy about him, she stopped having lunch and

taking breaks at work and socialised equally crazy hours, burning the candle at both ends. She fell asleep on him once over dinner in a busy restaurant.

'Such a compliment,' Rocco quipped.

When she appeared in photos by Rocco's side in the gossip columns, she began receiving pointed cracks and knowing looks from her male co-workers. One of the directors provoked a chorus of sniggers the day he thanked her for giving Woodlawn Wyatt so much free publicity. Her working environment was one where men lived in eager hope of seeing a manipulative woman using her body to get ahead. Having an affair with a wealthy and powerful international financier was not the ticket to earning respect.

'Why won't you give me the chance to meet Rocco?' Opal demanded of Amber repeatedly. 'A quick drink early some evening…an hour, no big deal, Amber.'

Amber viewed her sibling's pure, perfect face and her heart sunk for she knew she could not compete. Not in looks, not in wit, not in *any* field. 'It's not cool to confront guys with your family. It might give him the wrong message—'

'You're very insecure about him. I suppose you can't believe your good luck in attracting a male of his calibre and are still wondering what he sees in you,' Opal remarked with deadly accuracy. 'But if he's a commitment-phobe, better to find out now than later. Don't do what I once did. Don't waste five years of your life making excuses for him and chasing rainbows.'

And that was the surprising moment when Amber learned that her sister, whom she had naively assumed to be ultra-successful in *every* way, disabused her of that notion. Prior to meeting Neville, Opal had apparently been strung along by an older man she'd adored and then been ditched when she'd least expected it. That confession of vulnerability allowed Amber to feel close to her older sister for the first time. But the one person she could have trusted with her confidences, she refused to trust.

By the time she had been with Rocco an entire three months, Amber was literally bursting with the simple human need to verbally share her happiness with someone. It was sheer deprivation to have no friend in whom to confide the news that Rocco was the most romantic, the most wonderful guy in the world. Years of attending evening classes several nights a week and working long hours had left Amber without close friends. Dinah Fletcher had gone to school with Amber, made the effort to get Amber's phone number from Opal and rang up out of the blue to suggest a girly get-together, a catching-up on old times…

Deep in her disturbing memories of that disastrous

evening with Dinah, Amber hoisted herself up onto the low, sturdy branch of a giant conifer and braced her spine against the trunk. At least everything was still dry below the thick tree canopy, she reflected ruefully, staring up at the loose dead branch pointed out to her by her employer and wondering how best to dislodge it. Reaching down for the leaf rake, she clambered awkwardly higher.

Hearing the rustling, noisy passage of something moving at speed through the undergrowth, she stiffened in dismay, recalling her experience of being cornered by a very aggressive dog a few weeks back. The owner, a guest of the Wintons', had called the animal off, boasting about what a great guard dog he was, not seeming to care that Amber had been scared witless. But now when she peered down anxiously from her perch, she saw that it was Rocco powering like an Olympic sprinter into the clearing below. Her tension ironically increased.

'What the hell are you trying to do to yourself?' Rocco roared at her from twenty feet away. 'Get down from there!'

Amber assumed that now that the rain had quit he was the advance guard of a larger party getting the official tour of the woods, and her teeth gritted in receipt of that interfering demand. 'Why are you trying to make me look like a clown when I'm only trying to do my job?' she snapped in a meaningful whisper. 'Do you think I'm up here for fun?'

Lean, bronzed features stamped with furious exasperation, Rocco strode up to the tree, removed the leaf rake dangling from her loosened grasp and pitched it aside. 'If you knock that hanging branch down, it's going to smash your head in!'

'I'm as safe as houses standing here!'

'Don't be bloody stupid!' Rocco reached up and simply snatched her bodily off her perch. As he did so, the branch on which she'd stood bounced and sent a shiver up through the tree. With a creaking noise, the loose branch above them lurched free of its resting place and began to crash down.

Rocco moved fast, but not fast enough to retain his balance when he was carrying her. Sliding on the soft carpet of leaves below the trees, he went down with her on top of him. Weak with relief that neither of them had been hurt, Amber kept her face buried in his shirt-front, drinking in the achingly familiar scent of him that clung to the fibres, listening to the solid thump of his heartbeat.

'So how are you planning to say thank you?' Rocco enquired lazily.

Amber pushed herself up on forceful hands and scrambled backwards and off him as if she had been burnt. 'Thank you? When you almost killed both of us?'

'I saved your life, woman.' Raw self-assurance charging every syllable of that confident declaration, Rocco strode over to survey the smashed pieces of wood strewing the ground. 'Winton should have hired a forester or a tree surgeon for this kind of work—'

'He's too mean to pay their rates.' Her uncertain gaze followed him and stayed with him. In a dark green weatherproof jacket, his well-worn denim jeans accentuating his lean hips and long, powerful thighs, the breeze ruffling his luxuriant silver fair hair above his lean, dark, devastating features, Rocco looked so sensational, he just took her breath away. 'How come you seem to be out here on your own?'

'I'm escaping some *serious* Monopoly players.' Rocco leant back with fluid grace against the tree trunk and surveyed her with heavily lidded eyes, his gaze a golden gleam below dense, dark lashes.

'Monopoly? You're kidding me?' Amber said unevenly, wandering skittishly closer, then beginning to edge away again as she registered what she was doing.

'I'm not into board games.' He stretched out his long arms and captured her by the shoulders before she could move out of reach. 'You're pale...all shaken up.'

'Maybe...' Amber connected with his stunning

dark golden eyes and she wanted to say something smart, but all inventiveness failed her.

Rocco tugged her to him with easy strength. 'I'll be gone in a couple of hours.'

'Gone?' In the act of forcing herself to pull back from him, Amber stilled in shock. She wasn't prepared for that shock, either. Indeed the shock came out of nowhere at her like a body blow. He was a weekend guest, *of course* he was leaving. 'But it's only Saturday,' she heard herself muttering weakly.

'Twenty-four hours of the Wintons goes a long way, tabbycat.' Framing her taut cheekbones with long, sure fingers, Rocco extracted a hungry, drugging kiss as if it were the most natural thing in the world.

Amber was defenceless, all concentration already shot by the knowledge of his imminent departure. Leaning into him, she slid her hands beneath his jacket to rest against his crisp cotton shirt. Shivering, desperate hunger had her in a stranglehold. Going, going, gone… I can't *bear* it, screamed a voice inside her head. Her heartbeat racing at an insane rate beneath the onslaught of that skilful kiss, she blocked out that voice she didn't want to hear.

'While one minute of you doesn't last half long enough,' Rocco husked, and let his tongue pry between her readily parted lips, once, twice, the third time making her shiver as though she were in a force-ten gale.

He stopped teasing and devoured her mouth with plundering force. She pulled his shirt out of his waistband, allowed her seeking fingers to splay against the warm smooth skin of his waist, felt him jerk in response. He dragged her hand down to the hard, thrusting evidence of his very male arousal. Her fingertips met the rough, frustrating barrier of denim. He pushed against her with a muffled groan of frustration, angled his head back from her, feverish golden eyes glittering, to say with ragged mockery, 'No sheet to hide under out here, *cara*.'

'Rocco...' Cheeks flaming, she was assailed by bittersweet memories that hurt even as they made her shiver and melt down deep inside where she ached for him. And the combination released a flood of recklessness. She stretched up and claimed his sensual mouth again for herself and jerked at his belt with trembling fingers. He tensed in surprise against her and then suddenly he was coming to her assistance faster than the speed of light, releasing the buttons on his tight jeans.

The feel of Rocco trembling like a stallion at the starting gate was the most powerful aphrodisiac Amber had ever experienced. Her own legs barely capable of holding her up, she slid dizzily down his hard, muscular physique onto her knees.

She pressed her lips into his hard, flat stomach and then sent the tip of her tongue skimming along the line of his loosened waistband. His muscles jerked satisfyingly taut under that provocative approach and he exhaled audibly. 'Don't tease…' he begged her, Italian accent thickening every urgent syllable. 'I couldn't stand it…'

'Stop trying to take control…' Taking her time, she ran her hands up his taut, splayed thighs, loving every gorgeous inch of him, loving the way just touching him made her feel. As she eased away the denim, dispensed with the last barrier, Rocco was shaking, breathing heavily. Finding the virile proof of his excitement was not a problem. The extraordinary effect she was having on him was turning her so hot and quivery inside, she was sinking deeper and deeper into a sensual daze.

As she took him in her mouth, he groaned her name out loud, arching his hips off the trunk in surging eagerness. She felt like every woman born since Eve; she felt a power she had never dreamt she could feel. He was *hers* and he was out of control as she had never known him to be. It gave her extreme pleasure to torture him. He meshed his hand into her hair, urging her on, and then he cried out in Italian and he shuddered into an explosive release when she chose, not when he chose.

In the aftermath, the birdsong came back to charge

a silence that still echoed in her sensitive ears. She was so shaken up, her body so weak, she felt limp.

Rocco hauled her up to him to study her with dazed and wondering dark golden eyes and then he wrapped his arms round her, pulled her close, burying his face in her hair. He held her so tightly she could not fill her lungs with oxygen, but she revelled in that natural warmth and affection of his, which she had missed infinitely more than she had missed him in her bed. He muttered with a roughened laugh, 'So...I sack the gardener at my own country estate. I hire you...I get into rustic daily walks...no problem, *cara!*'

Amber went rigid and, planting her hands against his broad chest, she pulled free of him like a bristling cat.

'Joke...' Rocco breathed when he saw her furiously flushed face. 'Obviously the wrong one.'

Amber wasn't so sure: Rocco had a very high sex drive. Rocco was still surveying her with stunned appreciation. Rocco always just reached out and took what he wanted. But she wasn't available; she wasn't on offer and never would be again.

'No encore. Goodbye, Rocco.'

'So you weren't in a joking mood—'

Amber crammed her shaking, restive hands into the pockets of her jacket as she backed away from him. 'Your days of being stalked by me are over…OK?'

'I openly admit that I was stalking *you* today, *cara*.'

'Do you think I didn't work that out for myself?' She forced a jarring laugh for she was actually only making that possible connection as he admitted it. 'But I turned the tables—'

'Yes. You also turned *me* inside out…' Rocco rested his intense golden eyes on her, a male well aware of the strength of his own powerful sexual appeal.

Amber dealt him a frozen look of scorn that took every ounce of her acting ability. 'So now you know how that feels.'

CHAPTER FIVE

THE instant Amber believed she was out of sight and hearing, she broke into a run, her breath rasping in her throat in a mad flight through the trees.

It was only four but it was getting dark fast. As Neville had promised, he had had her car brought back. She blundered past it into the cottage, shedding her jacket in a heap, pausing only to wrench off her boots. Not even bothering to put on the lights, she was heading up the stairs when she noticed the red light flashing on the answering machine. With a sigh, she hit the button in case it was something urgent.

Opal's beautifully modulated speaking voice filled the room. Opal and Neville had gone to visit friends, were staying on there for dinner with the children and were planning on a late return. 'Freddy's getting loads of attention,' her sister asserted. 'He won't get the chance to miss you. I'll put him to bed for you when we get back home.'

The prospect of hugging Freddy like a comforting security blanket that evening receded fast. Eyes watering, Amber hurried on upstairs. In the tiny shower room, she switched on the shower and pulled off her clothes as if she were in a race to the finish line.

Stepping into the cubicle, she sent the door flying shut and stood there trembling, letting the warm water flood down over her.

What had got into her with Rocco? Sudden insanity? She didn't know what was happening inside her head any more and she was too afraid to take a closer look. All she remembered was feeling as if she were dying inside when Rocco had said he was leaving. So had she somehow had a brainstorm and imagined he was going to move in with the Wintons for ever? Rocco playing board games? Rocco, who was so full of restive, seething energy you could get tired watching him?

She sank down in the corner of the shower, letting the water continue to cascade down over her still-shivering body. What had come over her out in the woods? She didn't want to know. He was gone, he was history…he was *gone*. A horrendous mix of conflicting feelings attacked her. Rage…fear…pain. She hugged her knees and bowed her head down on them.

Rocco had come in search of her. He had admitted that. To say goodbye? Impossible to imagine the Rocco she remembered planning to take advantage of her smallest show of weakness and drag her down into the undergrowth to make love to her again. She would have said no anyway, she *definitely* would have said no, she told herself. He hadn't laid a finger on her, she reminded herself with equal urgency. But then, bombarded by erotic imagery which reminded her precisely why Rocco had been so unusually restrained, she uttered a strangled moan of shame. Rocco not having touched *her* was no longer a source of reassurance or comfort.

She hated him, she really did. She was over him, over him. She hadn't even been kissed in eighteen months, had conceived a violent antipathy for every male her brother-in-law had brought home to dinner in the hope she would take the bait and start dating again. Maybe that had something to do with how she had behaved with Rocco. Or maybe she just loved his body. *Yes.* Wanton, shameless…starved of him? *No*, she swore vehemently to herself. Just a case of over-charged emotions, confusion and an overdose of hormones out of sync. She stayed in the shower until the water ran cold.

Wrapping herself in a towel, she padded out of the shower room. She frowned at the sight of the dim light spilling from her bedroom out onto the landing. She hadn't even been in her bedroom yet. Had she left the bedside lamp switched on all day? If so, why hadn't she noticed it when she'd come upstairs earlier? Acknowledging that she had been in no state to notice anything very much and that she still felt hollow and sick inside, Amber pushed the door wider and walked into her room.

On the threshold, she froze. Rocco was poised by the window.

'How on earth—?'

'You didn't hear me knock and your front door was unlocked—'

'Was that an invitation for you to just walk on in?' Amber snapped, thinking how very lucky she was that he had not gone into Freddy's little room next door to hers first. Had he done so, he would hardly have failed to notice the cot and the toys in there.

He had changed out of his designer casuals. Sheathed in a formal dark business suit, his arrogant head within inches of the ceiling, Rocco looked formidable.

Agitated by the severe disadvantage of having a scrubbed bare face, dripping hair in a tangle and only an old beach towel between herself and total nudity, Amber added, 'And walk right up into my bedroom?'

Rocco gave her a cloaked look. 'Since I've already said my goodbyes to my host, I didn't think you'd want me to advertise my presence by waiting downstairs in a room that doesn't even have curtains on the windows.'

Amber flushed at that accurate assumption. 'I haven't got around to putting any up yet,' she said defensively.

'I think a woman living alone and secluded by a

big empty courtyard should be more careful of her own privacy and safety—'

Amber lifted her chin. 'You're the only prowling predator I've ever known. So what are you doing here?'

'When you turn me inside out, you take the consequences,' Rocco murmured with indolent cool.

'What's that supposed to mean?'

'That what you start, you have to finish.'

'We *are* finished,' she said breathlessly.

'I'm not hearing you...' Rocco sidestepped her and pushed the bedroom door closed like a guy making a pronounced statement.

'Rocco—'

'You want me...I want you. Right now, when I'm flying out to Italy for three days, everything else is superfluous.'

A tide of colour washed up over her heart-shaped face.

The expectant silence rushed and surged around her.

'Unless you say otherwise, of course,' Rocco spelt out with soft sibilance. 'I can't say goodbye to you again.'

Rocco wanted her back. She couldn't believe it. He had wrongfooted her, sprung a sneak attack, thrown her in a loop. She had had no expectations of him at all. She had said goodbye and she had meant it. But her saying goodbye had been kind of pointless when no other option had been on offer, an empty phrase that nonetheless could rip the heart out of her if she thought about it.

'You have incredible nerve...' she mumbled shakily, wondering what had happened to all that stuff about him never being able to trust her again, fighting to focus her brain on that mystery, utterly failing.

'No, I'm a ruthless opportunist.'

She saw that, could hardly miss that. Show weakness and Rocco took advantage. He had taught her that within twelve hours of their very first meeting. A brilliant, ruthless risk-taker whom she had once adored and could probably adore again, but the prospect terrified her. Freddy...what about her son, *their* son, Freddy? He didn't know about Freddy and she didn't think that it was quite the right moment to make that shock announcement. Rocco seemed to believe that the clock could be turned back and, dear heaven, she wanted to believe that too, *but*... A baby made a difference; Freddy *would* make a difference.

'So...' Rocco was studying her as she imagined he would study an opponent in the boardroom. With a cool, incisive intensity that sought to read the thoughts on her face. 'Do I go...or do I stay?'

No, it really wasn't the moment to ask him how he felt about being a father and, since it was his fault she had fallen pregnant in the first place, he was really just going to have to come to terms with Freddy. Oh, yes, Rocco, she thought with helpless tender amusement, unlike you once assured me, it *is* that easy to get pregnant. He might reign supreme in every other corner of his organised, fast-moving existence, but fate had had the last laugh in the field of conception.

'You've got a big smile in your beautiful eyes,' Rocco drawled with a wolfish grin that twisted her vulnerable heart.

He jerked loose his silk tie.

'You could be taking a lot for granted,' she said, trying to play it cool.

'I took you for granted until I had to get by without you. When I saw you last night, I became a very fast learner,' Rocco asserted, shimmying his wide shoulders back with easy grace and casting off his superb tailored suit jacket.

'No servants here, Rocco... I'm not picking up after you,' Amber whispered, heart hurling itself against her ribcage, making her feel dizzy.

Rocco vented a rueful laugh. 'So I'm not tidy.'

It had been so long since she'd heard him laugh like that, she wanted to tape him; she wanted to capture the moment, stop time dead, just look, listen, rejoice. She picked up his jacket; she couldn't help it. She couldn't bear to see expensive clothes treated like rags of no account. She hugged his jacket to her, happiness beginning to soar like a bird taking flight inside her. Thank you, God, she chanted with silent fervour, thank you.

As far as she was concerned, Rocco's slate of sins was wiped clean. Within the space of twenty-four hours, Rocco had transformed himself from being a stubborn, angry, unforgiving louse full of wild allegations back into the charismatic lover she had lost. Hadn't he just said that he had taken her for granted until he had had to get by without her? Had he been too proud to seek her out after his anger had ebbed?

He flung his shirt on the chair where she was draping his jacket. She gave him a sunny smile of approval. 'Did you drive yourself down here? Where's your car?' she asked.

'Parked in the back lane…this is like having an illicit assignation.'

She tensed. 'And how much do you know about that?'

'I don't mess around with married women.'

At that grounding admission, a little of her buoyancy ebbed. 'But you haven't exactly spent the past eighteen months *pining*…let's be frank.'

Stilling, Rocco sent her a slanting glance of scorching hunger.

She was vaguely surprised that her towel didn't go up in flames, but the pain she was suppressing wouldn't let go of her. 'Stop evading the issue…'

A faint rise of dark blood accentuated his fabulous high cheekbones. His equally fabulous mouth tautened. 'I was on the rebound...I was trying to replace you. I don't want to talk about that,' he completed with brooding abruptness, lush black lashes lifting, stormy golden eyes challenging her.

Was that guilt or regret she was hearing? Or back off, mind your own business? Amber turned away. A split second later, he was behind her, tugging her back against him with possessive hands. 'So how many other men have there been?' he said in the same tone he might have utilised to read a weather report, but his big powerful frame was so tense it betrayed him.

'Back off...mind your own business,' Amber heard herself say.

'But—'

'I don't want to talk about it.' She flung back the same words he had given her.

'Sooner or later you'll tell me,' Rocco forecast, and swept her right off her feet in a startling demonstration of his superior strength to carry her over to her own bed. 'You tell me *everything*.'

'Not quite everything...no one tells everything.'

He settled her down on the bed and then lifted her again to yank the duvet from beneath her. He came down beside her, like a vibrant bronze image of raw masculinity, and detached the tuck on her towel with long brown fingers. Smouldering tawny eyes scanned her hectically flushed face. 'I'll get it out of you, tabbycat.'

She lifted an unsteady hand to trace the course of one hard, angular cheekbone. 'Don't call me that unless you mean it,' she whispered helplessly. 'I don't want you hurting me again.'

He caught her fingers and kissed them, ridiculously long inky lashes screening his gaze from her. 'I would never set out to hurt you and I never say anything I don't mean.'

In receipt of those assurances, her attack of insecurity ebbed, but she was already very conscious of her own intense vulnerability. She had got by without Rocco by persuading herself that she hated him. Now the scary truth was blinding her. She was still crazy about him. Her barriers were down. Putting them back up would be impossible for her a second time.

CHAPTER SIX

'YOU'RE so serious, *cara*,' Rocco censured huskily.

And tonight, 'serious' was obviously not what was required, Amber interpreted without much difficulty. That *wasn't* like him, she thought uneasily, but she suppressed that suspicion and concentrated instead on being seriously happy.

'Smile…' Rocco urged, tumbling her back into the pillows and arranging himself over her, so that not one inch of her was bare of his potent presence.

Amber smiled brighter than the sun because she was with him again. He kissed her in reward. She even tried to smile under his marauding mouth and her heart sang, her senses flowering to the taste and the touch and the scent of him again. Every fibre of her being was on a knife edge of delicious anticipation.

He found her breasts with a husky sound in the back of his throat that was incredibly sexy. Her sensitised flesh swelled into his shaping palms and she trembled in response. He rested appreciative eyes on the full, pouting mounds. 'I swear that though the rest of you has got thinner, your gorgeous breasts…*per amor di Dio*—just looking at you makes me ache,' he ground out with thickened fervour. 'You're every erotic dream I have ever had, *cara.*'

Amber was aware that pregnancy *had* changed her shape. She tensed, but Rocco chose that exact same moment to give way to temptation and send his dark head swooping down to capture a throbbing pink nipple in his mouth. Her ability to think was wrenched from her at speed. Her eyes squeezed tight shut and her spine arched. As he teased at the stiff, tender buds begging for his attention, nothing existed for her for long, timeless moments but the all-encompassing surge of her own writhing response. She had always been intensely sensitive there. Pulsing waves of intense pleasure cascaded through her quivering body as she yielded to his erotic mastery.

'I *missed* you so much…' she gasped, mouth dry, throat tight, breathing a challenge.

He reclaimed her reddened lips with fierce, plundering passion, his hands knotting into her damp honey-blonde hair, lifting her to him as if he could never get enough of her. His tongue delved deep into her mouth and her thighs clenched together on a need that already felt shockingly intolerable. He kissed her until she was moaning and clinging to him and he only paused to catch his own breath.

He studied her passion-glazed eyes with intense

male satisfaction. 'When I saw you getting out of that car this morning, I felt violent,' he declared with raw force as he shifted with innate eroticism against her, acquainting her with the bold, hot proof of his hard arousal. 'I wanted to rip that guy out of his Merc and beat him to a pulp. Then I wanted to drag you off like a caveman and imprint myself so deeply on you that you would never look at another man again!'

'Neville's my brother-in-law,' Amber reminded him, aghast.

'They can't *all* have been relatives—'

As Rocco loomed over her, all domineering male, Amber ran worshipping hands up over his magnificent hair-roughened torso, adoring the hard strength and beauty of him, and he shivered, rippling muscles pulling taut. But shimmering stubborn golden eyes still gazed down into hers. 'I only want a number...I've no wish to talk about them—'

'No...someone as possessive as you are doesn't want a number either,' Amber whispered, a rueful giggle tugging at her vocal cords, even as his hand tightened on her hip and dragged her closer and her wanton body turned liquid as heated honey.

'Ballpark figure?' he pressed with roughened determination.

Amber exerted pressure on his big brown shoulders to tug him back to her again. It would be so easy to admit that there had never been anyone else, but the mean streak in her wouldn't let her tell him that yet. If, and when, he deserved that honesty.

'*Dio mio*…it's driving me crazy thinking about you with other—'

'Shush…' Amber came up on one elbow and pressed her tingling mouth to his again.

Rocco went rigid and then he vented a hungry groan and he responded with devastating, driving sensuality. She laced her fingers into his thick, tousled hair, weak and quivering with a hunger as unstoppable as a floodtide. Every time her sensitised skin came into glancing contact with any part of his lean, hard frame, the heat building inside her and the tormenting ache for fulfilment increased.

'Rocco…' she moaned as he thumbed the aching buds of her breasts and lingered there, giving her ruthless pleasure with indolent ease.

Skimming sure fingers through the silky fleece of curls at the junction of her thighs, he pressed his carnal mouth to the tiny pulse flickering at her collarbone, making every skin-cell leap. Her blood started roaring through her veins, her heart thundering in her own ears. As he explored the hot, damp welcome awaiting him, she could not stay still and all control was taken from her. There was only Rocco and what he was doing to her with such exquisite expertise, the burning need that sent her hips rising from the bed, the choked sounds wrenched from her with ever greater frequency.

'Please…' she sobbed.

He pulled her under him, spread her thighs with an urgency that betrayed his own urgent need. She collided with feverish golden eyes and a great wave of love infused her.

'I never thought I would *be* with you again…' Rocco groaned with raw, feeling intensity as he tipped her up and drove deep into her moist satin sheath.

She arched up to receive him, a stunned cry of response torn from her for she had forgotten just how incredible he could make her feel, forgotten that bold sensation of being stretched to accommodate him. He set a pagan rhythm and with every fluid thrust he excited her beyond bearing. Every hot, abandoned inch of her revelled in his strength and masculine dominance. His passionate force drove her wild with excitement until at last he allowed her to surge over the final threshold. That shattering climax felt endless to her, splintering through her writhing body in long, ecstatic waves of release. Utterly lost in him, mindless with delight, she whimpered and clung as he shuddered over her and slammed into her one last time with a harsh groan of very male pleasure.

'Nobody can make me feel like you do, tabby-cat…' Rocco vented an indolent sigh of satisfaction.

Smoothing her hair from her brow, he stole a tender, lingering kiss from her swollen lips and hugged her close.

She kissed his shoulder, drowning in the hot, damp smell of his skin, loving him. It felt like coming home. She could not credit that he had only come back into her life the night before, for it now felt to her as though they had never been apart…as though the whole dreadful nightmare of that cheap and sleazy spread in a down-market newspaper had never happened. 'When did you start appreciating that I must have been set up by Dinah Fletcher?' she murmured curiously.

His big, powerful frame tensed. Lifting his tousled fair head, he rested dark as midnight eyes on her, superb bronzed bone-structure taut. He was still in her arms but she recognised his instantaneous withdrawal by the impassivity of his gaze. It was as if he had slammed a door in her face. 'We haven't got time to talk. I have to be out of here in fifteen minutes.'

As Rocco rolled free of her and sprang out of bed, Amber was stunned. 'You have to be out of here in fifteen *minutes*?'

'What began as an excuse to extract me from this weekend early turned into the real McCoy,' Rocco quipped on his way out of the room. 'I have to work out a rescue package for a hotel chain which belongs to friends of mine by Tuesday.'

Obviously he had known that before he'd come to see her. She just wished he had mentioned how little time he had to spend with her. On the one hand, she felt hurt and disappointed, but she was also aware that Rocco's talents were always very much in demand. It was also exactly like him to drop everything to go to the assistance of a friend. She listened to the shower running, knew he would find very little, if any, hot water.

'I'm not a fan of primitive plumbing, *cara*,' Rocco commented with a feeling shudder on his return to the bedroom. 'I'll organise a car to move you out of here tomorrow.'

'Move me *out*…of here?' Amber prompted unevenly, immediately wondering if he was asking her to live with him and wondering how she would answer him if that was what he meant. Everything felt as if it was happening way too fast for common sense, but it had always been like that with Rocco.

Rocco dropped the towel wrapped round his lean brown hips. Attention straying, she swallowed hard. He was magnificent: the lean, muscular power of a very fit male laced with the overwhelming appeal of a very sexual animal. Her cheeks burned. He was drop-dead gorgeous but gaping at him made her feel embarrassed for herself in spite of the renewed intimacy between them.

'I *have* to come clean with you,' Rocco murmured with rueful emphasis. 'I'm afraid I overreacted when I first realised you were working for the Wintons yesterday…'

Amber nodded agreement, glad he was admitting that reality.

His expressive mouth tightened and then he breathed in deep. 'But by the time you came indoors to reason with me, I had *already* called Harris and warned him that you might only be marking time here in search of a story worth selling.'

Amber turned pale with horror at that most belated confession.

'I'm sorry.' Rocco spoiled his seemingly sincere apology, however, by adding, 'But it's not really a problem now, is it?'

'What did Mr Winton say?' Amber demanded tensely, only now recalling how cool the older man had been with her earlier in the day, but she hadn't even suspected that there might have been anything personal in his apparent preoccupation.

'He'll be looking for grounds to sack you and get you off his property as fast as possible.' Rocco followed that devastating assurance with a shrug of incredible cool. 'But since this is not a convenient neck

of the woods for you to live when I'm based in
London when I am in the UK, it hardly matters—'

'It hardly matters…' Amber parroted in a shattered
tone of disbelief. 'You tell me that you've virtually
got me the sack and that I'm likely to be kicked out
of this cottage…and you *think* that's no big deal?'

Rocco elevated a dark, imperious brow. 'Like you
really love that wheelbarrow and living in this
dump!' he derided.

'I won't even dignify that with an answer!' she
said in reproach, appalled by his seeming indifference to the plight he had put her in.

His white shirt hanging open on his bronzed, hair-
roughened chest, Rocco strolled over to the bed and
crouched down to her level. Tawny eyes rested on
her shaken and furious face. He closed his big hands
over hers, strenuously ignoring her attempt to pull
free of his grasp. 'It goes without saying that, from
this moment on, I will take care of *all* your expenses
so you really do have nothing at all to worry about.'

She stared back at him in astonishment.

Rocco released his hold on her and lifted lean
brown fingers to brush her hair back from one taut
cheekbone in a soothing, but nonetheless very confident, gesture of intimacy. 'It's the only thing that
makes sense and you know it—'

Pale as death, Amber compressed bloodless lips,

but she couldn't stop herself trembling. 'You never brought money into our relationship before—'

His lean, powerful face clenched. 'It was a different relationship.'

'Different?' Amber echoed and she could hear her own voice fading away on her, for this terrible fear was building inside her that she had entirely misunderstood what he had meant by coming back to her.

In an abrupt movement, Rocco vaulted back upright again.

The silence stretched into infinity.

'Explain that word ''different'' to me,' Amber whispered tightly.

'It would be hard to quantify it.'

'Oh, I think I can quantify it *for* you,' Amber muttered in an agony of humiliation, but she didn't speak her thoughts aloud. She had given him sex and he had come back for more sex and the foreseeable future would include only very much more of the same. Being a wanton in the woods had rebounded on her. He thought he could have her back on any terms now.

'We can't pretend the past never happened. Naturally things have changed. But there's nothing wrong with my wish to look after you.'

'Look after me…with a view to what in the future?' Amber asked shakily.

Rocco chose that exact moment to turn his back

to her searching eyes and duck down low enough to use the dressing mirror and straighten his tie. 'Whatever happens, I'll be there for you. I don't turn my back on my responsibilities. You're making a fuss about nothing.'

Amber was so crushed she couldn't think straight. She was thinking of Freddy: Freddy who was very much Rocco's responsibility. Somehow Amber did not think that Rocco would be quite so keen to reacquire a lover who had already given birth to his child.

'I won't be your mistress, your kept woman, whatever you want to call it,' she stated curtly. 'I thought you cared about me—'

'*Santo Cielo*…of course, I care about you! Stop dramatising the situation,' Rocco whipped back round to rest his stunning dark gaze on her in cool challenge. 'Be practical. Right now you're as poor as a church mouse!'

Amber lost even more colour and studied her tightly linked hands.

'No doubt if I was as poor as a church mouse and on the brink of being unemployed and homeless as well, *you* would offer to keep *me*!' Rocco continued in a very specious argument, attempting to present the unacceptable in an acceptable guise.

'You would starve sooner than take me up on the offer. Furthermore,' she countered tightly, 'you dug yourself into a hole when you phoned Harris Winton and screwed up my job security, so you can hardly walk away *without* having me on your conscience—'

'Couldn't I?' Rocco shot her an exasperated appraisal. 'I could have just handed you a cheque in compensation. Are you coming to London or not?'

She swallowed the thickness in her throat. *'No…'*

Rocco withdrew a gold pen from his jacket. 'I'll leave my phone number with you—'

'No…'

'I'm not about to grovel,' Rocco grated.

'You're refusing even to discuss that newspaper story last year!' Amber condemned.

'If we talk about it, I might just wring your neck!' Rocco sent her startled face a flashing look of censure. 'I did not appreciate being publicly labelled a five-times-a-night stud—'

'But I never *said* that…I didn't make one tiny mention of even sleeping with you!' Amber gasped strickenly.

'So how come it was true?' Rocco growled, unimpressed by that plea of innocence.

'Lucky guess?' she muttered chokily.

'The day after that trash was printed, I walked into a Mayfair restaurant with a client and a bunch of city traders at the next table stood up and gave me a slow handclap.' The banked-down rage in his stormy gaze at that unfortunate recollection flailed her.

Amber just cringed.

'But I could have got over that…it was the sense of betrayal I couldn't take,' Rocco spelt out fiercely. 'I trusted you. When you really care about someone, you're loyal and you don't discuss that person with anyone else!'

'If you still believe that I would've discussed our intimacy with anybody, then get out of here because I don't want you near me!' Amber told him feverishly, but she was horribly impressed by his definition of caring.

'If you can't take the heat, you should have stayed out of the kitchen, tabbycat,' Rocco responded with silken derision. 'Don't start thinking that giving me a great time in bed automatically wipes out what you did last year!'

Amber stood up on hollow legs. At that crack, an uneven laugh escaped her. 'I am *so* much more forgiving than you are—'

'What have *you* got to forgive?'

Just at that moment, Amber felt dead inside, as if he had killed all her feelings. 'You didn't love me enough. I can see that now…odd, how I refused to face that at the time. A man who *really* loved me would have given me the chance to explain myself.'

His darkly handsome features clenched, 'Amber—'

Amber turned away. 'Please leave—'

'I haven't got time for this right now,' Rocco delivered, his tone sufficient to tell her that he wasn't taking her seriously.

'So *go*!'

'You don't mean that.'

Amber breathed in so deep, she marvelled that she didn't explode and fizzle round the ceiling above him.

Rocco reached the door and spread fluid and confident hands. 'You'll be on the phone within twenty hours—'

Amber's teeth gritted together.

'You need me.'

'No, I needed you eighteen months ago,' Amber countered fiercely. 'But I *don't* need you now. I got by without you once and I will again. If I get in touch with you in the next few days, Rocco…I warn you, it won't be about *us*.'

Rocco sent her a sudden vibrant grin of amusement. 'I'll see you in London, tabbycat.'

Only if she went, she wouldn't be arriving alone, Amber thought heavily. She listened to the slam of the front door downstairs and hugged herself. He didn't listen; he *never* listened to what he didn't want to hear. It wasn't that he had a huge ego. No, Rocco had something much harder to deflate: immense and boundless confidence. In addition, he had once been tremendous at second-guessing her every move. Only this time, he was miscalculating because there was a factor he didn't know about. *I would never set out to hurt you.* Stinging tears burned her eyes. She felt even more alone than she had felt when she had finally appreciated that she was pregnant by a man who wouldn't even take a phone call from her. Why, oh, why had she been such a fool as to imagine that the clock could be turned back when Rocco had never loved her in the first place?

CHAPTER SEVEN

IT WAS ironic that Harris Winton could not conceal his dismay when Amber went up to the house and tendered her resignation without notice early the following morning.

'I'm not a media spy, Mr Winton, and I'm not leaving because I have some poison-pen article written either,' Amber declared with wry humour and, now that she was leaving, not caring what opinion she left in her wake, continued, 'Rocco gets a little carried away sometimes. I'm going because it no longer suits me to work here.'

After the turmoil of the night, a strange accepting calm settled over her as she drove over to her sister's house. It had been a pretty awful job and she hated being so dependent on Opal and Neville's charity and seeing so little of her son. Freddy was growing fast and he wouldn't be a baby for much longer. It was time to make fresh choices and leave pride and personal feelings out of the question. The guy who had sworn he didn't turn his back on his responsibilities was about to find out that he *had*. How he felt about that, she didn't much care at that moment.

Opal was rarely taken by surprise. Reclining on a

sofa in her elegant drawing room, looking very much like a fairy-tale princess with her flowing pale blonde hair and her exquisite face, she smiled with satisfaction when Amber announced that she had given up on gardening. 'You can move back in here immediately. It was very convenient having you here as second in command with the children. It suited you too. You saw much more of Freddy.'

'Thanks, but I've decided to move back to London.' Amber drew in a deep breath as Opal's fine brows elevated. 'I'm going to tell Rocco about Freddy—'

Her sister sat up with a start. 'Are you crazy?'

Amber would have much preferred not to admit that Rocco had been staying with the Wintons earlier that weekend but in the circumstances it wasn't possible. As she completed her halting explanation about having 'got talking' with Rocco and certain fences having been partially mended, while refusing to indicate *which* fences, her sister wore her most cynical expression of freezing incredulity.

Opal then looked at her in outright disgust. 'So Rocco Volpe just snaps his fingers and you throw up everything and go running—'

'It's not like that—'

'Isn't it? You didn't *tell* him about Freddy and we both know why, don't we? But what was the point of keeping quiet? The guy will laugh in your face if you try and pin a kid on him!' Opal forecast.

Amber paled.

'You'll humiliate yourself for nothing. He'll walk out on you and if you hear one more word from him, I guarantee it will be through his lawyer!' Opal continued.

'Maybe…but I'm doing what I should have done a year ago,' Amber declared tightly. 'Not for my sake, but for Freddy's. I want the right to tell my son who his father is and not have anybody laugh in my face *or* his.'

'Tell me, are you imagining that Rocco will open his arms to your child and turn into Daddy of the Year?' Opal demanded with total derision.

Amber studied her sister with hurt, bewildered eyes. 'I don't have *any* expectations at all. I don't know how he's likely to react. But I thought you'd think I was doing the right thing.'

'You're making yet *another* big mistake.'

'I don't think so.' It took courage for Amber to stand up to her sister.

'Why don't you tell Amber the truth about why you feel the way you do, Opal?' Neville had appeared in the doorway, his frank blue eyes pinned to the wife he adored with rare disapproval.

'Stay out of this, Neville—'

'I'm sorry, I can't.' The older man sighed. 'You're

too prejudiced. The man who let *you* down was a married man—'

Amber stilled at that revelation and looked at her sister in astonishment. 'The man you told me about, the commitment-phobe you were with for five years, was *married* to another woman?'

Twin highspots of furious colour now burned over Opal's cheekbones.

'And like most married men having an affair, he couldn't run far enough when your sister told him she was expecting his child,' Neville completed heavily.

'Is this true?' Amber questioned her rigid and silent sister. 'You were pregnant?'

'I miscarried…fortunately,' Opal admitted curtly. 'But those facts have no bearing on the advice I've given you.'

Amber could not have agreed with that appraisal. She had just seen in Opal's rigid face the depth of her sister's bitterness, her sister's own memory of humiliation and rejection at the hands of the married man she had loved. Naturally that experience had coloured the forceful opinions which Opal had given Amber. 'I'm sorry you got into a situation like that,' she said awkwardly. 'But I wish you had told me the whole story.'

Ten minutes later, Freddy crawling round her feet in pursuit of a wooden car, Amber called the number

Rocco had left with her. She got an answering machine and all she could do was leave a message.

However, within an hour Rocco called her back. Having answered the phone, her still-frozen-faced sister extended the receiver to Amber as if it were an offensive weapon.

'When do you want to travel?' Rocco asked, disconcerting her with that prosaic opening question, for she had expected a variety of greetings and that had not been one of them.

'The day you're coming back,' she said stiltedly. 'But I'll drive myself up—'

'You sound terrified. You won't regret this,' Rocco swore huskily.

'I think you *will*,' Amber muttered tautly. 'I'm just warning you…OK?'

'When did I contrive to forget that you're a pessimist, who nourishes negative expectations of anything new and different?' Rocco loosed an extravagant sigh.

'You haven't even told me where we…' She stumbled in dismay. 'I mean, *I'm* going to stay—'

'No, that's why you have to be collected and you can't drive yourself. I very much want to surprise you—'

'I don't like surprises.'

'Within a week of Christmas, that is *not* good news, tabbycat.'

'Don't call me that,' Amber told him woodenly.

'Whatever you say,' Rocco drawled with scrupulous politeness. 'We'll cancel Christmas too, shall we? Obviously you're not in the mood for it either.'

'Look, I've got to go,' Amber muttered, blinking back hot tears and swallowing hard. 'I'll see you when you get back to London.'

CHAPTER EIGHT

Two days later, a long, opulent limousine drew up to collect Amber from her sister's home.

The uniformed chauffeur was somewhat disconcerted to be confronted with a disassembled cot, a baby seat, a buggy, two bulging suitcases and a laundry basket full of toys and other unavoidable essentials.

'Will you get it all in?' Amber asked anxiously.

'Of course, madam.'

Before leaving for work, Neville had pressed a mobile phone on her. 'I think you should've given Rocco fair warning of what's coming. I'll be working late at the car showroom tonight. If there's a problem, wherever you are just call me and I'll come and collect you and Freddy.'

Opal had been even blunter. 'Don't be surprised if Rocco takes one look at Freddy and slams the door in your face! I cannot credit that you are doing this. It's *insane*…it's like something a foolish teenager would do.'

Amber only began to question what she was doing and how she was doing it on the drive to London. That was when she recognised her own bitterness and her own seething desire and need to confront Rocco. It would have been more sensible to tell Rocco about Freddy without Freddy around. But then, in such circumstances, there really wasn't a right or an easy way, was there?

When the limo headed for Holland Park and turned beneath an imposing arched gateway and came to a halt in front of a picturesque Georgian mansion set within lush lawned grounds, Amber at first assumed it was a hotel. Realising that it was a private residence, she was taken aback. Was this where Rocco now lived? Eighteen months ago, he had been living in a penthouse apartment, opulent and impressive if not remotely cosy, the perfect backdrop for a single male.

An older woman greeted her, introducing herself as the housekeeper. Freddy was much admired. Rocco had been held up in Rome, Amber was informed, and was not expected back before nine that evening. As it sank in on Amber that Rocco had had her brought to his own home, her nervous tension began increasing. Of course, it didn't mean that he had plans for her to stay under the same roof for more than one night.

By eight, Freddy was tucked into his cot in a charming guest room and fast asleep after a more than usually active day. Almost an hour later, Amber heard a car pulling up outside. She was wearing a fitted burgundy skirt suit and high heels, her hair conditioned within an inch of its life to fall round her shoulders in shining waves. She wanted to knock him hard with what he had done to her life, but she definitely didn't want him looking at her and thinking that dumping her again would be no great sacrifice.

Rocco strode through the door of the drawing room as Amber reached it. She had only a single enervating glimpse of his startlingly handsome dark features before he hauled her into his arms, clamped her to his big, powerful frame and crushed her startled mouth beneath his with a groan of uninhibited hunger.

That passionate onslaught knocked her sideways. The taste of him after a three-day-long fast was too much altogether for her self-discipline. Every prepared speech just went out of her head and she clung to him to stay upright on knees that had turned weak. As he sent his tongue delving between her readily parted lips to search out the moist, tender interior in explicit imitation of a much more intimate invasion, Amber's temperature rocketed into outer space. Her whole body went into sensory overload in reaction, her breasts pushing against her bra, straining peaks pinching into taut, erect buds, a stirring desperate ache making her clench her trembling thighs together.

'It's a torment to stop and breathe, *cara*,' Rocco

growled against her reddened mouth, gazing down at her with smouldering golden eyes. 'I just want to jump you like an animal. Three days can feel like half a lifetime, especially when I wasn't *sure* until the very last minute that you would come here.'

'Weren't you?' Blinking rapidly, Amber studied her clinging hands, which were pinned to his shoulders, and dragged them from him in an abrupt guilty motion, face burning.

'I would've driven down to fetch you if you had backed out on me. In any case, I ought to meet your sister and her husband,' Rocco stated without hesitation.

Amber stiffened and dropped her head at that unwelcome announcement. Why on earth did she have this terrible fear of Rocco meeting Opal? And then the answer she had long avoided out of her own reluctance to face it came to her. Opal would set out to charm and enchant and hog centre stage because Opal always did that with men. Neville's adoration alone wasn't enough to satisfy her sibling's ego.

'And right now,' Rocco continued as she focused on him again, 'there is nothing I want to do more than carry you upstairs and make mad, passionate love to you *but—*'

'Rocco…' Amber was back on track again and striving to muster the words for her big announcement, and then she just blundered on into it before she lost any more momentum. 'When you ditched me, eighteen months back, I was *pregnant*!'

His black luxuriant lashes semi-screened his intent dark gaze, but his bone-structure had clenched hard. He stared at her with riveted attention. 'You can't have been—'

'I was actually two months pregnant by then, but I'm afraid I had no idea. I was losing weight, I wasn't eating properly or even sleeping enough, and my cycle had never been that regular. When we were still together, it didn't even occur to me that I might be pregnant because I never had the time to stop and think and worry,' Amber said in a driven rush. 'My life then was just one mad whirl.'

Rocco had been listening to her with an intensity as great as the stunned light growing in his dark as midnight gaze. 'Pregnant…'

It seemed to her that he could hardly bring himself to speak that word out loud and she could see for herself how appalled he was.

'But you were taking the contraceptive pill,' he continued hoarsely.

'I had only been taking it for a couple of weeks,' Amber reminded him uncomfortably. 'And if you cast your mind back—'

'I don't *need* to have my mind cast back,' Rocco interposed tautly, pacing over to the window to stare out at the street lights glowing behind the belt of

trees surrounding the house, his wide back and powerful shoulders taut with strain beneath his tailored
dove-grey suit jacket. 'You warned me that the doctor had said you needed to take extra precautions. It
was the middle of the night and I had nothing left to
use and *I* said that it wasn't that easy to get pregnant.'

Amber had certainly not expected such perfect recall of events.

'Famous last words,' Rocco conceded in a dark,
roughened undertone. 'Famous *stupid* last words.
Even as I spoke them I was wincing for myself, but
I couldn't resist temptation long enough to do what
I should have done. It was always like that with you,
bella mia.'

'I could have said no,' Amber found herself pointing out in all fairness. 'But I didn't. I was irresponsible too.'

'I was your first lover and I'm seven years older
and a lifetime more experienced,' Rocco countered
harshly, swinging back to face her. He had turned a
sort of ashen shade beneath his bronzed complexion
and his strong facial bones were rigid. 'But after a
few weeks had passed and you showed not the
slightest sign of concern, I assumed we'd got away
with our recklessness and I didn't think of the matter
again.'

Amber flushed. 'I thought about the risk even less than you did.'

'It's not a risk I've ever taken with any other woman,' Rocco muttered heavily, his lean, strong hands clenching into fists and then slowly unclenching again as if he was willing himself into greater calm. 'So this is what changed in you, this is why you told me I might regret you coming here…everything is falling into place. *Porca miseria*…I have been incredibly slow on the uptake. Your bitterness and your anger were there for me to see. But there I was, believing like a plaster saint that only I was entitled to such feelings.'

'Rocco…'

Rocco lifted his hands and spread them in an almost aggressive silencing motion. 'I need a drink.'

He had already worked it all out, Amber registered. And although she had not expected him to react as if he had received the good news of a lifetime, she had equally well not been prepared for him to turn pale as death and head for the drinks cabinet.

'Do you want one?'

'No…'

'Neither do I.' With a hand that was noticeably unsteady, Rocco set the glass he had withdrawn back into the gleaming cabinet and thrust the door shut again as if he was warding off temptation. He settled sombre dark eyes on her. 'I'm afraid I don't know what to say to you—'

'You're speaking pretty loudly without saying very much.' Amber thought that his shock, horror and pallor gave her a fair enough indication of his feelings on finding out that he was a father. Certainly, a woman with a young child was no candidate for a free-wheeling affair and frequent foreign travel. But then she wasn't about to have an affair with him, she reminded herself urgently.

'Shock… I think I could have better stood this happening with anyone but you—'

As that statement sank in on Amber, the seemingly ultimate rejection, her tummy gave a sick somersault. 'How can you openly say that to me? *How?*'

'How *not*? Do you think I can simply shrug off what you've told me as if it never happened? Don't you think that just like you I'm going to be remembering this for the rest of my life?' Rocco demanded, more emotional than she had ever seen him.

Her brain fogging up in her efforts to understand what he was telling her, Amber gazed blankly back at him.

'Well, maybe *not* just like you,' Rocco adjusted, meeting her questioning eyes with frowning force. 'But surely taking such a decision was deeply upsetting?'

Amber had had just about enough of trying to follow a bewildering dialogue in which Rocco appeared to have lost his ability to put across clear meaning. 'Would you please pause for a moment and just tell me in plain English what you're talking about?'

'*What?* I was trying to be tactful. I didn't want to distress you,' Rocco ground out between clenched white teeth. 'But you don't seem to be that sensitive on the subject, do you? No, scratch that. I *didn't* say it…you *didn't* hear it. I swear I am not judging you. I wasn't there to offer support. I know that. I accept that—'

Amber tilted her honey-blonde head to one side and stared at him with very wide but no longer un-comprehending eyes. 'Tell me, is the word you're dancing all around but avoiding…abortion?'

Rocco went sort of sickly grey in front of her, a sheen of perspiration on his skin. He nodded jerkily and breathed in very deep.

'Did I accidentally speak that word without real-ising it?' Amber prompted on a rising note of incre-dulity.

Rocco shook his head in negative.

'So you just *assumed* that if I fell pregnant I would *naturally* rush off for a termination, did you?'

The silence sizzled like a live electric current.

His full attention welded to her, Rocco's brows pleated. 'Didn't you?'

'Didn't I?' Amber sucked in a vast amount of

oxygen like a woman ready to enter a pitched battle with extreme aggression. 'No, I darned well didn't go off and have an abortion! You have got some *nerve* just arrogantly assuming that that's what I chose to do!'

'Right…right,' Rocco said again, evidently getting his brain back into gear but not, it had to be said, at supersonic speed. 'You didn't have an abortion…you gave birth to our baby?'

He was recovering a more natural colour and straightening his shoulders again, Amber noted. Huge relief was emanating from him in perceptible waves. Amber was utterly transfixed and fascinated. She had never been able to read Rocco as easily as she did that moment.

'For that, I am very grateful,' Rocco asserted thickly at nowhere near his usual pace and making a visible effort to shake free of his shock. 'The other conclusion…it would have haunted my conscience for ever and we might never have come to terms with it. So, obviously, you gave our child up for adoption—'

'Excuse me?' Amber's temper was on a knife edge because she was so wound up.

'The thought of that breaks my heart too…' Rocco's dark, deep drawl shook slightly as he made that emotive admission.

'Really?' Amber was back to being fascinated and paralysed to the spot again.

'But it was very brave of you to go through the pregnancy and face that alone and a situation I will simply have to learn to live with,' Rocco framed like a guy picking every word while walking on ice likely to crack under him and drown him at any minute. 'I can...I will, but it is such a terrible loss for both of us, *bella mia*.'

'Yes, I suppose it would have been...at least, it would have been for me, certainly,' Amber heard herself mumbling. 'And I'm beginning to get the message that it would have been a terrible loss for you too. *So*—'

Rocco raised and spread fluidly expressive hands in an appeal for a pause in revelation. 'No more until I have had a drink. I am all shaken up.'

Amber watched him pour a brandy with a great deal less than his usual dexterity 'So you like children.'

'I think so...I haven't met many,' Rocco said hoarsely, carefully, and passed her a drink without being asked. 'But that time I thought I might have got you pregnant, I liked the idea.'

'Oh...did you?' Amber studied his clenched profile, recognised that he was still firing on really only one cylinder, and her heart overflowed. 'That's good, Rocco. Because, for what it's worth, your idea of what I would do when I found myself unexpectedly pregnant and without support is very badly off target.'

He focused on her with grave dark eyes, his strain palpable. 'How…off target?'

'Well, I didn't go for abortion and I didn't go for adoption. Oh, and before you make yet another wild deduction, I did not abandon my baby either or have him placed in foster care,' Amber informed him gently. 'In fact, my baby—*our* baby is upstairs right now…OK?'

The balloon glass dropped right out of Rocco's hand and fell soundlessly to the carpet. But it smashed noisily when he stood on it in his sudden surging step forward.

'If that is a joke, it's a lousy one,' he breathed raggedly.

Amber folded her arms. 'Unlike you, I don't crack jokes at the most inopportune moments. Freddy's upstairs sleeping in one of your guest rooms.'

Rocco gazed at her as if she had taken flight without wings before his eyes. He was totally stunned. 'Say that again…*Freddy*?'

'Your son, Freddy…I called him after my grandfather, who was about the only role model I wanted him to follow in my own family,' she said shakily.

'Upstairs…*here*?' Rocco shot at her incredulously,

suddenly recovering his usual energy without warning. 'In my own home? I don't believe you!'

'You want to see him?'

Rocco wasn't waiting He was already striding out
into the hall. Amber followed his forceful surge up
the stairs. 'Room at the foot of the corridor... Rocco,
if you wake him up before midnight, he'll scream
blue murder. After midnight...even around two or
three in the morning, he's bouncing about his cot and
positively dying to socialise.'

'I'm not going to wake him up...OK?'

Amber insinuated herself between him and the
door which had been left ajar. She pushed it wider.
Light spilled in from the landing and, in concert with
the nightlight Amber had brought with her, it shed a
fair amount of clarity on the occupant of the cot.
There Freddy lay in his all-in-one sleeper which was
adorned with little racing car images.

Rocco mumbled something indecipherable in his
own language and peered down into the cot, lean
hands flexing and then bracing again on the side bars.
Freddy shifted in his sleep, looking incredibly an-
gelic with his dark curls and fan-shaped lashes.
Rocco's expression of sheer, unconcealed wonderment filled Amber with enormous pride, but there
was no denying that she was in a stupor of shock at
the way matters appeared to be panning out.

Like a man in a dream, Rocco was slowly sinking

down to crouch by the side of the cot so that he could get an even closer look at his sleeping son. 'The throwback gene didn't get him,' he muttered absently.

'Sorry?'

'His hair is dark. He's not going to get the life teased out of him at school as I did,' Rocco extended with pronounced satisfaction. 'He has my nose and your mouth.'

Amber nodded in silence at news that was not news to her, but which she had not expected him to pick up on quite so quickly.

'Also my brows—'

'He got your eyes too.' Amber was in a total daze. Where were the doors slamming in her face, the denials of paternity, the demands for birth certificates, DNA testing and all the other supporting evidence she had somehow expected? Well, maybe not all of that, but at least one or two elements, she conceded dizzily.

'Where was Freddy when I was stalking you in the woods?' Rocco murmured.

She explained about her sister's nanny.

'Freddy is *really* something else,' Rocco declared of his son.

'He won the beautiful baby competition at the village fête last summer,' Amber heard herself saying with pride. 'Opal was furious and couldn't hide it.

She was expecting her daughter…my niece, Chloe, to win.'

Rocco sprang fluidly upright again and cast her a veiled appraisal. 'We need to talk.'

CHAPTER NINE

Rocco only walked to the big landing above the stairs and cast open a door there.

'You've accepted Freddy's yours, haven't you?' Amber enquired nervously. 'He's a year old next week but he was born prematurely... I had an awful pregnancy.'

'How awful?'

Scanning the spacious bedroom as he switched on the lights, Amber wondered why they weren't going downstairs again and asked.

'I want to hear Freddy if he wakes up.' Rocco studied her with stunning dark golden eyes. 'Awful...you were saying?'

'Well, I wasn't exactly fighting fit to begin with,' she pointed out, edgily pacing away from him. 'I was sick morning, noon and night as well, so I lost more weight. I couldn't find another job and I couldn't afford the rent on my flat either, so I had to move into a bedsit. I didn't have blood running in my veins by that stage, I only had stress.'

She spun back. Rocco was really pale, his bone-structure rigid.

'Had enough yet?' Amber prompted.

'No...' he framed doggedly.

'Well, my blood pressure was too high and I ended up in hospital because I was threatening to miscarry. So there I was flat on my back and not allowed to do anything for weeks on end. It was like a living nightmare. No privacy, no visitors, no nothing, just me and my thoughts—'

'What about your sister?'

'If you knew Opal like I know Opal, you wouldn't have been in any desperate hurry to contact her and confront her with your messy mistakes either.' Amber sighed. 'But I finally had to call her because I needed my bedsit cleared out and she was really wonderful.'

'And I was nowhere—'

'I started hating you in that hospital bed,' Amber admitted.

'Am I allowed to ask why you didn't contact me?'

Amber surveyed him in outrage. 'After you accused me of stalking you?'

'Did you know you were pregnant at that stage?'

'No.'

Rocco just closed his eyes and swung away. 'I was a bastard. On Saturday, you said I wouldn't discuss that newspaper story and that that wasn't fair. You were right, so let's get it out of the way now and then never talk about it again.'

Unprepared for that subject to be raised, Amber

groaned. 'I went to school with the journalist who wrote that story.'

In astonishment, Rocco froze. 'You went to *school*—'

'With Dinah Fletcher, yes.' Amber explained how the other woman had contacted her. 'She said she had only recently moved to London to start a PR job—'

'A *PR* job—?'

Amber kept on talking. 'She was always great fun at school and I was delighted to hear from her. She came over with a bottle of wine. I told her about you but I never gave her a single intimate detail. It was girly gossip, nothing more—'

Rocco sank down heavily on the foot of the bed. 'She got in touch with you because she already knew that I was seeing you. She set you up,' he breathed in a raw undertone.

'Yeah and I fell for it.' Amber could feel the tears threatening because she still felt sick at the awareness that she had actually enjoyed that evening. She had had no suspicion that Dinah was a junior reporter, ambitious to make her mark, regardless of who got hurt in the process. 'A couple of days after the story appeared, she phoned and said she hoped that there were no hard feelings and that she was only doing her job. I asked her if it was also her job to tell lies about what I'd said but she just put the phone down on me.'

Rocco viewed her with haunted dark eyes and vented a distinctly hollow laugh. 'I was planning to tell you tonight that I was now big enough to take a joke—and that at least you hadn't informed the world that I was lousy in bed and you had to fake it all the time…' His deep, dark drawl faltered. 'Now I don't know what I can say.'

'Not a lot in your own defence,' Amber agreed in a flat little tone, but the most appalling desire to surge across the room and put her arms round him was tugging at her. He was badly shaken and suddenly she was no longer feeling vengeful satisfaction. Only as she saw that within herself did she appreciate that she had so badly wanted revenge. The nasty part of her had enjoyed hammering him with all the bad news.

'I was naive…I was indiscreet and probably I deserved to get dumped because I caused you so much embarrassment,' Amber conceded in a sudden rush. 'But it was the way you *did* it—'

Brilliant dark eyes shimmering, Rocco sprang upright again. 'I was on the brink of asking you to marry me. Then that sleazy article hit me in the face and I really thought you'd been taking me for a ride!'

Amber's feet had frozen to the carpet. It was her turn to go into shock.

'Nothing had ever hurt me so much and I couldn't face seeing you again. I saw no point,' Rocco admitted heavily. 'I could see no circumstances in which that story could've been conceived without your willing agreement and participation.'

Amber stared at him with shaken eyes. 'You were going to ask me to marry you?'

Rocco pushed a not quite steady hand through his bright silvery fair hair and shrugged, but it was a jerky movement that lacked his usual grace. 'I felt you'd made such a fool of me. There I was ready to ask you to be my wife... I was in the process of buying a house, I even had the engagement ring...and then *bang*! It all fell apart in my hands.'

'But couldn't you have once stopped and thought that I wouldn't have done such a thing to you?' Amber pressed helplessly, if anything even more aghast at the discovery that she had lost so much more than she had ever dreamt. Rocco had loved her, planned to marry her. Rocco would have been pleased about Freddy. Rocco would have been there for her every wretched step of the way had not that newspaper story destroyed his faith in her.

'When I'm hurt I lash out and nothing I can do or say can alter the past. You will say I didn't love you enough...I would say I loved you *so* much, I was afraid of being weak and ending up back with you again,' Rocco bit out in a roughened undertone.

'Would you?' A glimmer of silver lining appeared in the grey clouds that had been encircling Amber until he spoke those final words. 'And all those other women?' she asked on the strike-while-the-iron's-hot principle.

'Anything to take my mind off you and it didn't work. I didn't sleep with anyone else for a very long time...and that was lousy too. In fact...' Rocco hesitated and then forced himself on, dark blood rising to accentuate his carved cheekbones. 'Everything was lousy until I looked out Harris Winton's front window and saw you and felt alive again for the first time since I dumped you.'

'I just love you saying that when you couldn't *wait* to phone the man and talk me out of my job!' Amber exclaimed, and then her shoulders slumped, the stress and strain of it all suddenly closing in on her, making her realise all at once how absolutely exhausted she was. 'I'm almost asleep standing up.'

'You should be in bed.' Never in her life had she seen a guy leap so fast for an escape route, or at least she thought that until Rocco lifted her up into his arms and carted her over to the divan and settled her down on it with pronounced care and absolutely none of his usual familiarities.

'Are you staying?' she asked in a small tense voice.

'Not if you don't want me.'

Her teeth gritted. 'Is this your bed?'

Rocco nodded slowly.

'OK…you can stay so I can nag at you until I fall asleep,' she muttered.

'I can live with that.'

Filching a rarely worn nightdress from her case, she headed into the bathroom. Her head felt as if it were spinning with the number of conflicting thoughts assailing her, but one emotion dominated. She loved him. It didn't stop her wanting to kick him but she couldn't bear to leave him alone with his guilty conscience. Regret was just eating him alive and furthermore, on a purely practical side, Rocco was telling her things that torture wouldn't have extracted from him eighteen months ago. If he wanted to talk more, she didn't want to miss out on a single syllable. So he had planned to surprise her with a house and an engagement ring? Rocco and his blasted surprises! If only she had known, she would've crashed into his office in a tank and pinned him down to make him listen to her eighteen months ago.

She crept into bed, wondering if the nightie was overkill, but she knew that taking it off would be noticed. She listened to him undress.

'How do you feel about getting married on Christmas Eve?'

Amber blinked and then came up over the edge of

the duvet to stare at the male ostensibly entranced in the shape of his own shirt buttons, but so tense she was anything but fooled. Her heart hit the Big Dipper and kept on hurtling higher. Well, he had his flaws *but*…

'Christmas Eve?' Amber echoed rather croakily. 'Well, I'm not doing anything else…'

'Like I said to you before, you won't regret it.'

It sounded like a blood oath. 'What about you?'

'I get you as my wife,' Rocco murmured, smooth as silk. 'I also get part-ownership on Freddy. Those facts will then become the only things in my life I don't have to feel bad about.'

'You're just killing me with your enthusiasm.'

'How much enthusiasm am I allowed to show?'

'Major moving on to maximum,' Amber muttered, leaning heavily on the encouragement angle. 'Fireworks, Fourth of July, whatever feels right.'

'Would you have married me eighteen months ago?'

She would have left a smoke trail in her haste to get to the church. 'Possibly…'

Rocco slid into bed. She was waiting on him mentioning love; she was praying on him mentioning love.

'You were such a workaholic then that we hardly saw each other,' Rocco remarked tautly, dimming the lights but not putting them out.

'It was such a boring job too—'

Rocco took her aback by hauling her across the bed into his arms and studying her with scorching dark golden eyes of disbelief. 'You put that *boring* job ahead of me every time!'

Amber winced, shimmied confidingly into the hard heat and muscularity of his big, powerful body and whispered softly, 'But I surrendered my wheelbarrow for you, didn't I?'

He captured her animated face between long brown fingers, gazing down into dancing green eyes that had miraculously lost the dulled look of exhaustion. 'Not without argument, *cara*.'

'I had Freddy's security to consider.' She shivered against him, drowning in the sexy depths of his stunning eyes.

'Of course…' Something cool in Rocco's agreement, a dry note, tugged anxious strings deep down in her mind, but then Rocco possessed her mouth with a raw and hungry sensual force that electrified her. He took precisely ten ruthless seconds to remove the nightdress.

'Are you angry with me?' Amber whispered, sensing a tension in him that troubled her and easing back with a furrowed brow.

'With myself…*only* with myself,' Rocco swore with roughened fervour, his spectacular gaze resting with an intensity she could feel but no longer read on her anxious face.

She edged back to him, weak not only with hunger but also with a desperate need for reassurance that everything was all right. It felt so much *more* than all right to her. She was so happy she could have cried. She didn't want him to be angry with himself. But he curved an exploring hand over the straining rosy bud crowning one pouting breast and, that fast, she was sucked down into a place where thinking was more than she could manage.

It was as though the stressful day had built up an incredibly urgent need in both of them. There was a wildness in Rocco, a wildness that was gloriously thrilling and fired her every response to fresh heights. He slid down over her quivering length, pausing to make passionate love to every promising curve and hollow he encountered in his path. Before very long, all she was remotely aware of was the thunderous crash of her own heartbeat, her breath sobbing in her throat and a level of sensation which seemed to transcend earthly existence.

'I want this to be amazing...' Rocco rasped.

She was half out of her mind with an intensity of pleasure at that point, which made it impossible to tell him that amazing did not *begin* to cover the excitement of what he was making her feel. Writhing with utterly mindless and tormented delight, she moaned his name like a mantra, clutched at his hair, grabbed his shoulders and surrendered to her own abandonment while being pleasured within an inch of her life.

'Amazing…' she managed when she could speak again but only just.

'It's not over yet,' Rocco husked in a tone of promise.

And if the beginning and the middle had been totally enthralling for her, the conclusion was an even more ecstatic and long-drawn-out affair. In the aftermath she was too weak to do anything but lie in his arms. She had a dazed sense of having seen, experienced and revisited paradise more than once and she was awash with tender love and wonderment that he was finally, actually and for ever hers.

That was the inopportune moment when Rocco shifted away from her and breathed flatly like a male to whom paradise was an utterly unknown place, 'At least I know you're not faking it now…'

I'm not going to say anything, screeched the alarm-bell voice inside her shaken head. She hadn't got the energy for a row, she told herself weakly, and she curved into a comfy pillow like a hampster burrowing into a hiding place. They could row *after* they got married.

CHAPTER TEN

AMBER focused on her own reflection in the cheval dressing mirror.

It was Christmas Eve and it was her wedding day and she was wearing the most divine dress she had ever seen or ever worn. The delicate gold-and-silver-embroidered boned bodice hugged her to the waist, where the full ivory rustling skirt flared out, overlaid at the back by an elaborate train with matching embroidery. She pointed her toes to see her satin shoes adorned with tulle roses, tipped up her chin the better to allow the light catch the superb contemporary gold and diamond tiara and the elegant short veil that hung in a flirty froth from the back of her head.

But it was no use! No matter how hard Amber tried to lose herself in bridal fervour, she had to emerge again to be confronted by an awful truth: Rocco *wasn't* happy! She was wilfully marrying a man who didn't love her, but who very much wanted to be a father to their son. Her nose tickled as she fought to hold back welling tears. It had honestly not occurred to her until after she had said yes to his marriage proposal that his most likely motivation had been sheer guilt and Freddy.

It had been days since Rocco had even kissed
her—not since that very first night. The next day, she
had returned from her shopping trip for her wedding
outfit and a slight difference of opinion had resulted
in her hot-headedly transferring her possessions into
the guest room next to Freddy's. She had kind of
shot herself in the foot with that relocation: Rocco
had neither come in search of her nor betrayed the
slightest awareness of the reality that she had gone
missing from his bed. Separate bedrooms and they
weren't even married yet, she thought wretchedly.
Just when she had believed that every cloud on her
horizon had vanished, a brick-wall barrier had come
up out of nowhere and divided them. Since then
Rocco could not have made it clearer that Freddy
was his biggest source of interest.

He had spent that whole day with Freddy while
she'd been shopping. When she'd got back, Freddy
had been in his bath. Rocco had been dive-bombing
Freddy's toy boats with pretty much the same enjoy-
ment that Freddy got from loads of noisy splashes
and sound effects, but her entrance to the fun and
frolics had cast a distinct dampener on the proceed-
ings.

'Did you find a dress?' he asked with scrupulous
politeness.

'Yes…it cost a fortune. Thanks,' she said with the
semi-guilty, semi-euphoric response of a woman who

had managed to locate her dream wedding gown, her dream veil and her dream shoes, not to mention a set of lingerie that had quite taken her breath away.

'Odd how being a kept woman within marriage doesn't seem to bother you quite the way it bothered you *before* I mentioned the wedding ring,' Rocco drawled in a black-velvet purr.

Screening her shaken and hurt eyes at that cutting comment, which she was absolutely defenceless against, Amber murmured, 'Would you like me to go and mow the lawn to justify my existence?'

'You picked me up wrong, *cara*…'

Like heck, she had misunderstood! So that was why she had shifted into a guest room but doing that had made it even easier for Rocco to distance himself from her. There he was surging home every evening to spend time with Freddy, perfectly charming and polite with her, but the instant Freddy had fallen asleep, Rocco had excused himself to work. It was as if they had already been married ninety years and he had nothing left to say to her!

Amber straightened her bowed shoulders, took a last longing, lingering look at her reflection in her dream wedding gown and faced facts. Nearly all week, she had refused to let go of her fantasy of becoming Rocco's wife. Hiding her head in the sand, she had shrunk from acknowledging that Rocco was showing as much enthusiasm for matrimony as the proverbial condemned man.

She could ring him on his mobile before he arrived at the church. Better a misfired wedding than the misery of a marriage that was a mistake, she told herself. Blinking back tears, Amber stabbed out his number and waited for Rocco to answer.

'Rocco? Where are you?'

'*En route* to the church. What's wrong?'

'I want to call it off,' Amber whispered.

'Call…what off?' Rocco breathed jerkily.

Amber gulped. 'I don't think we should go through with the wedding. You've been so unhappy for days—'

'And *this* is the magic cure? I'm a bloody sight *more* unhappy now!' Rocco launched down the line at her with incredulous force. 'You've got cold feet, that's all. Now pull yourself together. We're getting married today!'

'But you don't really want to marry me—'

'Where did you get that idea? I really, really, *really* want to marry you,' Rocco murmured intensely, changing both tack and volume. 'I want to be stalked by you every day for the rest of my life—'

'But you couldn't even stalk *me* as far as one of your own guest rooms!' A sob caught at Amber's voice.

'Cards on the table time,' Rocco muttered with

fierce urgency. 'I somehow got the impression that you were only marrying me for Freddy's benefit—'

'Don't be stupid...' Amber winced and then confided in a small voice, 'Actually I was thinking the same thing about you.'

'Freddy's wonderful, but he's not so wonderful that I'd sentence myself to a lifetime with a woman I didn't want,' Rocco swore impressively.

'I also thought that maybe you were just marrying me because you felt guilty—'

'No, I think most guys run the other way if they feel *that* guilty. I can handle guilt, but I'm not at all sure I can handle not having you...'

Amber blossomed from a nervous wreck into a happy bride-to-be again. 'See you at the church—'

'You've made me really nervous now—'

'Well, you shouldn't have ignored me for so long in favour of Freddy,' Amber told him dulcetly.

Neville was waiting downstairs to accompany her. Opal had arrived with her husband early that morning to help Amber into her bridal regalia and had then gone on to the church in company with Freddy and Freddy's new nanny, a lovely friendly girl, whom Rocco had insisted on hiring to help Amber.

Amber negotiated the stairs with the housekeeper holding up her train. Her brother-in-law gave her a smiling appraisal. 'You look incredible, Amber. Rocco won't know what's hit him.'

Amber rather thought Rocco *would* know what had hit him after that emotional phone call they had shared. They were each as bad as the other, she reflected ruefully. Neither of them had shared their deepest fears over the past few days. She had been pretty tough on Rocco that first night in London. But she was really surprised that a male as confident as he was had entertained the lowering suspicion that she might only be marrying him for Freddy's benefit and for security. Somehow, she recognised, she had subconsciously assumed that Rocco *knew* she was still madly in love with him. Now she knew he *didn't* know and was amazingly subject to the same insecurities as she was. A sunny smile spread over her face at that acknowledgement.

The church was absolutely miles away, right outside London. Amber thought Rocco had picked a very inconvenient location but then she had had nothing to do with *any* of the arrangements: Rocco had assured her that he had everything organised. Feeling that he could at least have consulted her about her own wedding day, she had rigorously refused to ask questions.

The Rolls finally drew up outside a charming rural church surrounded by cars. As Amber got out her emergence and her progress into the church were minutely recorded by a busy bunch of men wielding all sorts of cameras. The press? she wondered in surprise. Then she looked down the aisle and saw Rocco waiting for her at the altar and all such minor musings evaporated. There he was, six feet four inches of devastatingly handsome masculinity, and her heart started racing. She might have generously offered him his freedom back, but she had never been so grateful to have an offer refused.

Stunning dark golden eyes scanned her, stilled and just stayed locked to her all the way down the aisle. It wasn't at all cool bridegroom behaviour, but Amber loved that poleaxed stare. He didn't have to speak: she knew he thought she looked spectacular. He reached for her hand at the altar. She was so happy that her eyes stung a little. The plain and simple words of the ceremony sounded beautiful to her. Freddy, however, let out an anguished wail at the sight of both his mother and his father disappearing out of view to sign the wedding register. Amber darted back to retrieve their anxious son from his nanny's knee and take him with them.

'You look incredibly gorgeous,' Rocco told her as he lifted Freddy from her arms to give him a consoling hug. Back where he felt he ought to be in the very centre of things, Freddy smiled.

Loads of photos were taken on the church steps and Rocco swept her off into the waiting limo as soon as he could.

Amber gave him a teasing look. 'Do you think you

could tell me now where we're having our reception?'

'Wychwood House.'

A slight frown-line indented her brow. 'I've heard that name before somewhere.'

'Let me jog your memory.' A wolfish grin was now tugging at the corners of Rocco's expressive mouth. 'When we were together last year, do you remember the way you always used to devour the property sections of the Sunday newspapers?'

A slow tide of hot pink crept up over Amber's face, but she lifted her brows in apparent surprise. 'No…'

'Married an hour and already lying to me,' Rocco reproved with vibrant amusement. 'Did you think I didn't notice that while I was deep in the business news you were enjoying a covert thrill scanning the houses for sale?'

Feeling very much as though an embarrassing secret habit had been exposed, Amber bristled defensively. 'Well, just glancing through the property pages is not a crime, is it?'

'*Just glancing?*' Rocco flung his handsome head back and laughed out loud at that understatement. 'You were in seventh heaven rustling through those pages. So when you finally went to the lengths of removing an entire page from a newspaper, I knew it was a fair bet that you'd found your dream house.'

Just then, Amber recalled ripping out that particular page while Rocco had been in the shower. A sudden, barely considered impulse after reading an interesting article about the history of a gorgeous country house that had been about to come on to the market.

'So after doing some investigation to find out which house it was, I bought it for you.'

'Honestly?' Amber was going off into shock. 'B-but I thought it was the house in London that you bought for us last year!'

'No, that was a much more recent acquisition. I bought Wychwood for you a week before we broke up.'

'But...' Amber was just transfixed with disbelief.

'I told you that I had a country estate,' Rocco reminded her gently.

Recalling the context in which that statement had been made and taken by her as a most unfunny joke on her gardening status, Amber swallowed with difficulty. By then the Rolls was already powering up an imposing winding drive that led through a long sweep of beautiful rolling parkland adorned by mature oak trees.

'Not all my surprises go wrong, tabbycat,' Rocco commented with the kind of rich self-satisfaction that she usually set out to squash flat in him.

However, as the magnificent Palladian mansion

came into view round the next bend Amber was too dumbstruck to do anything other than nod agreement in slow motion.

'Although I have to confess that this particular surprise felt like it had gone *very* wrong when I got Wychwood without you included,' Rocco confided ruefully.

In normal mode, Amber would have told him that that was the direct result of his having dumped her and that he had deserved to have had his surprise backfire on him. But the truth was she was so thunderstruck by the sheer size of the house *and* the surprise, she was feeling generous.

Rocco lifted her out of the Rolls and up into his arms. It was just as well: she honestly didn't believe her legs would have held her up. 'Rocco...?'

She collided with dark golden eyes that filled her to overflowing with joyful tenderness and what felt fearfully like adoration, so she didn't tell him she loved him, she said instead, 'I think you're totally wonderful.'

Was it her imagination or did he look a little disappointed?

'Absolutely fantastic...the most terrific husband in the world?' she added in a rush.

Evidently she finally struck the right note of appreciation because he took her mouth with hungry, plundering intensity. As excitement charged her every skin-cell, she realised just how miserably long a few days without Rocco's passion could feel.

'Incredibly sexy too,' she mumbled, coming up for air again as he carried her over the impressive threshold of Wychwood House.

A towering Christmas tree festooned with ornaments and beautiful twinkling lights took pride of place in the wonderful reception hall where a log fire burned. 'Oh, my…' she whispered, appreciation growing by the second. 'Rocco, please, please tell me we're going to spend Christmas here.'

He smiled. 'The day after Boxing Day, we set off for warmer climes.'

All the photographers then sprang out from behind the tree to take loads more pictures of them and she tried not to let her jaw drop too obviously. 'Really conscientious, aren't they?' she whispered to Rocco when they had to stop to load more film.

'I told them I didn't want a single second of this day to go unrecorded.'

Freddy was belatedly fetched out of the Rolls where he had been abandoned because he was fast asleep. Reunited with his nanny when she arrived, he was borne upstairs to complete his nap in greater comfort and Rocco and Amber were free to greet their guests. Some of them she had met when she'd been seeing Rocco the previous year. Others were strangers. And then there were the Wintons: Harris coming as close to a grin when he wished her well as he was ever likely to come, and Kaye with her gutsy smile, not one whit perturbed by any memory of having warned Amber off Rocco only a week earlier.

Neville and Opal joined them at the top table in the elegant dining room where the caterers served a magnificent meal. Amber watched for Rocco getting that glazed look men usually got around Opal, but if he was susceptible he was very good at concealing it.

'My sister's very beautiful, isn't she?' Amber was reduced to fishing for an opinion when they were walking through to the ballroom where a band was playing.

'Do I get shot if I say no…or shot if I say yes?' Rocco teased.

Amber coloured hotly at his insight into her feelings.

Rocco curved an arm round her taut shoulders in a soothing gesture. 'She's lovely and very fond of you, but I have to confess that listening to her talk to you as if you are a very small and not very bright child is extremely irritating.'

Amber paled.

'Now what have I said? You know you rarely mention your family—'

She forced a rueful laugh. 'My parents were very clever, just like Opal—'

'Research scientists. I remember you telling me that.'

'By their standards I *wasn't* very bright. I'm average but they made me feel stupid,' Amber admitted reluctantly. 'I felt I was such a disappointment to them—'

'So that's why you always pushed yourself so hard. If your parents had seen how hard you'd worked and how much you had achieved by the time I met you, they would have been hugely impressed,' Rocco swore vehemently.

'You sound like you really mean that, *but* I remember you offering me employment and behaving as if the job I had was nothing—'

'Give me a break.' Rocco laughed softly. The protective tenderness in his gaze warmed her like summer sunlight. 'All I was thinking of was being able to see more of you and you *were* wasted in the position you were in then.'

Amber stood up on tiptoe and whispered playfully, 'Go on, tell me more, tell me how bright I am—'

Rocco caught her to him with a strong arm, making her urgently aware of him and the glinting gold of his smouldering scrutiny. 'You picked me didn't you?'

'Is that really one of the brighter moves I've made?'

Rocco looked down into her animated face and murmured with ragged fervour, 'I hope so because I love you like crazy, *bella mia*.'

Amber stilled. 'Honestly?'

'Why are you looking so shocked?'

She linked her arms round his neck and sighed helplessly. 'You let me go, Rocco…you never came after me—'

A dark rise of colour had accentuated his fabulous cheekbones. 'I *did* come after you. It took me two months to get to that point. Two months of sleepless nights and hating every other woman because she wasn't you. I told myself I just wanted to confront you…which is pretty much what I told myself when I saw you with your wheelbarrow as well—'

'You *did* come after me?' Amber gasped in delight, finally willing to believe he might still truly love her. 'So why didn't you find me?'

'You'd moved out of your flat without leaving a forwarding address and I had no relatives or anyone else to contact,' Rocco ground out in frustration. 'I even got a friend to run your Social Security number through a computer search system…that's illegal, but it didn't turn up anything helpful.'

'I forgive you for everything…I love you, I love you, I love you!' Amber told him, bouncing up and down on the spot, so intense was her happiness and excitement.

'For goodness' sake, Amber…remember where you are,' Opal's voice interposed in pained and mortified reproof.

'She's in her own home and I'm enjoying this tremendously, Opal. If you'll excuse us,' Rocco murmured with a brilliant smile as he whirled his ebullient bride onto the floor to open the dancing.

At three in the morning, Amber and Rocco came downstairs with Freddy to open some Christmas presents.

Freddy was in the best of good humour. It was Christmas Day and it was also his first birthday. He was truly aware of neither occasion but was enthralled by the big tree and all the twinkly lights and the shiny ornaments. He played with the card he was given and he played with the wrapping paper, watching while his parents struggled to get the elephant rocker out of its box, and then struggled even more on the discovery that it was only part-assembled. He sat in the rocker for about one minute before crawling off it again to head for the much more exciting box he wanted to explore.

'I think the rocker just bombed,' Rocco groaned. 'He's happier with the paper and the packaging.'

'As long as he's happy, who cares?' Amber said

sunnily, entranced in watching the lights send fire glittering from the superb diamond engagement ring Rocco had slid onto her finger. 'I bet I'm the only bride for miles around who got an engagement ring *after* the wedding and it's really gorgeous!'

'Just arriving eighteen months late, tabbycat.' Rocco surveyed her with loving but amused eyes as she whooped over the matching eternity ring she had just unwrapped. 'That's for suffering all those weeks in hospital to have Freddy.'

'Well, perhaps it wasn't as bad as I made out…if I'd had you visiting, I'm sure I wouldn't have been feeling sorry for myself. Next time—'

'*Next* time? Are you kidding?' Rocco exclaimed in horror. 'Freddy's going to be an only child!'

As Freddy had crawled into the box and now couldn't get out of the box and was behaving very much as if the box were attacking him, Amber rescued him and put him back on the rocker. After that disturbing experience, the elephant's quieter charms were more appreciated.

'I'll be fine the next time,' Amber told him soothingly.

'I love Freddy, but I value your health more, *bella mia*.'

'Yes…you worship the ground I walk on,' Amber reminded him chattily as she measured the huge pile of presents still awaiting her and looked at Freddy and Rocco, especially Rocco. Rocco who was so incredibly romantic and passionate and hers now. Rocco winced. 'Did I say that?'

'And lots of other things too…you got quite carried away around midnight.' Confident as only a woman who knew she was loved could be, Amber gave him a glorious, wicked smile.

Rocco entwined his fingers round hers and hauled her back to him with possessive hands. 'You're a witch and I adore you—'

'I adore you too…so I didn't buy you the book on how to pleasure a woman in two hundred ways in case you thought I was dropping hints,' she said teasingly. 'I mean, I might die of exhaustion if I got any more pleasure. So I got you this instead. Merry Christmas, Rocco.'

Rocco unwrapped his miniature gold wheelbarrow and dealt her a vibrant grin of appreciation, which just turned her heart over. 'I'll keep it on my desk, *cara.*'

Freddy was slumped asleep over the elephant's head.

'You and Freddy are the best Christmas presents I have ever had,' Rocco confided with touching sincerity as he cradled his gently snoring son.

'Well, I did even better,' Amber pointed out, resting back beneath his other arm, blissfully content as she stared into the glowing embers of the fire. 'I got you, a fantastic wedding and this is going to be the most wonderful Christmas because it's our first together—'

Rocco urged her round to him and claimed her mouth in a sweet, delicious kiss that left her melting into his hard, muscular frame. 'Magical,' he groaned hungrily, and only Freddy's snuffly little complaint about being squashed got them back upstairs again.

A SPANISH CHRISTMAS
Penny Jordan

Dear Reader,

I have always been fascinated by my fellow human beings and the way they live. And this fascination becomes even stronger when it involves people from another country and culture. It was a chance remark by a friend of mine concerning a certain New Year's Eve custom in her home city of Madrid in Spain that led to me writing this particular story.

I don't want to give away here and now just what the custom is, but I'm sure when you come to it in the story you will recognize it and understand just why, as a lover of love and romantic gestures, I had to use it.

Spain itself has always seemed to me to be a very romantic country—the first romance books I myself read often had a Spanish hero, and I hope that today you will find my particular "Spanish hero" as compelling as I did those in the books I read over three decades ago.

Happy reading.

Penny Jordan

CHAPTER ONE

'OH, THIS must be our car.'

Carefully parking her patient's wheelchair amongst the throng of people besieging the all too few taxis pulling up to collect the departing airport passengers, Meg hurried towards the sleek chauffeur-driven limousine which was just in sight and which, after the long wait they had had, just *had* to be the hire car they had pre-booked in London before leaving for Seville.

Her patient, Elena Salvadores, was an elderly sixty-something and still very frail following the accident whilst she had been on holiday in London, which had resulted in the operation to her knee. This in turn had necessitated her hiring a private Spanish-speaking nurse from the agency for which Meg worked, to accompany her back to Seville and to remain there with her until after the Christmas holiday. Meg had taken to the Señora as soon as they had met and the Señora on her part had been almost embarrassingly grateful to Meg for the care she had given her.

Perhaps it was because of her own accident that she was so easily able to empathise with the anxiety and pain suffered by her patient, Meg acknowledged. As a busy young theatre sister who loved her job, the last thing she had been prepared for was to be attacked late at night in Casualty by a knife-wielding drunk who had inflicted such serious injuries on her unprotected hand and arm that they would never again be strong enough for theatre work.

The pain of losing her career as well as the complications and physical suffering her injuries had caused might have daunted someone less strongly grounded than Meg, even embittered them, but Meg had firmly told herself and everyone else who asked that working for an agency as a private nurse was helping her to become multi-functional. It had been the fact that she was fluent in Spanish which had gained her her present job.

When she had been growing up her father had managed an exclusive marina in Spain and she had spent her holidays there with her parents, quickly learning the language. Her parents were retired now and living in Portugal, where her father could indulge his twin passions of sailing and golf.

The limousine had pulled into the kerb now, a huge highly polished black beast of a car which was attracting the discreetly awed attention of the crowd on the pavement—and no wonder. Personally Meg would have thought that her request for a car suitable to take a wheelchair-bound patient and her luggage might have resulted in something rather more modest, but as she already knew Elena Salvadores was an extremely wealthy woman.

They had flown out from Heathrow first class, and the Señora had insisted that there was no way she wanted to have Meg wearing a uniform, which was why now, as she hurried to speak to the driver of their car, she was wearing a pair of warm trousers along with a toning butter-soft leather jacket. The trousers, with their fine blending of wool and cashmere, like the leather jacket, had been a birthday present from her parents.

She had reached the car now, and was just about to lean forward to speak to the driver when— 'Excuse me!'

A note of icy warning entered Meg's voice as she drew herself up to her full height of almost but not quite five feet four inches—six if you included the heels of her boots—and confronted the arrogantly imperious Spaniard who had appeared out of nowhere to try to lay claim to 'their' car.

Tall, he dwarfed *her*, Meg recognised, and had to be a good two inches over six foot, and broad-shouldered—he was practically blocking out what little winter light there was. Everything about him commanded—*demanded*—that Meg give way to him, to his maleness, his *arrogance*—and that she allowed him to take 'their' hire car.

Thoroughly infuriated by him, as well as concerned for her patient, who she had sensed had not enjoyed the flight and who was now looking tired and unwell, she opened her mouth to tell him what she thought of his bad manners. But before she could say a word the Spaniard was addressing *her*.

'*Madre de Dios*,' he stormed. 'Are you a *thief*, that you *dare* to try to steal *my* car?'

His car?

Pink-faced with anger and disbelief, Meg turned to face him. His eyes were the colour of obsidian and as cold as ice, his hair thick and black, and as for his face! Meg could all too easily imagine that hawkish, far too good-looking profile impressing *some* women, but fortunately *she* was not one of them, she congratulated herself as she exclaimed in righteous indignation, '*Me* steal *your* car. *I* was here *first*.'

It was ridiculous, Meg knew. She was not normally given to making impulsive judgements about people on first sight, but there was just something about this particular man that infuriated and antagonised her. Her heart was jumping with emotion, thudding almost painfully against her chest wall—not because he was too good-looking but simply because he was too arrogant, she assured herself.

'First?' He stopped her, scanning her smooth pale skin and wide-spaced turquoise-blue eyes, speaking to her in English, Meg suddenly realised, as she had done to him, forgetting in the heat of the moment just where she was.

Was it her imagination or was he staring rather longer than necessary at the silky length of her dark red hair? It obviously *was* her imagination, Meg acknowledged ruefully, when he began smoothly, 'For your information—'

He broke off suddenly as Meg gave a soft exclamation of concern and, ignoring him, hurried towards her patient, who she could see was looking tired and stressed. But as she did so the arrogant Spaniard who was so determined to hijack their transport stared after her, suddenly exclaiming, to Meg's shock, 'Tia Elena! What on earth...?' at the same time striding past Meg to reach her patient ahead of her.

'Christian,' Elena Salvadores was exclaiming in pleasure as he reached her. 'What a surprise. What are you doing here?'

'I'm just on my way home from a business trip to South America,' Meg heard him answering. 'But what on earth has happened to you?'

'I had an accident in London,' Meg's patient was explaining in Spanish. 'Fortunately nothing too serious, and I am on the mend now, but they would not allow me to return on my own, and since my leg still has to be dressed and bandaged Meg here has accompanied me. She is a trained nurse,' she added, giving Meg a fond smile. 'But I'm afraid she will find it very dull here in Seville with only me for company, especially since it will be Christmas.'

She gave a small sigh.

'I miss my Esteban so much, even though it is over ten years now since he died. Your mother and I were both widowed in the same year, but she has the good fortune to have her children.'

'I'm afraid she does not always consider us to be ''good'' fortune.'

The rueful smile that illuminated his whole face as he spoke did decidedly dangerous and unwanted things to Meg's heartbeat, things she had no wish to so much as acknowledge, never mind go to the risky lengths of trying to analyse.

So he was good-looking, *very* good-looking. So what? Without realising she was doing so, Meg gave a small toss of her burnished hair, unwittingly causing the object of her thoughts to break off his conversation to look at her. And Meg, although she was too modest to know it herself, was very well worth looking at from a male point of view.

Small, slender, but with a deliciously curvaceous female shape. The harmonious toning of her hair and skin colouring with her caramel clothes allied to the unexpected brilliance of her spectacular eyes set in a soft heart-shaped face, guaranteed to bring out the hunter in even the mildest of men.

Unable to break the contact his gaze was deliberately locking her into, Meg felt her heart start to race whilst tiny flutters of anger-edged nervousness infiltrated her body. It was as though he was silently, subtly taunting her, telling her that of the two of them he had the more power, the power over her as a female, the power to do whatever he wished with her, *to* her.

Abruptly he looked away, breaking the spell, addressing her patient for all the world as though that oh, so male look of domination and power he had just given her had never existed.

'You look tired, Tia Elena,' he said softly, his voice warm with sympathy and concern. 'You shouldn't be waiting out here in the cold like this. Your nurse should—'

Once again he was looking at her, this time with very evident disapproval, Meg recognised wrathfully.

'It isn't Meg's fault,' Elena Salvadores insisted, immediately coming to Meg's rescue. 'We ordered a hire car but so far it hasn't arrived.'

'Allow *me* to give you a lift,' came the swift and firm response, followed by a very sardonic look in Meg's direction before Christian added, 'I have *my* car here.'

Unable to help herself, Meg glared at him. A quick fresh look at the waiting limousine had conveyed to her what she should have recognised much sooner: namely that it was far too expensive and exclusive a vehicle to be anything other than privately owned. However, there was no way she was going to acknowledge her error to *him*! Instead she pointed out grandly, 'This is a public taxi rank, and private cars are not allowed.'

Before she could finish what she was saying Elena was informing her gently, 'Christian has special status, Meg. His diplomatic duties mean that he is allowed to park wherever he wishes.'

His *diplomatic* duties? Meg was struggling not to betray her chagrin, refusing to be impressed even when her patient introduced them formally. So the Spaniard was titled, a member of the Spanish nobility. Don Christian Felipe Martinez, el Duque de Perez!—and her patient's godson. So what?

His suave, 'You may call me Christian,' made Meg's eyes shoot sparks of brilliant angry fire, but somehow she managed to hold her tongue, busying herself instead with ensuring that the chauffeur who was helping her patient did not inadvertently add to Elena's discomfort in any way.

But it wasn't the chauffeur, it was Christian himself who took charge and helped Elena into the car, making sure she was comfortably settled inside it—whilst Meg, who had been about to do exactly that herself, was forced to stand back and look on in helpless indignation. How dared he both pre-empt her and at the same time manage to subtly imply that he

didn't trust her ability to take proper care of her patient?

Stiff-backed with growing hostility towards him,
Meg allowed the chauffeur to usher her into the car,
which had to be the most luxurious she had ever been
in—a huge Mercedes with black leather upholstery,
and a far cry from her own little compact at home.

For the first ten minutes of their journey Meg listened in silence whilst her patient talked to Christian
about his family and various shared friends, but when
Elena started to tell him she was concerned that Meg
would be lonely and bored in Seville, with only her
for company, Meg started to frown.

However, before she could interrupt to remind
Elena that the purpose of her being in Seville was
for her to nurse Elena, she heard Christian telling the
older woman very much the same thing, his voice
becoming crisp and rather cool as he looked pointedly at Meg and then away again.

Infuriated by the fact that he dared to disapprove
of *her*, Meg did some interrupting of her own, telling
him pointedly in Spanish that she could both speak
and understand his language.

Instead of recognising that she had been warning
him against discussing her, Christian reacted to her
interruption by telling her sharply, 'I am relieved to
hear it, since Tia Elena does not speak English very
well. You should really have told us about your ac-

cident.' He turned away from Meg to gently scold Elena. 'I could have come to London myself to bring you home. My mother will be very cross that you did not let us know.'

'I didn't want to bother any of you,' Elena was admitting. 'I know how busy you are, Christian. Your mother told me the last time we met that this charitable work you have taken on for our government is taking more and more of your time.'

Christian was shrugging. 'As my late uncle's representative, it is my duty to ensure that the orphanage he founded in Buenos Aires is properly administered and if, whilst I am there, I can represent the views of our country on certain matters, then it is also my duty to do that as well.'

Unable to stop herself, Meg murmured sardonically under her breath, *'Noblesse oblige.'*

But to her dismay she recognised that Christian had overheard her. 'You think it a matter for mockery that a person should acknowledge a sense of obligation and duty?' he asked her coldly. 'You surprise me, given your choice of career—but then, perhaps I should not be surprised since you obviously choose to sell your services to the highest bidder rather than work in the public services, as so many other nurses do.'

The arrogance and sheer unfairness of his comment took Meg's breath away, but she knew that her hot face and angry eyes betrayed her feelings, even if his comment had been said too softly to reach Elena's ears. Let him think what he liked, Meg decided furiously. There was no way she had any need to justify herself to him, or to explain just why she could only now work as a private nurse.

At her side Elena was saying wistfully, 'I envy your mother so much, Christian. It has always been a deep sadness to me that I never had children, and I especially feel the lack of them at times such as Christmas. You will all be going to the *castillo*, of course. Christian owns a most beautiful estate,' she informed Meg. 'It was given to his family by King Felipe in the sixteenth century, but Christian can trace his ancestry right back to the Moors.'

'I am sure your nurse does not wish to be bored with the history of my family,' Christian chided Elena, though the smile he gave her and the warmth in his voice robbed his words of any unkindness and instead made Meg feel as though somehow she was the one who was not worthy to receive such information. But Elena was totally oblivious to the underlying note of antipathy and sarcasm in his voice, and was already assuring him innocently, 'Oh, no, Christian, you are wrong. Meg is very much interested in our history and culture, and very knowledgeable about them,' she added, giving Meg an approving smile before continuing fretfully, 'I would have liked to have shown her something of our city whilst she is here, but of course with my knee the way it is that is out of the question.' Her face brightened as she suddenly exclaimed, 'But you are an expert on our local heritage, Christian. Perhaps you—?'

'No.'

Meg's face reddened when both Elena and Christian turned to look at her as she voiced her sharp denial.

'I...I'm here to work,' she pointed out, trying to alleviate the emotional intensity of her exclamation as she saw the bewilderment in Elena's eyes.

Quite what she might see in Christian's eyes if she could bring herself to meet them, she suspected she already knew. It was so unlike her to let a man get so immediately and so dangerously under her skin, but then Christian was no ordinary man. Meg's heart gave a small frantic jump as she recognised the dangerous allure of her thoughts.

Sexy, high-born Spanish aristocrats were not her type, she reminded herself firmly. She liked her men good-humoured, tolerant, compassionate and down to earth, not the embodiment of a female sexual fantasy.

'Ah, here we are.'

Meg jumped guiltily as she realised how little attention she had been paying to her patient whilst she wrestled with her rebellious thoughts. The limousine was pulling up outside an impressive building which Elena had already explained to her had been a grandee's private home prior to its conversion into several large apartments.

'Elena, if you will give me your keys, my chauffeur will go ahead and open the doors for us whilst I escort you inside.'

As Christian handed the keys the older woman gave him over to his chauffeur, he began to frown, his voice taking on its now familiar harshness as he addressed Meg.

'Elena's apartment is on the top floor. There is, of course, a lift, but it is not large. I trust you have checked that it will accommodate her wheelchair.'

'Of course.' Meg was pleased to be able to answer him with crisp efficiency. 'I took the precaution of telephoning the concierge before we left London, to give him the precise measurements of the chair, and he assured me that the lift could accommodate it.'

'I trust you also took the precaution of ensuring that it would accommodate you as well,' was his dulcet response. 'Otherwise my poor godmother will be travelling up and down in the lift, waiting for you to either ascend or descend the stairs.'

Meg took a deep breath, but for once her training deserted her. 'I am not exactly unfamiliar with the necessity of travelling in a lift with my patient, Don

Christian,' she informed him with formal hauteur. 'As a theatre sister I once worked in a hospital which had its operating rooms several floors below its wards; I am used not merely to standing in a lift with a patient but also to ensuring that his or her various drips and drains are not dislodged.'

'A theatre sister?'

She could see him starting to frown, but Meg was not interested in whatever it was he was going to say. She had her patient to attend to.

As she had guessed, it was a far more painful process for Elena to get out of the car than it had been for her to get in, and Meg was particularly careful to make the transition to her waiting wheelchair as easy as she could for her.

'It's all right,' she quietly reassured her at one point as the older woman winced and cried out in pain. 'Your leg will have stiffened up during the flight and that's why it's hurting so much now. Once we've got you in your apartment, I'll massage it for you.'

Instinctively Meg touched her own hand. The damaged tendons still caused her a good deal of pain at times, although she was far too professional to say so whilst she was working. She had forgotten, though, just how much those steely obsidian eyes saw, and suddenly Christian was at her side demanding, 'Is something wrong?'

'No, nothing,' Meg fibbed, and to prove it she reached into the boot of the car to remove her medical bag. To her consternation, as she did so it slid from her grasp when her stiff tendons refused to react as quickly as she had wanted.

Christian caught the bag before it reached the ground but it was Elena's sharp exclamation of concern that caused her cheeks to redden as much as her own clumsiness as her patient sympathised,

'Oh dear, is it your hand?' and then, before Meg could say anything, she was telling Christian emotionally, 'Poor Meg has been so brave, Christian. She was attacked in the hospital where she worked by a man with a knife, when she was trying to protect his girlfriend...'

'I was just doing my job,' Meg started to protest. The look Christian was giving her was making her heart bump heavily along the bottom of her ribcage and she fought to regulate her betrayingly unsteady breathing.

'Leave the luggage. I shall see to it,' she heard Christian instructing her sharply as she returned to the boot of the car whilst he manoeuvred the wheelchair.

'I can manage,' Meg insisted, and then gave a gasp of shock as he left Elena to stride towards her, lean brown fingers manacling her wrist as he lifted her hand away from the case she had been reaching for.

Turning it over, he studied her palm, his eyebrows snapping together as his gaze absorbed the extent of her scars. But the shock she had felt when she had seen him bearing down on her was nothing compared to what she felt now as his thumb brushed slowly along the length of the scar that disfigured her wrist.

Totally unable to bring herself to meet his eyes, and equally unwilling to suffer the humiliation of an undignified struggle to remove her wrist from his imprisoning grip, she fixed her gaze straight ahead which, unfortunately, meant she was staring at the shirt-covered expanse of a male chest which she could see all too plainly possessed the kind of muscular physique normally only found on a sportsman. Wretched man. Surely there must be *something* about him which she, as a woman, could disdain?

'He must have virtually severed your wrist.'

The quiet words, uttered in a tone of voice that seemed to rumble towards her from the depths of the chest she had just been unwillingly studying, shocked her into lifting her unguarded gaze to meet his.

'No... Well, not... I was lucky in that our hospital had the country's top microsurgical team. They—the surgeon...' She stopped and bit her lip, remembering how shocked she had been when Michael Lord had told her compassionately that he had done everything that he, as a surgeon, could do for her and that the

degree of movement she would recover was down to
her own determination and, as he had put it, 'the
goodwill of the angels'.

She had been lucky, very lucky—due in the main,
she was convinced, to his skilled repair work. So far
as most things went, she was perfectly able to operate
normally, but theatre work was not 'most' things, and
the risk that she might be too slow to hand an in-
strument over to a surgeon or, even worse, might not
be able to react at all to instructions, had closed the
door on theatre work to her for ever.

'Oh, darling, I'm so very, very sorry,' her mother
had tried to comfort her, adding, 'Look, why don't
you come and stay with Daddy and me for a while?'

But Meg had refused, signing on instead with the
private nursing agency for whom she now worked.

She felt Christian's grip on her wrist slacken and
immediately she bent back towards the boot of the
car, stubbornly determined to remove her *own* luggage. But Christian moved in the same direction at
the same time, so that their heads were close together
and he was still holding her wrist.

A sensation of intense awareness and sensitivity to
his proximity filled her, making it impossible for her
to breathe or think properly. Every protective urge
she possessed screamed at her to move away from
him, but something deeper, stronger and far more
elemental, was refusing to let her do so.

Christian was looking at her mouth and she…she was letting him, feeling her lips moisten and part, feeling too her eyes growing heavy and her breathing becoming unsteady.

What was the *matter* with her? Just because he was totally and undeniably male…just because…just because her head felt dizzy and her legs felt weak and her heart was pounding—*bounding* helplessly from one beat to another like a newborn foal finding its legs—that didn't mean…that didn't…

'Christian, is Meg all right?'

Elena's voice seemed to reach her from a long way away. Like a drowning man, Meg clung to it, forcing herself to remember where she was and why.

If this was a film, right now its audience would be in no doubt at all about what would happen next. But it *wasn't* a film, she reminded herself fiercely as she realised that Christian had released her wrist and she was free to escape from him and the dangerous sorcery of the spell his proximity had woven around her.

Get a grip, for goodness' sake, she berated herself mentally as she hurried towards Elena's wheelchair. It was totally unlike her to react like this and she couldn't understand why she was behaving so idiotically.

CHAPTER TWO

'THERE, how do you feel now?'

'Much better.' Elena thanked Meg gratefully as she finished massaging her patient and smiled at her.

It was less than two hours since their arrival at the apartment, which had proved to be even more luxurious and elegant than Meg had expected.

The bedroom she had been shown to by Elena's elderly housekeeper was more of a small suite than a mere room, complete with its own luxurious marble bathroom and a small sitting room as well, but Meg had been more concerned about her patient than the luxury of her new surroundings, insisting on making Elena comfortable before settling herself in.

The telephone beside the ornately luxurious bed rang just as Meg was slipping the covers back over Elena, and discreetly she left the room to allow Elena to speak to her caller in privacy whilst she made her way back to her suite.

She was, of course, fully familiar with the Spanish custom of eating late at night, but hunger pangs were now beginning to gnaw faintly at her tummy. It seemed a long time since she had eaten the delicious meal they had been served in the First Class cabin on the plane.

Presumably she would eat her meals in the kitchen with Elena's housekeeper, Anna, whilst Elena herself either dined alone or with friends—or her godson… Meg's heart gave a betraying thump. But, no, he would not be visiting whilst she was here, Meg reassured herself. Hadn't Elena herself mentioned the fact that he and his family would be spending Christmas at his family estate in the country?

His family… Was he married? Her heart gave another sharp thump. Meg guessed that he must be in his early thirties and, although he had made no mention of a wife, a man with a background like his would surely want to have a son to continue the family line.

The intercom telephone on the table next to Meg rang, making her jump. When she answered it, she heard Elena's voice excitedly asking her to come to her room.

When Meg got there, her patient was sitting up in bed, looking pink-cheeked and happy.

'My telephone call was from Luisa, Christian's mother. She has invited us both to spend the Christmas holiday with them. Christian must have told her how concerned I was that you would find it dull here on your own, with just me for company.

Oh, I am so pleased. You will love Christian's family, I promise you.'

Valiantly, Meg tried not to show her own consternation. The mere thought of *seeing* Christian again, never mind spending time in his home, was doing the most alarming things to her nervous system. But Meg knew there was no way she could refuse to go. Elena's wound still needed careful cleaning and bandaging, and her surgeon had been insistent that she had to have proper nursing care for at least three weeks after her operation.

Meg had always taken her professional responsibility very seriously and there was no way she was going to stop doing so now, just because of a mere man.

A *mere* man? *Christian?* A delicate hint of pink colour tinged her skin as certain unassailable facts forced themselves in front of her.

Christian bore just about as much resemblance to being a 'mere' male as a medical student did to a senior consultant, which was to say that when it came to quantifying 'maleness' Christian was in a class of his own.

What was *she* doing, boosting the wretched man's already far too high opinion of himself with her foolishly treacherous thoughts?

Anyone would think that she was in danger of finding him attractive—which she most certainly did not, she assured herself vigorously, as Elena started to plan what she was going to need to pack for their visit, suddenly becoming far more animated and happy than Meg had previously seen her.

'This is all Christian's doing. He really is the most thoughtful person. But then all the men in his family have been known for their benevolence to others. Christian's uncle, the one he mentioned, was so affected by the plight of the street children in Buenos Aires that he set up and financed a special home for them and left money in his will for its continued maintenance. Christian's family have had business links with South America for many generations, and now our government has requested his help when it comes to any kind of delicate negotiations.'

It was obvious to Meg just how much Elena admired her godson and how much she was looking forward to spending Christmas with his family. No doubt he was used to women doting on him. Well, *she* certainly wasn't going to become one of his besotted admirers!

'So, if you will wait here with the luggage, Meg, I shall take Tia Elena down to the car in her wheelchair and see her safely installed in it, whilst I send Esteban up to collect the luggage.'

'Oh, but *you* will make sure that the apartment is

securely locked up, won't you, Christian.' Elena in-
tervened anxiously.

'Of course,' he told her.

Gritting her teeth, her hackles already rising in an-
tagonistic response to the lordly mantle of control
Christian had assumed since his arrival at the apartment ten minutes earlier, Meg tried not to notice how
sexually male he looked wearing a pair of casual
snug-fitting jeans and a soft cotton shirt, the top couple of buttons of which were unfastened.

Meg was forced to swallow hard against the taut
feeling of female awareness threatening to sabotage
her determination not to find him in the least bit attractive.

So why on earth was her tummy fluttering, just
because as he'd turned towards her patient she had
glimpsed the disturbingly male darkness of his body
hair where his shirt lay open? And, even more dis-
concertingly, why was she having to control that up-
surge of female wantonness that said so clearly and
mortifyingly that it wanted to see more?

Naked male bodies were nothing new to her, as a
nurse, so why should the thought of *this* particular
male body turn her into a quivering, dithering mass
of desire?

Meg had no idea. She was just relieved that
Christian was finally wheeling Elena out of the apart-

ment, leaving her to await the arrival of his chauffeur, Esteban.

The amount of luggage Elena deemed it necessary to take with her for a fortnight's stay with friends for what she had told Meg would be a 'family Christmas' had reduced Meg to awed silence as she had watched Anna pack, reverently wrapping everything in layer after layer of tissue paper.

The addition of a large, old-fashioned leather jewellery case had been the final confirmation, if Meg had needed one, that the rich were indeed different.

Everything *she* needed for their two-week stay had taken less than half an hour to repack into her one single case and, indeed, she had spent longer packing her medical bag—not just with everything that she felt Elena would need, but with the basic medical essentials without which she never travelled.

Esteban arrived and then departed with Elena's cases, whilst Meg waited in trepidation for Christian to return to release her to go down to the car with her own luggage, whilst he made sure the apartment was securely locked.

The apartment door opened and Christian strode in, giving Meg an inimical, sweeping glance.

'You have everything?' he asked her, the tone he used to her far more curt and abrasive than the soft affectionate one he used to his godmother, Meg noticed.

Simply nodding her head tersely, she bent to pick up her two cases, intending to make her way to the lift and then down to the waiting car, leaving him to lock the flat on his own.

She was wearing the clothes she had travelled to Spain in, but today she was carrying her jacket over her arm, deeming the soft cashmere sweater she was wearing warm enough for the car journey. Just to be on the safe side, she had also swathed a toning honey-coloured pashmina around herself.

As she leaned forward to pick up her cases, Christian stopped her, telling her, 'I'll carry those.'

It was on the tip of Meg's tongue to remind him sharply that she was not a sixty-year-old invalid like his godmother, and was more than capable of carrying her own bags, but the truth was that her injured wrist and hand were feeling stiff and painful. She knew that she would have to carry each of her bags out into the hallway individually, and that her medical bag was particularly heavy.

Even so, her eyes smouldered with the feelings caution told her it would be unwise to voice and, for a moment, as their glances clashed, Meg could see in Christian's an answering smoulder daring her to defy him, before it was banished to be replaced by a look of coolly thoughtful consideration.

In silence, he placed her bags outside the apartment door in the elegant hallway, then told her,

'We'll go down in the lift together, if you will just wait until I have secured the apartment.'

Only the fact that she was wary of trying to carry her medical bag prevented Meg from going down to the car on her own. Not that he kept her waiting long… She had barely had time to do more than chide herself for the way she was reacting to him when he was locking the outer door to the apartment and striding past her to summon the lift.

As Meg had already discovered for herself, the lift to the apartments was not exactly generously proportioned. It held Elena's wheelchair with Elena in it and herself—just—which meant that it allowed two fully grown adults, especially if one of them was over six foot in height and with the breadth of shoulder surely more appropriate for a top-scoring polo player than a businessman, just about enough room, provided they did not mind sharing their own personal 'space'.

Even with her two cases in the lift between them, Meg still discovered that her body felt that Christian was standing very intimately close. But that was still no excuse for it to start reacting as though it liked that proximity rather than objected to it.

Determinedly, Meg stared forward, her soft lips clamped tightly closed. There was no way she was going to allow Christian to guess how idiotically her body was behaving. But suddenly the lift jolted to a halt, throwing Meg off balance and into Christian and, of course, it was only natural that he should reach out to steady her. Field her was probably a more appropriate term, Meg recognised, the breath whooshing out of her lungs as she collided with the impressive hardness of his chest.

The lift had stopped and they did not appear to have reached the ground floor, but Meg was only aware of *that* fact with the periphery of her consciousness. Something far, far more important was occupying virtually all her attention.

Pressed up against Christian's body, held there not just by the weight of his arm but also by the dangerous intensity of her own reactions to him, Meg could feel herself starting to tremble, a fine quivering female response to Christian's maleness rocketing through her.

'Don't be afraid. This lift *is* sometimes temperamental,' she heard Christian murmuring, his voice, somewhere close to her temple, a deep rumbling sound she could feel as his chest vibrated against her own.

As she lifted her head to deny that she was afraid the lift moved sharply, causing her to squeak in protest instead and instinctively steady herself again against its unexpected lurch by clinging to the front of Christian's shirt. Now that she had lifted her head she could see his eyes... and his mouth... and, whilst the lift might have stilled, her heart most certainly had not followed suit.

Here it was, the knowledge she had been fighting to reject ever since she had first seen him. Despite everything that her common sense and her instinct for self-protection had told her, right now, more than anything else, what she wanted was...

As though he had somehow tuned into her feelings, Christian started to lower his head, one hand braced against the lift wall behind her and the other resting on her waist so that she felt totally, sensually enclosed by him, totally sensually in thrall—not just to him but to what she herself was feeling.

She could see his knowledge of her feelings in the fiercely male glitter of his eyes, feel it in the aura of power and sexuality that seemed to emanate from him and engulf her.

Helplessly she gave in to it, swaying against him, her head tipping back against the arm he had lifted from her waist to hold her. The kiss that burned a trail of life-defining sexuality against her lips was so far outside her known experience that her eyes opened briefly in betraying bemusement, hot pools of sensuality, their gaze enmeshing with the heart-rockingly exciting male danger of his.

As though he had somehow whispered a soft command to them, her lips parted, her eyes closed, and her body softened in wanton pleasure, her tongue-tip delicately exploring the alien shape of his mouth. A small soft sound of female approval purred in her throat as the sexily hard shape of his lips responded to the delicate probe of her tongue, opening, daring her to explore further…deeper…

It took the sudden sharp jerk of the lift as it started to move to bring her back to reality. Face pink with mortification, she pulled agitatedly back from Christian.

What on earth was she doing? What on earth was *he* doing—or could she guess?

Meg had sensed his arrogant superiority from the moment they had met and she guessed that this was his way of underlining it, reinforcing it, of asserting his sensuality and tormenting her with his knowledge of just how vulnerable she was to him.

As the lift continued on its journey towards the ground, Meg tried to convince herself that the shakiness she was experiencing and the breathlessness she was suffering were the result of being momentarily trapped in the lift, rather than the effect of being so intimately trapped in her own sensual response to Christian's kiss.

The lift came to a halt; the doors opened. Quickly, Meg hurried out, not daring to allow herself to look at Christian. Anger was beginning to take the place of her original shock and confusion. Anger not just against Christian but against herself as well. No doubt his ego had been extremely pleased by her intense response, but she was in Spain to work, not to fall for some arrogant aristocrat. He was simply amusing himself. Esteban was standing beside Christian's car, holding the front passenger door open for her.

As she hesitated, the Señora informed her from inside the car, 'You are to sit in front with Christian, Meg. He is to drive us to the *castillo* whilst Esteban returns to his family to spend Christmas with them.'

A hundred objections fought for utterance inside Meg's head, but all of them died unspoken as she suddenly heard the totally unexpected sound of two very young male voices from the back seat of the car.

She and the Señora were not to be the limousine's only passengers, she realised, her stomach plunging with icy shock as she studied the two young, boyish faces so similar to those of their father.

Christian was *married*. He had *children*! Now her anger burned white-hot, fuelled not just by her disgust at Christian's behaviour but also by her own guilt. For a second she was tempted to refuse to get in the car, but the discipline of her nurse's training grimly forced her to rethink her emotional reaction. She had a professional duty to remain with her patient and that *must* take priority over her personal feelings, no matter how strong they might be.

Christian and his chauffeur had finished loading
the luggage into the boot of the car, and out of the
corner of her eye Meg could see Christian heading
towards the driver's door.

As he opened it he turned towards Meg, but she
refused to make eye contact with him. How *could* he
sit there, calmly fastening his seat belt, for all the
world as though he had done nothing wrong? But
then perhaps to him kissing someone other than his
wife was such an everyday occurrence that it didn't
bother him at all. It bothered *her* though—and not
just because she now felt consumed with guilt, Meg
recognised, torn between anger and anguish. From
the back seat, one of the boys leaned forward and
made a laughing comment to Christian.

'Yes, indeed,' Christian concurred, speaking in
Spanish as he turned sideways to give Meg a deliberately speculative look, accompanied by a little curl-
ing smile that made her heart start to somersault before she clenched her muscles against such
waywardness. 'Meg does have very pretty hair.'

Pretty hair!

Meg could feel the colour creeping up under her
skin. Christian had no right to give her that kind of
deliberate, explicitly erotic look. No right whatsoever. He was a married man. He had children…a
wife… What was *she* like? Meg found herself won-

dering. Did she *know* how carelessly, how recklessly her husband treated his marriage vows?

For some unfathomable reason, Meg began to feel tears burning the backs of her eyes. Turning in her seat to check on the comfort of her patient, she managed to blink them away. What on earth had she got to cry for? No doubt Christian's poor wife had already had the occasion to shed many tears over him. The occasion and the right.

Another wave of frighteningly strong and totally unwanted anguish rolled over her.

What was the matter with her? Anyone would think she had done something impossible, like falling in love with the man instead of just being stupid and unguarded enough to share a kiss with him. What was a kiss these days, after all?

Nothing!

Nothing and *everything*, a despairing inner voice whispered warningly.

They were clear of the city now. Christian was a good driver, Meg was forced to recognise, his hands controlled and firm on the wheel, his concentration not just on his own driving but on everything and everyone else on the road. He even seemed to know instinctively just when the two boys in the back were going to start play-wrestling just a little bit too fiercely for the Señora's comfort.

A father's instinct. Immediately Meg tried to shut down on her feelings.

The winter-bare countryside they were driving through had a sombre, stately beauty that somehow touched her senses. Seville and its environs were unfamiliar territory to her and she was glad of the Señora's gently informative travelogue, not just because of what she was learning but also because it prevented her from allowing the man seated next to her to dominate her thoughts.

'You're very quiet, Meg,' the Señora suddenly commented from the rear seat. 'I hope you are not feeling unwell with travel sickness...'

'Mama has that,' the younger of Christian's sons suddenly chimed in.

'No, silly,' the older one corrected him immediately, 'Mama is sick because of the baby she is going to have.'

Christian's wife was *pregnant*!

A sharp wave of revulsion attacked Meg, causing her to utter a small sound of distress.

Immediately Christian turned towards her, the car slowing down. He was frowning as he demanded, '*Are* you unwell?'

'No,' Meg denied fiercely.

She couldn't bear to look at him, couldn't endure to be *anywhere* near him. How *could* he have kissed her like that when...when...? Her patient had already told her that Christian had Moorish blood in his veins from the days when that race had ruled this part of Spain. Perhaps it was from those long-ago ancestors that he had inherited his arrogant belief that he had the right to make his own rules, live his life by his own laws.

Meg gave a small shudder and closed her eyes, opening them again as she heard Christian saying sharply, 'You are cold. Why did you not say so?'

Almost immediately the air inside the car grew noticeably warmer, his unwanted attention to her comfort causing Meg's face to crimson with anger. The raw sharpness of the pain she was enduring was far too dangerously intense. Why should she care about Christian's duplicity, his deceitfulness? She cared because, like his wife, she was a woman and because...

They were climbing into the hills now, the terrain around them becoming more rugged and the road decidedly tortuous, narrowing so much in some places that Meg found she was holding her breath and squeezing herself in.

And then one of the boys called out excitedly from the rear of the car, 'There it is. I can see the *castillo*.'

Sure enough, as Meg looked past Christian, she too could see it. Like a fortress it rose magnificently from the rock on which it was built, and the Moorish influence in its architecture was evident in its towers and turrets. The winter sun was burning its stone escarpment rose-gold and Meg stared at it in awed disbelief.

She had expected it to be large, dominating its surroundings in the same way that Christian dominated his, but she had not been prepared for its beauty, like a fairy-tale fantasy.

They were approaching the *castillo*, driving into a large sun-splashed paved courtyard filled with the musical sound of water from its ornate fountain. The car was stationary. Christian was climbing out and going to the assistance of his godmother whilst the two boys scrambled out of their seat and hurried towards an open door, through which a darkly elegant older woman—who Meg guessed must be Christian's mother—was approaching them.

Mindful of her responsibilities, Meg went to help Christian with the Señora. He had already removed her wheelchair from the boot of the car and now, as they gently helped her into it, between them, his fingers brushed against Meg's.

Immediately she gave a small, low cry, snatching her hand away, and the gaze she turned on him was full of reproach and angry disdain.

He was frowning, glancing immediately at her hand as he apologised formally. 'I'm sorry... Is it your hand?'

Her *hand*. Storm signals flashed in Meg's eyes.

How dared he pretend not to know why she couldn't bear him to touch her? His poor wife. How sorry Meg felt for her, being married to such a heartless man.

Christian's mother had reached them now, and greetings were being exchanged. Meg watched as mother and son embraced with uninhibited tenderness.

Releasing her son, Christian's mother then embraced her friend with warm affection before turning to welcome Meg herself.

'I have put you in rooms next to one another,' she informed the Señora and Meg as Christian gave discreet orders to the two men who were efficiently removing the luggage from the boot of the car.

'Meg isn't here just to nurse me. I want her to have fun as well,' the Señora was saying firmly, much to Meg's own embarrassment.

'Well, we shall certainly do our best,' Christian's mother laughed, turning away from them to tell her son, 'Juanita is already here, but she is resting. She said to thank you for bringing the boys.'

Meg frowned, indignation clouding her eyes as she listened. Why on earth should Christian's wife have to *thank* him for taking charge of his own sons?

The car was fully unloaded now, and instinctively Meg went to pick up her medical bag, but Christian got there before her, his hand on her arm.

'Don't touch me,' Meg spat fiercely at him.

'Don't *touch* you?'

She could see the angry, almost shocked look in his eyes.

'That's not what your body was saying to me only a very short time ago, *querida*...'

Querida... He had *dared* to call her *that*, when he was married?

Meg had spent enough time on the Spanish resort coast to know what kind of opinion many Spanish men had of British womanhood, those unknowing heedless girls who flocked to the *costas* for two weeks of reckless wanton behaviour, unaware of the reputation they were attracting. If Christian thought that *she* was like that intent on having 'fun'...

'How dare you call me that?' she demanded, white-faced. 'You might be a duke, but to me you are *lower* than the poorest beggar!'

'It was only a kiss, *querida*,' Christian was almost drawling, his voice soft, but his eyes were as cold as sin, promising retribution. 'If you did not want it, then perhaps you should have told those soft, inviting lips of yours so at the time. Instead...'

He paused and then flashed her a long lingering look that made her face and body burn and her toes curl protestingly inside her shoes.

'I don't think I have *ever* kissed a woman whose

mouth was more sweet and ripe with promise,' he told her softly.

Meg had had enough.

'You have no right to speak to me like that,' she told him furiously. 'No right at all. And if you do I shall... I shall...' She stopped as her own feelings overwhelmed her.

'Be careful,' she heard Christian warn her savagely. 'When a woman challenges me, I react like any other man, especially when I know she—'

'Christian...'

As his mother appeared round the side of the car Meg made her escape—without her medical bag.

CHAPTER THREE

'DO YOU know something?' the Señora commented conversationally to Meg as Meg helped her into her wheelchair prior to them both going downstairs for dinner.

That the *castillo* was equipped with a lift had been a bonus Meg hadn't been expecting and one she was extremely grateful for.

'I know lots of somethings,' she responded teasingly, starting to push the wheelchair towards the bedroom door.

'You have such a lovely sense of fun, Meg,' the Señora laughed. 'But, no, what I was going to say was that I believe that Christian is *very* attracted to you…'

She said it so approvingly and happily that Meg was glad she was standing behind her and that the Señora couldn't see her own bleakly shocked expression.

'He's a very good-looking man, and so kind and so—'

'—so *married*,' Meg put in sharply, unable to keep back the words any longer.

'Married? Christian?' She could hear the be-

188 A SPANISH CHRISTMAS

musement in the Señora's voice. 'But, no! What on *earth* makes you think that? Christian has no wife.'

'No wife? He *isn't* married?' Meg questioned disbelievingly. 'But what about the boys—his sons?'

'His *what*? They are not *his* sons; they are his nephews—the sons of his sister Juanita and her husband Ramon, who you will meet at dinner tonight.'

Christian's nephews... So he *wasn't* married. He *didn't* have any children. He *didn't* have a wife to be unfaithful to... Dazedly, Meg tried to digest what she had just learned. Christian was completely free to... To what? she asked herself grittily. To flirt with her; to kiss her; to treat her as though...?

That surely wasn't relief and happiness she was feeling—was it? Surely she was far too sensible to mistake a male ego-boosting bit of sexual flirtation with her for something meaningful, wasn't she? Especially when the male in question was the impossibly arrogant Christian.

But she had allowed him to kiss her, and she had... A girl was allowed to enjoy a kiss, wasn't she, in these enlightened days, without having to go into lengthy self-analysis about the whys and wherefores of it?

The lift stopped and she wheeled the Señora out of it and across the hallway towards the room her patient was indicating.

'I am so happy that we have been invited here,'

she confided to Meg. 'Christian's mother has been the kindest friend to me.' She gave a small sigh. 'When we are young, we think all that matters is being with the one person we love. My husband was everything to me,' she added quietly. 'But since I have lost him, I have realised how much one needs to be part of a family.'

For some reason, her words touched a sensitive chord in Meg's own emotions.

'At least you and your husband shared love,' she tried to comfort her patient.

They had reached the door now, but before Meg could open it it opened for them and Christian was standing there.

'Ah…I was just about to come and find you.'

He was addressing the Señora and not *her*, Meg warned herself. After all, he had not even looked at her.

As he smiled down at his godmother Christian refused to give in to the temptation to look at Meg. From the moment he had set eyes on her at the airport, she had both infuriated and enchanted him. Right now, the temptation to turn his head and drink in the unique combination of physical attributes that made her so dangerously special was overpowering. The way she could turn from being furiously hostile to him one minute to so passionately and sensually responsive another made him feel…made him want…

His mouth compressed in cynical self-judgement as he silently acknowledged just what Meg *was* making him want *and* how fiercely. She had kissed him so passionately in the lift. But throughout their drive to the *castillo* she had virtually ignored him.

Unable to stop himself, he turned his head and looked at her.

What was that look supposed to do? Meg wondered shakily as she felt the hard, silent pressure of Christian's gaze on her. Was he deliberately trying to intimidate her with his power, his sexuality?

Somehow she managed to look away from him, firmly taking charge of the Señora's wheelchair as she pushed her into the salon.

It was a large room, furnished with items that Meg suspected had to be priceless antiques, but in such a way that her first impression of it was that it was a room of immense comfort and warmth. A huge log fire burned in the equally huge grate, and seated on one of the large sofas drawn up close to it were the two boys who had travelled to the *castillo* with them, and a young woman who was quite plainly their mother, Christian's sister.

A man was standing behind the sofa with one hand on her shoulder, and Meg guessed that he must be her husband. The younger man who was engaging the boys in a game Meg could not place, until Christian's mother introduced him to her as her daughter's brother-in-law.

As he bent low over Meg's hand and then raised it to his lips with a theatrical flourish, Meg recognised that Sancho was a practised and expert flirt—and perfectly harmless. He was typical of the many young Spaniards who had frequented the marina her father had run and who had tried, always unsuccessfully, to convince her that their flirting was serious. The feelings he aroused in her were completely different from those she had experienced on meeting Christian.

Sancho might be a very attractive young man, but Meg knew she was in no danger whatsoever of being anything other than amused by the long languorous looks he was giving her, or the way he deliberately kept hold of her hand, only relinquishing it when Christian asked Meg with crisp pointedness, 'Perhaps you might help my godmother to get settled comfortably on the sofa? It will be warmer for her there, out of any draughts.'

Meg could hear the Señora demurring that she was perfectly comfortable in her chair, but neither that nor the knowledge that she was in no way to blame for the manner in which Sancho had kept hold of her hand had the power to stop Meg's face from burning with betraying colour, whilst her eyes flashed storm signals of furious resentment in Christian's direction.

She had no need of *him* to remind her of what her duties were or of her responsibility to her patient.

Seething with fury, she missed the speculative look Christian's sister gave her brother, although she did see the frowning, gentle sympathy in Christian's mother's eyes as she made room on the sofa for her friend.

Having made sure her patient was comfortably settled, Meg was tempted to make her exit, but before she could do so Juanita was inviting her to sit down next to her.

'My sons tell me that you speak Spanish.' She smiled. 'And that you have beautiful hair,' she added with a mischievous laugh.

She was so friendly that Meg couldn't resist cautiously responding to her questions. As she did so she could hear the younger of Juanita's sons demanding excitedly, 'Tio Christian. The tree is here and Pedro is fixing the lights on it. Can we help him decorate it?'

Breaking off from her conversation with Meg, Juanita said firmly, 'Tomaz and Carlos, you are not to go near that tree on your own.' Ruefully, she explained to Meg, raising her voice over her son's protests, 'Every year we have an enormous tree in the drawing room. It is a tradition. Last year, Carlos tried to climb it...' She raised her eyebrows.

'I was very brave. I didn't cry,' Carlos informed Meg importantly.

'*You* may not have done, but Maria nearly did when she saw the mess you had made of her newly cleaned salon,' Christian informed his nephew. 'We shall all decorate the tree together after dinner,' he added, and the warmth of the smile he gave his nephews as they both hurled themselves into his arms made Meg blink three or four times. Not because her emotions had been stirred, she denied. No, it was just...it was just that it was almost Christmas and she was a long way from her *own* family.

In her ear Sancho was murmuring provocatively, 'Decorating a Christmas tree is all very well for children, but I cannot help but feel that it will be very dull and boring for you. If you would permit me, I could drive you into Seville. There is a nightclub there...'

'I don't think—' Meg began, but before she could explain that she had come to Spain to work Christian, whose hearing had to be demonically sharp, was answering for her.

'Meg is not here to visit nightclubs, Sancho,' he said sternly. 'My godmother is employing her to ensure that the wound on her leg is properly cared for.'

'Oh, but surely she is allowed *some* time off?'

Sancho was protesting, completely unabashed, whilst Meg writhed inwardly in a fury of righteous anger and discomfort.

'I'm sure she is,' Christian was agreeing scathingly. 'But since she has only just arrived here, I hardly think she is likely to want to make the journey to Seville and back again tonight—and, of course, she will be spending the night *here*, and not in Seville.'

There was no doubt about what he meant, but before she could demand that she be allowed to exercise her own moral judgement—did he really think she was likely to want to spend the night with Sancho? Was his opinion of her really that low?— Sancho himself was responding angrily to Christian's embargo.

'Meg is an adult. She…'

Meg knew she had to defuse the situation. Quietly she told Sancho, 'It's very kind of you to invite me out, but in all honesty I am rather tired.'

To her relief, Sancho took her refusal goodnaturedly, waiting until Christian had turned his back to whisper softly to her that there would be other nights, but it was Christian's remark that she could not forgive.

A question from his elder brother, Juanita's husband, drew Sancho away from Meg's side, leaving her free to concentrate on her patient and the gentle

PENNY JORDAN 195

conversation of Christian's mother, and to throw a
murderously resentful look at Christian's back.

As in all Spanish households, they didn't sit down
to dinner until quite late. The elegance of the dining
room initially took Meg's breath away.

'There was a Hapsburg connection to the family,'
Juanita explained, rolling her eyes in wry amuse-
ment. 'A cousin of a cousin of the then ruling family.
It was at that time that many renovations were made.'

The dining room did have a distinctly baroque air
to it Meg acknowledged.

'We don't normally dine in such style,' Juanita
was further explaining with a wide smile. 'This dining room is only used for special occasions.'

Her smile widened even further when she saw the
look Meg was giving the dinner service on which
their meal was being served.

'It was a wedding present to the Hapsburg bride.
It's Sèvres...'

Sèvres and priceless, Meg guessed, swallowing
hard, but as though she had guessed what Meg was
thinking Juanita told her, 'Christian insists that it is
used. He says if it is not then it might as well be
placed in a museum. And whilst I agree with him—'
she grimaced as she glanced at her sons '—I confess
I am always a little nervous that the boys might accidentally break a piece.'

It was impossible not to warm to Christian's sister,

Meg acknowledged. And oddly, despite the awesome magnificence of her surroundings, Meg was actually beginning to feel very much at home with the family.

With Christian's family, perhaps, but most certainly not with Christian *himself*.

As they all eventually made their way from the dining room to the room where the huge tree was standing, bedecked with tiny fairy lights and waiting for its final clothing of shiny baubles and decorations, Meg hung back. Bending down, she murmured to the Señora, 'If you are feeling tired, perhaps we should—'

'Tired? No…I am enjoying this *so much*,' she told Meg, her eyes sparkling. 'It reminds me of when I was young—and look, Meg, in the corner of the room, Christian still has the traditional crib display I remember his parents having when *he* was a child.'

Juanita, who had overheard her comments, informed Meg, 'Some families these days do not bother so much with the Christmas crib, but Christian is very much a traditionalist and likes to do things in the old way. Tomorrow night it is Christmas Eve, and then the children will open some of their presents, but as with most Spanish families we shall keep others back for the Night of the Three Kings on the fifth of January.

'We shall celebrate that in Seville, though, where there is the Epiphany Festival. There will be floats in the streets and much merry-making. You will enjoy it. It is a good opportunity for our young people to be allowed to let off steam.'

She broke off her conversation with Meg to shake her head when her younger son urged her to climb the step-ladder and hang some decorations on the tree. 'Perhaps Meg will help you,' she suggested, smiling at Meg as she patted her stomach. 'Whenever I am pregnant I seem to lose my head for heights, along with my waistline.'

Her husband and Christian had left the room a few minutes earlier, Christian taking Ramon to his office so that he could use his computer.

'I am sure that Sancho will be only too pleased to hold the ladder for you,' Juanita gently teased her brother-in-law.

Feeling that it would be churlish of her to refuse, Meg made her way over to the Christmas tree, taking the baubles Tomaz was holding out to her and mounting the ladder.

She had just finished hanging them to his satisfaction when Sancho announced, 'Perhaps we should place Meg at the top of the tree instead of the angel. She is certainly pretty enough,' he added admiringly, giving Meg a long lingering look.

Sancho was obviously determined to flirt with her, but Meg suspected that she was only the focus of his attention because he was bored and she was the only unmarried woman available. Shaking her head reprovingly, she descended the ladder calmly, distancing herself from him to rejoin Juanita. However, her coolness deserted her when she realised that Christian was standing in the doorway and that he was watching her with grim disapproval.

It wasn't her fault that she was here in his family home, where he so plainly did not want her to be, she was thinking indignantly, when suddenly Juanita called out in alarm, 'No, Tomaz, you must not go on the ladder.'

Immediately Meg swung round and started to hurry back to the tree. Tomaz, in the manner of all small boys, was gleefully enjoying himself, unaware of any danger as he tried to reach for the top of the tree.

'I have the star. I will put it at the top,' he was calling out happily, but as he spoke the ladder started to sway a little.

As she heard from behind her Juanita's anxious maternal gasp Meg reacted instinctively, closing the gap between herself and the swaying ladder and reaching out to steady it. But Christian had got there before her, and instead of holding the ladder Meg discovered that it was Christian's body she was embracing as he in turn held the ladder secure and commanded his nephew sternly to come down.

'But I want to put the star at the top of the tree,' Tomaz was insisting stubbornly.

'Tomaz. Come down. You can't reach the top,' Juanita instructed. Eager to prove her wrong, the little boy insisted determinedly, 'Yes, I can. Look...'

Grateful for the diversion he was causing, Meg hoped that no one had noticed her embarrassment as she quickly removed her hands from Christian's torso. Her relief was short-lived, though, when Christian turned his head and looked sharply at her. Unable to drag her gaze away from his, Meg prayed that he wouldn't see in her eyes the shock the action of touching him had given her. He was just a man, flesh and blood, and there was no need, no reason why she should feel so strongly aware of him in a way that was wholly female. Her fingertips were still tingling a little, as though she had received a small electric shock, and...

'Tomaz, that is enough. I shall put the star in place for you.'

The calm firmness in Christian's voice as he turned away from her and back to his nephew had the desired effect on Tomaz's rebellious behaviour, but the effect it was having on her equally rebellious emotions was far from desired, Meg admitted as Christian firmly removed his nephew from the ladder and placed him on the floor, taking the star from him as he did so.

Meg was just about to move away when Christian stopped her, saying quietly, 'If you wouldn't mind holding the ladder for me I shall put the star at the top of the tree so that both it and the ladder can cease to be a cause of further temptation.'

Silently Meg steadied the ladder, waiting for Christian to climb it.

He had only climbed a couple of rungs when he paused, apparently to straighten one of the baubles but in reality to lean down towards her and say in a cool undertone that only Meg could hear, 'It's a pity that there isn't an equally simple way of removing Sancho from his temptation.'

Both his tone and the look he was giving her made it very clear what he meant, and Meg knew that the angry colour sweeping her face was betraying her own reaction to his obvious disapproval of Sancho's interest in her.

What gave him the right to criticise her, to disapprove of her? She longed to say as much to him but she reminded herself, as he continued to climb the ladder and reach out to put the star in place, that she was here under his roof in her professional capacity. This surely should mean that he ought to know she was not in a position to respond to Sancho's flirting, even if she wanted to do—which she most certainly did not.

Refusing to look at him as he descended the lad-

der, she barely waited until he had reached the floor
before relinquishing her steadying hold on it and
walking away.

'Meg—a word with you, please.'

Meg paused warily as Christian addressed her.
They were alone in the hallway. Juanita and Ramon
had taken the boys upstairs to put them to bed and
Meg herself was just on her way back to the salon,
having gone upstairs to get Elena's painkillers, sensing that the older lady was in some discomfort.

Christian was frowning, his voice terse, and Meg
could feel her body tensing defensively.

'Sancho is a young man who lives a very much
more...' He paused and looked at her, and Meg's
heart turned over inside her chest before lurching cra-
zily against her ribs, helplessly out of control. 'More
modern lifestyle than that of my godmother's and
mother's generation. Of course the way he behaves
outside my home is no concern of mine, but he is
under my roof. My sister claims that I am a traditionalist and old-fashioned, and I suspect she may be
right. I am sure you are already worldly-wise enough
not to need any warning from *me* about encouraging
the attentions of a young man such as Sancho, but
whilst you *are* both beneath my roof—'

Meg had heard enough—more than enough.

'What are you trying to say?' she demanded, incensed. 'That if I am not careful Sancho will take advantage of his position and kiss me—perhaps in the lift?'

She knew from the sound of Christian's savagely indrawn breath that he understood what she meant.

'I did *not*—' he began angrily and then stopped, muttering something she could not catch beneath his breath before telling her thickly, 'Just what is it about you that drives me to such insanity? It is *impossible* to reason with you. You are… Perhaps there *is*, after all, only one way for me to deal with you…'

Meg gave a shocked gasp as she was suddenly hauled into his arms and held tightly there, his heart thudding erratically against her body as his mouth took her own captive.

Immediately it was as though somehow, somewhere deep inside her, something had thrown a switch. At the touch of his mouth on hers all her antagonism left her and in its place she felt the most incredible sense of piercing longing, aching need, combined with a sense of rightness…of completeness, almost.

Without her having any say in what was happening, her body seemed to melt into Christian's. Blindly, Meg opened her mouth to him, wanting to breathe him, sense him, *feel* him within her deepest, most secret places. A shudder ran through him as his hand cupped the back of her head, his fingers stroking and caressing.

She was trembling herself as she recognised what was happening to her—what *had* happened. Helplessly she lifted her hands to draw him closer, and then, as the realisation struck fully home, instead to push him away, fleeing from him when he released her as though he were the devil and not stopping until she had reached the sanctuary of her room.

Once there she stared accusingly at her reflection in the mirror, searching for something—*anything*—she could see there to explain to her just why she had been so stupid.

She was old enough to know the danger of falling in love with a man like Christian—a man who would never share her feelings. A man who quite obviously regarded her with a mixture of angry contempt and some unfathomable cruel brand of male desire, which he seemed to think he had every right to indulge in whenever he chose.

The Señora's bottle of painkillers was still in her hand. She would have to return downstairs with them. She knew it was going to take every ounce of strength and courage she possessed to get through the next two weeks of their visit to the *castillo* without betraying what had happened to her. Mentally, she prayed that she *would* be able to do so. The humiliation she would suffer if Christian were to guess how she felt about him made her feel physically sick.

But still, heart-achingly, there was a part of her that yearned to relive the sensation of his mouth on hers, the shocking thrill of that heartbeat of time when she had known that she loved him. Her desire to recreate those feelings, to rewrite the whole scene, editing out the harsh realities of it and substituting them instead with her own dangerous fantasy of love and longing was so strong she had to will herself to resist it.

Downstairs in the silent hallway, Christian gritted his teeth. His hand was already on the ornate banister, the urgency of his need to follow Meg a physical pain.

Watching Sancho flirt with her earlier in the evening had made him feel…had made him *want*… The pain that engulfed him was savage and explicit. He considered himself to be a civilised man, but right now there was something very uncivilised about exactly what he wanted to do.

The thought of Meg responding to Sancho's kisses in the way she had to *his*—the thought of her responding like that to *any* other man, in fact—

He *couldn't* go after Meg. He would despise himself if he did, just as he would despise *any* man who attempted to force himself on a woman.

*   *   *

Upstairs in the privacy of their bedroom Juanita smiled at her husband, shaking her head when he asked her if she wanted to go back downstairs.

'Do you know, Ramon?' she commented. 'I think at last that Christian is following our family tradition.'

Ramon's frown told her that he had not followed her quick intuitive thinking. Sighing, she explained, 'You know that it is the tradition in our family for its men to fall immediately and lastingly in love only once in their lives? Up until now, Christian has not done so, but now I think…' She paused. 'I do so like Meg!'

'*Meg*? You think that your brother has fallen in love with *Meg*…' Ramon looked bemused. 'But they have only just met.'

'As had we, when I knew that you were the one for me,' Juanita reminded him lovingly.

'But he is so very cold and formal towards her.'

'Exactly,' Juanita agreed, giving him a secretive female smile.

CHAPTER FOUR

MEG couldn't believe it. It was already two days after Christmas. From her bedroom window she could see Juanita's sons playing in the garden below.

Earlier that morning, Juanita's husband and his brother had had to return to Madrid to attend to some business matters, and Meg suspected that Juanita had been rather relieved to see her brother-in-law go.

Charming though he could be, there was no doubt that Sancho was also extremely irresponsible. For once, Meg had found herself totally in accord with Christian when he had expressed disapproval and anger at the way in which Sancho had encouraged his nephews' excitement and interest in the air rifle he had carelessly brought to the *castillo* with him.

'I like to hunt, and this is the country.' Sancho had shrugged. 'You of all people should surely support such a tradition.'

'Hunting in the days when it was necessary to do so for food was one thing,' Christian had replied curtly. 'But...' His mouth had tightened as he'd looked from Sancho's openly taunting expression to the absorbed faces of his nephews as they had begged to be allowed to handle the gun.

Meg had seen how much Christian wanted to step in and demand that Sancho did not allow them to do so, but she suspected that he, like her, knew that Sancho would enjoy deliberately flouting his authority.

Later, when Juanita had firmly ushered the boys away, quietly reminding Sancho that they were far too young to be allowed to 'play' with something so potentially dangerous, Meg had seen Christian take Sancho on one side, no doubt to remonstrate with him for being so irresponsible.

She was on her own at the *castillo* today, apart from Christian and the boys, Christian's mother having persuaded the Señora, as well as Juanita, to join her on a visit to an elderly relative living some miles away.

At the Señora's insistence, Meg had stayed behind. She deserved to have some time to herself, the Señora had insisted, suggesting that Meg might enjoy walking round the *castillo*'s extensive gardens.

Too much time on her hands wasn't something Meg really wanted, though. It could lead all too easily to the dangerous self-indulgence of thinking about Christian, and from *thinking* about him it was one very easy and short step to remembering the way he had kissed her.

From her bedroom window she could see Christian walking across the courtyard to join his nephews.

Hungrily she studied him. It was a sunny day and the sunshine burnished the darkness of his hair. The small ache which had taken up permanent residence in her heart grew to a tormented yearning. Suddenly Christian turned to look up towards her bedroom window. Flushing, she drew back from it.

She had come upstairs to write a letter to her parents but half an hour later she was still nowhere near finishing it. There was so much that she could *not* tell them, so much that she did not *want* them to read between her lines.

'Meg?'

The totally unexpected sound of Christian's voice calling her name urgently from outside her bedroom door shocked her into wary immediacy. What did he want? Why was he there?

'Meg.'

The sharp, impatient insistence in his voice as he repeated her name made her hurry towards the door.

As she opened it he stepped quickly inside, shouldering the door shut behind him.

Something in his expression told her immediately that something was very wrong.

He had a cloth over his right arm, which he was holding in place with his left hand, and as she glanced at it Meg saw that blood was seeping through it. Instantly her professional training overrode her emotions.

'What's happened?' she demanded as she hurried towards him, focusing her attention on his arm.

'Somehow the boys managed to get hold of Sancho's rifle—I warned him about making sure it was safely locked away. I was afraid there might be an accident and I went to get it from them, but unfortunately...'

He gave a small shrug and then winced in obvious pain as Meg urged him towards her bathroom. The cloth was bright red with blood now. Soon it would be dripping on the bedroom floor, and the no doubt priceless rug that covered it, and besides her medical bag was in the bathroom and she wanted it to hand when she removed that cloth.

'The gun went *off*. You were *hit*?' she demanded sharply.

'Unfortunately, yes,' he agreed. 'The boys are very shocked. Maria is taking care of them.'

Maria was the *castillo*'s housekeeper and Meg nodded her head as she took hold of his arm and removed the cloth.

The pellet from the air rifle had gouged a deep furrow along the length of Christian's forearm and Meg winced as she saw the extent of his wound.

The pellet would have to be removed and the wound cleaned and then stitched, and that was a job for a doctor, not her—a doctor who, she was sure, would immediately prescribe a course of strong antibiotics just in case the wound should become infected.

'You need to see a doctor,' she told Christian quietly.

'It is just a scratch, a flesh wound,' Christian insisted with a small shrug. 'You are a nurse. Surely you can do *something*.'

'*Something*,' Meg agreed. 'But—'

'Then do it,' Christian commanded. 'Unless you would prefer that I attended to it myself?'

He sounded serious enough to have her reaching anxiously for her medical bag. She knew what had to be done, of course, and quickly set about doing it, having first insisted on bringing a chair from her bedroom for Christian to sit on.

'In case I get bored,' he mocked her.

'In case you pass out,' Meg corrected him briskly, starting to sterilise her hands and the area of the wound. The length of the furrow was bad enough, but it was also worryingly deep. Her work as a theatre sister meant that she was thoroughly familiar with the sight of blood, bone and tissue, but even so on this occasion she found she was having to grit her teeth and steel herself as she parted the edges of the wound to inspect the damage and look for the pellet.

Her stomach churned nauseously when she saw it, a small dark object buried into the flesh it had torn and perilously close to a main artery. If she tried to remove it there was a danger she might drive it deeper, to puncture the vein—but if she left it it could move of its own accord and puncture an artery anyway.

'I can see the pellet and I think I can remove it,' she told Christian, keeping her voice as even as she could. 'But…' She paused.

'But what?' he encouraged her.

'It's very close to a main artery,' she told him honestly.

For a moment they looked at one another. There was something in his eyes, in their expression, that made her heart jolt and her pulse race feverishly. She was imagining it, she told herself sternly. He was already bleeding rather more than she liked, but she was concerned that if she insisted on him sending for a doctor the situation could deteriorate before one could arrive—the *castillo* was, after all, remote.

'It will hurt,' she warned him.

The grim look he gave her made Meg flinch a little. Did he think that she would enjoy hurting him?

'You have—' he began in a clipped voice and then stopped. 'You must do what you have to do,' he continued after a brief pause. Meg could sense his determination not to betray any sign of pain.

Even so she felt him wince as she probed his flesh to remove the pellet.

Fighting back her own nausea, Meg pressed on

and then paused as, out of the corner of her eye, she saw Christian beginning to sag. Her hand ached with tension—she prayed it would not let her down.

'Nearly there,' she told him with a determined cheerfulness she was far from feeling. 'Just another few seconds…'

The seconds stretched into minutes as she carefully worked her way round the pellet, dreading that it might break into pieces before she could safely remove it.

'There…'

She had it. Meg held her breath as she very carefully extracted the pellet, easing it away from the artery. She could feel the trauma of what she was doing sending a small tremor through Christian's arm—and no wonder. Meg was no stranger to physical pain herself, and she knew that her hand would ache badly for days after the strain she had just imposed on it.

The pellet safely removed, she started to clean up the wound. It would have to be stitched and for that he would need to see a doctor.

Christian watched her as she worked, forcing himself to concentrate and not to give in to the nauseating waves of weakness that were breaking over him. She was half turned away from him, her face in profile, intent, professional, her concentration on what she was doing almost a force-field around her.

Before attending to his wound she had tied her hair up out of the way, but a few small strands had escaped and he had to fight the impulse to reach out with his uninjured arm to touch them, touch her...

Perhaps his pain had somehow intensified his senses. Could it do so? He didn't know, but for some reason he was acutely aware of everything about her—the soft delicate scent of her skin, the way she was breathing, the tension in her body as she worked and the relief once she had removed the pellet. He had even felt that small second of hesitation before she had started to clean his flesh.

He winced as something suddenly stung the rawness of the wound, his ears buzzing with the intensity of the pain, his vision blurring. He gritted his teeth against the verbal protest his body wanted him to make.

Meg was biting down hard on her own bottom lip, praying silently that Christian wouldn't faint. He had said nothing, made no sound, but her experience told her that his body was in shock. Mindful of her operating theatre experience, she began to talk to him. Having to listen gave a patient something to focus on other than their pain. She spoke quietly, almost hypnotically, her voice soothing and calm.

'I'll bandage your arm but I'm afraid it is going to need stitches and I can't do that—not without a local anaesthetic. It will have to be seen by a doctor,

Christian, and you will need a course of antibiotics, just to be sure that no infection has got in—and as soon as possible.'

'Then in that case you will just have to drive me to Seville.' The strength and purposefulness of his voice caught her off guard. He had looked so close to losing consciousness that she had half-expected him either not to reply at all or simply to mumble something, but here he was, speaking as irritatingly authoritatively as normal. In fact, anyone listening to their voices would probably assume that of the two of them *she* was the one in shock.

'I... I can't do that,' she protested. As she spoke she looked towards Christian and immediately wished she hadn't.

Despairingly she recognised that these last few days of telling herself that she was simply not going to allow herself to love him had been a total waste of time.

'I'm afraid you're going to *have* to,' Christian informed her tersely. 'There *is* no one else.'

Meg knew that it was true. Christian's mother, the Señora and Juanita were not due to return until much, much later in the evening and, of course, Christian's chauffeur was with them. Sancho and Ramon were away on business.

There is no one else... Somewhere deep down in her most private and secret emotions, his words

touched an aching chord. If only he were saying them
to her in another context…an emotional context…as
her lover, the man who *loved* her, the man for whom
there could never be anyone else but her.

Christian frowned as he saw the look of raw anguish in Meg's eyes. Instinctively he started to stand
up, wanting to comfort her, but he had forgotten
about his arm. A momentary surge of dizziness made
him sway slightly. Immediately Meg's professional
instinct overturned her private feelings and she was
standing beside him, using her body to steady and
support him as she placed her arm around him.

'It's all right,' she reassured him gently. 'You've
lost quite a lot of blood and that's bound to make
you feel a bit weak…'

Weak?

He was feeling *that*, all right, Christian acknowledged, and not just because of his injury. No, it was
Meg's proximity that was knocking him off balance,
her proximity and the sweetly sensual feel of her
body next to his, her arm protectively around him.

He turned his head to tell her that he was all right
and caught his breath as he saw that she was looking
up at him, her eyes brilliant with concern.

'Oh, Meg.'

He said it so softly that Meg thought she must
have misheard the aching note of tenderness in his
voice and then, unbelievably, he was lowering his

head towards her, brushing his lips against hers in the lightest and sweetest of caresses. Instinctively she reached up to curl her hand around his neck; the skin felt warm and smooth, his hair silky-soft.

'Thank you,' he whispered as he released her mouth.

Desperate to conceal what she was feeling from him, Meg immediately became fussily professional, reminding him sharply, 'You still need to get to see a doctor and—'

'—And the only way I'm going to be able to do that is for you to drive me to Seville,' Christian repeated.

She had released him now and was turning away from him, and he had a sudden violent urge to take her back in his arms and tell her how he felt about her, tell her too about his family's tradition and beg her to give him the opportunity to teach her to share his love.

The last thing Meg wanted to do was to spend several hours alone in the close confines of a car with Christian, but her professionalism and her sense of responsibility and duty insisted that she had no other choice—the *castillo* was so remote that it would probably take just as long to obtain the services of a local doctor as it would to drive Christian to Seville.

Giving a small sigh, she nodded her head in silent acceptance.

*   *   *

Not unnaturally, perhaps, it took Meg rather longer to drive along the tortuous mountain route to Seville than it had done Christian, but unexpectedly Christian did not show any impatience or irritation with her cautious handling of his large four-wheel-drive vehicle. On the contrary, he was calmly reassuring, even taking the trouble to boost her confidence by praising the way she was driving.

They had left Juanita's sons in the charge of the housekeeper—the rifle had, of course, been confiscated and locked away—and Meg had been filled with unwanted admiration for the gentle way in which Christian had handled his nephews' guilt and anxiety over the accident, making light of his injury. Fortunately, both of them were too young to be fully aware of what *could* have happened, although Meg's blood ran cold when she thought of how easily a real tragedy could have overtaken them all.

A brief message had been left with the housekeeper, explaining what had happened, although here again Christian had insisted that Juanita was to be protected from being shocked.

'There was a miscarriage before she conceived this baby,' he had explained quietly to Meg, 'and whilst her pregnancy is past *that* danger point now…'

Meg had nodded her head, immediately understanding and acquiescing with his decision.

And now, here they were, driving into Seville.

As she followed Christian's directions Meg glanced at his arm. The wound was still bleeding, the bandage showing a spreading crimson stain; her heart started to thud anxiously.

'Could we go straight to the hospital?' she asked him. 'Their casualty department will be able to deal with you immediately.'

'If you think that's best,' Christian agreed, deferring to her judgement so easily that her anxiety increased.

She had noticed him holding his bandaged arm surreptitiously whilst she was driving and she knew it must be hurting him. Her own hand was aching with tension, the damaged ligaments tightening. The four-wheel-drive was equipped with power steering and an automatic gear box, but the long winding bends on the mountain road had still taken their toll.

Frowning in concentration, she followed Christian's directions through the city, thankfully relatively empty of traffic. Her shoulders and her chest ached with tension and concentration and she had never been more relieved to see a hospital building.

She parked the vehicle and they both climbed out. Thankfully Christian was perfectly steady on his feet, although he looked a little paler than normal.

It was only a short distance to the Accident and Emergency entrance to the hospital, and they had almost reached it when Christian suddenly reached out with his left hand, stopping Meg from going any further.

'What is it?' she asked him anxiously. 'Are you feeling faint? Sick? Shall I go and get…?'

Christian shook his head, ignoring her anxious questions to demand brusquely instead, 'Your hand—you keep rubbing it. You should have said something. You're obviously in pain!' The brusqueness in his voice deepened. 'I shouldn't have allowed you to drive.'

'There wasn't any other way we could have got here,' Meg reminded him. For some reason, her throat felt constricted with stupid tears. What for? Because, despite his own pain, he had noticed *her* discomfort?

'We could have telephoned for the local doctor to visit, but I know he has a large practice and it seemed unfair to add to his workload, especially at this time of the year.'

'We're here now,' Meg responded. 'My hand will soon recover.'

She was so stoical, so independent, and Christian was furious with himself for being the cause of her discomfort. He wanted to take hold of her hand and wrap it in the warmth of his, to take hold of *her* and wrap her in the protection of his love.

Reluctantly he let her go, falling into step beside her as she hurried towards the hospital entrance.

Angry with herself, Meg blinked away her foolish emotional tears. Just for a second she had been so tempted to fling herself into Christian's arms, to tell him how afraid for him she had been, to feel him hold her and reassure her...to feel him *love* her!

They were inside the hospital now. Bracing her shoulders, Meg reminded herself of her professional responsibility.

CHAPTER FIVE

'MISS SCOTT?'

As she heard her name Meg looked up. A white-coated doctor was hurrying towards her.

'Christian? The Duque?' she began anxiously.

'He is fine,' the doctor assured her. 'My nurse is just finishing bandaging his arm. May I congratulate you on a very neat piece of work? Had you not had the skill to remove the pellet, it could quite easily have become lodged more deeply and dangerously by the time he got here. I understand from the Duque that you trained as a theatre sister.'

'Yes,' Meg admitted, more anxious to discuss Christian's injury than her own past history.

'We have stitched the wound and administered an antibiotic injection, but I should like to see him again in the morning. His temperature is a little raised and he could develop a fever.'

'In the morning?' Meg began. 'But…' She stopped as she saw Christian himself walking towards them.

It was plain that he had overheard the doctor's comment, because before she could say anything he was telling him smoothly, 'That will be no problem. We shall stay overnight at my apartment here in

Seville since it isn't feasible to drive back to the *castillo* tonight.' Thanking the doctor for what he had done, he placed his left hand on Meg's arm, gently but determinedly drawing her away.

They had reached the exit before she could manage to speak.

'*Why* isn't it feasible to drive back to the *castillo*?' she demanded. Her heart was racing frantically and she knew that her face must be flushed with the dangerous mixture of excitement and longing that was rushing through her veins.

To spend the evening *alone* with Christian… She didn't think she could bear to, but she knew that she could not bear not to. She was an idiot, storing up even more pain for herself, she told herself fiercely, but it was no good and she could see that Christian was not going to change his mind.

He confirmed this when he said crisply to her, '*I* certainly do not feel up to undergoing the drive back to the *castillo* now, only to have to drive all the way back here again tomorrow morning—even if *you* do. No—' he shook his head decisively '—we will spend the night here in the city at my apartment.'

He paused and looked down into her eyes, his gaze so intense that Meg thought she might suffocate from the tension gripping her own body.

'It seems that I have a great deal to thank you for. The doctor told me that the pellet was perilously close to the main artery and that if you had not re-moved it...'

Meg couldn't say anything. She knew she would remember for the rest of her life the horror of that sickening second when she had realised how vitally important it was both that she removed the pellet and that she didn't accidentally push it further into the wound in doing so. Never had she regretted so des-perately her own injury, never had she prayed more fervently that her hand wouldn't let her down.

Christian's apartment was just as grand in its own way as the *castillo*. A whole floor in a beautiful old building overlooking its own private garden.

The guest room Christian had indicated she was to use was equipped with virtually everything an overnight guest might need.

'I'm afraid we shall have to raid the freezer for something to eat,' Christian had informed her. 'Un-less you would prefer to go out?'

Meg had shaken her head. She suspected that once the local anaesthetic wore off the stitches in his arm would make him feel distinctly uncomfortable. The doctor had given her some painkillers for him, in addition to a course of antibiotics to be taken once he was back at the *castillo*.

The long drive had left her feeling gritty-eyed and slightly grubby, and she looked longingly towards the luxurious marble bathroom attached to her bedroom.

Christian had told her that he intended to ring the *castillo* and explain what had happened. The temptation to indulge in a long luxurious soak was too much for Meg to resist.

Half an hour later she was seated at the dressing table, wrapped in a thick white fluffy towel just finishing blow drying her hair, when the bedroom door opened and Christian walked in.

The shock of seeing him made her drop the hairdryer, and as she made to pick it up so did Christian, apologising as he did so. 'I'm sorry... I did knock but obviously you didn't hear me.'

As he picked up the hairdryer he switched it off and put it down. He was looking at her in a way that made sensual awareness burn along Meg's veins. Unable to stop herself, she moistened her suddenly dry lips with the tip of her tongue, her heart slamming against her chest wall in shock as she saw his reaction to what she was doing in Christian's eyes.

He wanted her... Because she was a *woman*, she fought to remind herself, not because she was *her*. He was a very male man—a very *sexual* man—she already knew that. A man who no doubt was not used to living a celibate life. A man... A man she loved and wanted, and whom she ached and longed to have touch her, stroke her, slide the towel away from her body and slowly and thoroughly caress every inch of her flesh with his hands and then his mouth whilst she—

Yearningly, she stepped towards him, and then stopped as he raised his hand and she saw the bandage on his arm.

She wasn't here because he *loved her*, she reminded herself harshly.

As she stepped determinedly back from him, Christian cursed himself under his breath. This was going to be so much harder than he had imagined and he wasn't sure he had the self-control to keep his distance from her.

'I've checked the freezer,' he told her curtly. 'I hope you like fish.'

'I do,' Meg confirmed. Did her voice sound as shaky and huskily vulnerable to him as it did to her?

'I make a pretty fair paella,' Christian informed her. 'But on this occasion I'm afraid I'm going to need your assistance.' As he spoke he gestured to his arm. 'Are you hungry yet?' he asked, 'Or...'

She *was* hungry, Meg discovered, to her own surprise, but then the last meal she had eaten had been breakfast, and now it was six o'clock in the evening.

'Give me half an hour to freshen up,' Christian began.

'Remember that you have to keep your dressing dry,' Meg warned him, her professionalism coming to the fore, but it wasn't her professionalism that brought a hot surge of colour to her face seconds later as she closed her eyes briefly, trying not to imagine him standing naked beneath the hot wet pulse of a shower. What was she doing to herself, *tormenting* herself like this?

To her relief, Christian hadn't seen her betraying reaction, and was turning away from her and heading towards her bedroom door.

Half an hour. She had half an hour to bring herself back to some semblance of sanity and reality. Then she and Christian would be working together in his kitchen, preparing a meal for themselves, for all the world as though they were a couple, as though they were *lovers*…

Lovers… How tormentingly sweet and dangerous the word sounded, felt…*tasted*… She said it out loud, just for the forbidden pleasure it gave her. Lovers…

The apartment's kitchen was unexpectedly modern and well equipped. Christian was already busily removing items from the freezer when Meg walked in. Unlike her, *he* had been able to get changed. As though he could guess what she was thinking, he told her ruefully, 'I'm sorry. I cannot offer you a change of clothes. The best I can do is to give you one of my shirts, but I'm afraid it would drown you!'

One of his shirts… Was her expression giving her away? Meg wondered. Could he see in her eyes just what the thought of having one of his shirts, impregnated with the unique scent of *him*, to hold and cling on to was doing to her? She prayed not.

To her surprise, it soon became obvious that Christian was perfectly at home in his role of chef, carefully defrosting the items he had removed from the freezer in the microwave before starting to cook them. However, Meg kept a watchful eye on how much he was using his arm, insisting on taking over when she could sense that it was beginning to hurt him.

A mouthwatering scent of cooking food soon filled the kitchen.

Christian had opened a bottle of wine, pouring them both a glass which he insisted they should drink whilst they were cooking, giving her a rueful look when Meg reminded him that it might not be wise to drink very much whilst he was having antibiotics.

'Always the nurse,' he told her.

'Well, that *is* why I'm here,' she reminded him defensively.

The look he gave her made her curl her toes up inside her shoes. As he turned away from her he muttered something in Spanish that sounded like 'Don't remind me,' but Meg suspected she must have misheard him.

*   *   *

Guiltily Meg smothered a small betraying yawn, but it was too late; Christian had seen her. They had finished their meal and cleaned up after themselves, and at Christian's suggestion they had walked around the elegant nightscape-lit garden. These Spanish gardens had a very special magic that was all their own, Meg had acknowledged, as she paused to admire the fountain at the centre. But now they were back inside and, even though it was still not yet midnight, early by Spanish standards, she was feeling tired.

Christian had refused the painkillers she had offered him earlier in the evening, insisting that he felt fine. He wouldn't need his oral antibiotics until later tomorrow, and she suspected that the doctor at the hospital would give him another intravenous antibiotic when he checked him over in the morning.

'You're tired. Why don't you go to bed?' he was suggesting to Meg now.

Reluctantly Meg got up. He was morally if not technically her patient—in her eyes at least—and her nursing instinct urged her to ensure that he was safely ensconced in *his* bed before she sought her own. But before she could say anything the telephone rang.

As he answered it, Meg heard him say warmly, 'Juanita… No, everything's fine, I promise. A small flesh wound, that's all. No. I promise you, I'm fine… Yes. But that was just a precaution…'

Quietly, Meg headed towards the door, not wanting to eavesdrop on his conversation with his sister.

The huge double bed in her room looked blissfully inviting. Her hand was aching quite badly. She had her own prescription painkillers and she knew she ought to take one. As she padded into the bathroom for a glass of water she realised that she had nothing to sleep in. Her underwear would have to be rinsed and left to dry on the bathroom's heated towel rail. She could, perhaps, wrap herself in a towel, she mused.

Ten minutes later, having showered and brushed her hair, she decided that such modesty was unnecessary, and when she slid into her bed between the cool deliciousness of its pure cotton sheets she was glad she had decided against doing so. There was something almost wickedly sensual about the feel of cool, pure cotton against naked skin.

Wearily she closed her eyes. The events of the day had drained her more than she had recognised. Behind her closed eyelids she kept seeing Christian's arm, the ugly little pellet buried in his torn flesh. For the rest of her life she would remember that moment when she had started to examine the wound and recognised how close it was to his vein, and how careful she would have to be to remove it…

On his way to his own bedroom Christian paused outside Meg's bedroom door. She had tried to hide it from him but he had seen how much pain her hand was causing her earlier. *His* fault… If she hadn't had to drive him here to Seville…

The doctor at the hospital had made it plain to him just how lucky he had been, castigating whoever it was who had been foolish enough to give a young boy an air rifle.

Christian had deliberately played things down when he had spoken to his sister, assuring her that there was nothing for her to worry about and that she would see for herself when he and Meg returned to the *castillo*.

'When will you be back?' she had asked him.

'I'm not sure,' he had told her. 'I have to go to the hospital again in the morning.'

'Again? But why?'

'It is just a precaution…nothing more…' he had soothed her. He had spoken briefly to his mother and to his nephews, both of whom had sounded chastened.

What had happened had not been their fault, and he had said as much to Juanita.

'Thank goodness Meg was there,' she had told him emotionally.

Meg.

Christian realised that he was still standing outside her bedroom door like a lovelorn fool… Meg… He closed his eyes and allowed the pain of what he was feeling to thud through his veins, greater by far than the pain of his injured arm. *That* would heal, fade and be totally forgotten, but what he felt for Meg—that would be with him for the rest of his life.

Somehow there must be a way for him to break down the barriers between them, for him to show her how good things could be between them.

Somehow—but how?

Bleak-eyed, he headed for his own bedroom.

CHAPTER SIX

CHRISTIAN groaned as the pain in his arm intensified. He had been awake for over an hour, his arm throbbing increasingly uncomfortably as the effects of the anaesthetic wore off.

His body felt hot and his head muzzy. He wanted a drink of water and a cooling shower, but more, much more than either of those, he wanted Meg.

Unsteadily he pushed back the duvet and slid his feet to the floor.

Meg had always been a light sleeper, and her eyes were open the moment Christian turned the handle of her door. The sight of him standing inside her room wearing a short robe tied loosely and open to his waist made her heart pound, her stomach cramp with longing.

But then her professional eye saw the hot flush staining his face and recognised the slightly disorientated look in his eyes.

He was clasping his right arm and, even in the dim light of her bedside lamp, Meg could see how swollen it looked.

'I'm sorry to wake you,' he was telling her. 'Those painkillers—I think I may need one…'

Meg had put them in her bathroom.

'I'll get them for you,' she told him. 'Come and sit down.'

She wanted to take his temperature, which she was sure would be higher than it should be. Even though he had been given antibiotics, there was no guarantee that the wound had not become infected.

As he reached the end of her bed, and slumped rather than sat down on it, she pushed her bedclothes back anxiously and got out—and then realised too late what she had done. She was completely naked, and that Christian was looking at her as though he wanted…as though he felt…

He made a low sound somewhere between a moan and a growl deep in his throat.

'Meg…*querida*…' His voice sounded raw with longing and pain, totally transfixing Meg to where she stood as he came towards her.

Helplessly she felt his arms close around her whilst his mouth sought hers with hungry male determination.

What was happening was wrong and oh, so very, very dangerous, but the touch of his mouth on hers was fulfilling her deepest, sweetest fantasies as he caressed her lips over and over again, stroking them with his tongue, absorbing the taste of her and drawing from her a desire, an urgency to give herself completely to him.

Passionately she returned his kisses, her lips parting, her tongue seeking his, her hand sliding inside his parted robe and spreading possessively across the silky heat of his naked skin. His left hand curled around her neck, holding her a willing captive to his desire. His hand moved, his fingertips tender against her face, before he groaned, bringing his hot face against the soft curve of her throat.

The breath that shuddered from him made her tremble in response, and moan—a soft, acquiescent sound of love. Christian's reaction was immediate, his mouth caressing, devouring the exposed curve of her throat.

As the passion they had both been suppressing exploded into life everything else was forgotten. The pain which had brought Christian into Meg's room no longer existed; the barriers Meg had been so determined to erect against him had totally disintegrated. They were two people being consumed by a need they were powerless to deny.

'*Querida…querida*, you cannot *know* how much I have wanted this…*you*…' Christian was muttering fiercely against her skin as he kissed her.

Meg closed her eyes as she drank in the words whilst her flesh absorbed the sheeting pleasure of his touch. Her whole body felt as though suddenly it had come to life... She ached with him and for him, wanted him with an intensity that was shockingly raw and elemental.

Savagely, her hands pushed aside his robe, her body shuddering in delight as she drank in the fierce dark male beauty of him. Tiny whorls of sweat-dampened body hair lay pressed flat against his torso. In his arms and shoulders she could see the powerful definition of his muscles, the warm gilded beauty of his flesh. Hungrily, her gaze absorbed the physical reality of him.

'You're so beautiful.'

As she whispered the awed words she saw his chest rise and fall with laughter.

'No, *querida*,' he told her softly. '*You* are the one who is that. Here...' he told her, cupping her face with one hand and gently kissing her mouth. 'And here...' His hand dropped to hold her breast, his lips caressing its taut peak slowly savouring its response to him. 'Here...' His voice became deeper, thicker as he dropped to his knees in front of her and placed a small circle of kisses around her navel.

Meg held her breath and tried not to tremble.

His hand was covering her sex, as though he knew how shy she suddenly felt.

'And here,' he told her as he slowly started to caress her, his gaze holding her eyes as his fingers slowly stroked her body, 'you are the most beautiful of all.'

Meg could hear the harsh disjointedness of her own erratic breathing, feel the frantic pounding of her heart, feel too the sweet melting heat that was running through her veins.

She closed her eyes as Christian lifted her onto the bed. She had been wrong about the feel of cool cotton being the most sensual pleasure she had ever felt. *This*... Christian's hot naked flesh against her own...was what *real* sensual pleasure was all about. She felt...she wanted...

As he touched her she cried out her feelings to him, reaching for him, aching for him.

Somewhere in the tiny corner of her mind that was not wholly consumed with love and longing, a warning registered that the heat coming off Christian's body was not just caused by the sensuality of their lovemaking, but she was too enthralled by what was happening to pay any attention to it.

Christian was kissing her with a ferocity of passion that totally obliterated all the vague, pale beliefs she had previously held about what she wanted from a lover. There was an intensity about the way he was touching her, *loving* her, that made her shudder in semi-shocked pleasure. His hands, his touch on her breasts, her belly, *everywhere*, his kisses, seemed to trigger a thousand tiny bolts of pleasure through her body.

She ached so to have him deep, deep inside her, filling her, taking her to a special place that would be uniquely theirs, completing her and completing the awesome cycle of love they had begun.

Lost, rapt with the intensity of her feelings, Meg cried out her thoughts to him.

Through the hot haze of his own desire Christian heard her, smothering and silencing the words of love his heart was pouring out to her against her mouth as he took it in a kiss of totally elemental possession in exactly the same moment as he filled her with his body—and his love.

The pleasure seemed to last for ever, and yet at the same time it reached its peak so swiftly that Meg felt dizzy and breathless. She cried out and heard the sound of her own fulfilment, a sharp gasped sound, quickly followed by Christian's fierce cry of male triumph.

As she lay trembling with aftershock in his arms, Meg felt Christian gently kiss her closed eyelids and then her mouth. His tenderness brought a hot burn of emotional tears to her eyes and she lifted her hand to touch him. He was burning up with heat, his skin slick with sweat.

Alarm replaced her euphoria. She opened her eyes and turned to look at him. That was surely a febrile feverish glitter in his eyes. Immediately her professional instincts swung into action. She guessed that he had a temperature and a fever, which ominously suggested that, despite the antibiotic shot, his wound had become infected.

'What is it?' he was demanding huskily. 'You look so serious…too serious…' He was reaching for her, obviously intending to take her back in his arms, his lips brushing her temple.

She wasn't imagining it, she was sure; their touch was far, far hotter than it had been before.

'Querida…'

Even his voice sounded different, slower, huskier and disorientated. Her anxiety increased. Gently easing herself away from him, she slid out of the bed. She needed to take his temperature, even though instinct and experience told her what she would find when she did.

She was gone less than five minutes—two minutes had been wasted in the bathroom, where she had inadvertently caught sight of her own reflection as she'd opened her medical bag. The face staring back at her from the mirror had indubitably been her own and yet, somehow, the face of a stranger, another Meg who, until tonight—until *Christian*—she had never realised existed. A Meg who looked as though…who looked like a woman who… Pink-cheeked, she had turned away and hurried back to the bedroom.

In the short space of time she had been gone Christian had fallen into a feverish sleep. He was moving restlessly, a hot flush plainly discernible beneath his tan, his body drenched with a fever-induced sweat.

Anxiously, Meg looked at his arm, her heart sinking as she saw how swollen the flesh was around the bandage. There was as yet no tell-tale red line of potential blood-poisoning creeping upwards towards his armpit—thankfully.

Grimly, she knew that at this stage the only thing she could do was to make him as comfortable as possible and hope that the antibiotics he had been given would be able to fight the infection until he was able to see the doctor in the morning.

'Meg?'

The shock of Christian's eyes suddenly opening whilst his lips framed her name held her motionless.

'Oh, you are there…' His eyes had the glazed look of someone not totally fully aware. His voice dropped, becoming softer so that she had to lean closer to him to hear him. 'Closer…'

His command made her instinctively lower her head to catch what he wanted to say, but instead of speaking he curled his left hand round her neck and began to kiss her.

He was her *patient*, Meg tried to remind herself. He wasn't *well*…wasn't even really *aware* of what he was doing. But the aching sweetness of his kiss fired her vulnerable emotions like a match to dry tinder. And yet, somehow, she managed to find the strength of will to pull away from him. Had *any* of what had happened been real for him? Had he *known* who she was when they had made love? Had he really wanted *her*, or…?

He had lapsed into a deeper and less feverish sleep. Mentally, she crossed her fingers, hoping that the antibiotics were now taking effect.

It was three o'clock in the morning. There was no way she was going to spend the rest of the night sleeping in a bed beside him.

Why not? an inner voice tempted her. It's what you *really* want to do, isn't it?

Of course it was, but she couldn't. He wasn't fully aware of his actions.

So where was she going to sleep—in *his* bed?

To her relief, a quiet inspection of the apartment revealed another empty guest room. But, despite the luxurious comfort of its bed, Meg knew she was unlikely to get much sleep in it.

She was right. At six o'clock she had had enough and was up and dressed, a jittery nervousness invading her stomach after she looked in on Christian and ascertained that he was sleeping restfully and apparently fever-free.

As she paced the floor of the apartment's huge reception room she nibbled worriedly at her bottom lip. Would Christian say anything about last night? Would he even *remember*? And, if he did, would he just dismiss what had happened as an unimportant one-night stand?

She swallowed hard. What was the code of behaviour governing such occurrences? She had never... *would* never... To her own disgust, she discovered that she was having to blink hard to keep her eyes free of self-pitying tears.

That's what you get, my girl, she told herself derisively, for giving in to your emotions for a man who doesn't share them.

She would wait until seven o'clock before waking Christian, she told herself, and once he was awake she would not make any reference at all to their lovemaking. If Christian chose to raise the subject...

Agitatedly, she paced even faster. Perhaps if she made herself a cup of tea...

She was in the kitchen, waiting for the kettle to boil, when, to her consternation, Christian suddenly walked in. Engrossed in her thoughts, she hadn't heard him, and the sight of him fully dressed and quite plainly recently shaved—and, she guessed, in full possession of all his faculties—caused her hand to tremble as she held the kettle.

'Careful' Christian warned her.

He was frowning, Meg recognised, and as she turned away from him to busy herself with her tea-making—and, more importantly, so that she wouldn't have to look at him—she could almost *hear* the frown in his voice as he demanded, 'Are you all right?'

'Of course. Why shouldn't I be?'

Confronted by her back and the sharpness of her voice, Christian hesitated. It was quite obvious that she didn't want to talk about what had happened between them. To wake up in the bed that should have been hers but in which he had quite plainly slept alone had told him that, no matter how wonderful the lovemaking they had shared had been to him, Meg did not want him as a permanent feature in her life.

And yet, last night, he could have sworn that she returned his feelings. The way she had touched him, *spoken*…whispering those soft sweet cries of incitement and longing. But although his memories of their lovemaking were sharply etched into his heart, there was a muzzy confusion over just why and when she had left him.

Last night she might have been his lover, his beloved, the embodiment of everything he had ever

wanted or would ever want in a woman, a partner, a
wife. But this morning she was very definitely distancing herself from him.

'You were very feverish in the night,' she was
saying to him, her back still to him. 'I was concerned
that an infection might have set in.'

'I remember having a hell of a pounding pain in
my arm,' Christian acknowledged.

'Yes. You came to my bedroom to ask for a painkiller,' Meg confirmed.

She felt sick with nerves as she waited for his response. *Could* he remember anything about what had
happened between them, or had his fever totally
obliterated the event?

Behind her back, Christian wondered how she
would react if he were to tell her the blunt truth—
which was that whilst he *might* have gone to her
room seeking a painkiller, what he had really *wanted*
had been her. And he still wanted her—right
now…right here…more than he could find the words
to say.

'Meg…'

There was something in his voice that made Meg's
heart thump heavily into her ribcage, but before she
could say anything the telephone started to ring.

Was she imagining it or had Christian started to
make a move towards her before the strident sound
of the telephone had called him away?

What if he had?

He was a man, after all. A man who quite plainly thought nothing of having sex with a woman he didn't love purely to satisfy his own basic sexual needs.

Trying to whip up her own defensive anger against him, Meg felt her lips tremble as she began to drink her tea.

'That was Juanita,' Christian informed Meg as he came back into the kitchen. 'She insists on blaming herself for what happened—totally unnecessarily, as I have already told her. If anyone is to blame it's Sancho,' he added, his voice hardening.

Meg had guessed already that Christian did not have a very high opinion of Juanita's brother-in-law, and she certainly agreed that to show the boys a gun had been totally irresponsible—but for some contrary reason she found herself defending the younger man.

'Oh, of course, I had forgotten that *you* are quite an admirer of him—as he is of you,' Christian replied with ruthless contempt.

In any other man she might almost have suspected that his savage response was motivated by jealousy, Meg decided—but that, of course, was impossible.

No, given Christian's low opinion of Sancho, he probably thought that he and Meg deserved one another.

CHAPTER SEVEN

'I PROMISE you that I am fine and fully recovered,'
Christian reassured his assembled family for the
umpteenth time since he and Meg had arrived back
at the *castillo*, to be greeted by their anxious enqui-
ries.

'We are really sorry, Tio Christian,' Tomaz and
Carlos had apologised solemnly.

Kneeling down beside them, Christian hugged
them both, telling them gently, 'It was an accident,
but now you see what a very dangerous thing a gun
can be.'

There was a lump in Meg's throat as she watched
this tender little scene.

Before they had left Seville, after their second visit
to the hospital, where the doctor had reassured Meg
that Christian's wound was healing nicely, Christian
had insisted on making a visit to a toy shop, where
he had purchased gifts for the two boys.

And today it was New Year's Eve, and the family
were celebrating the event with a dinner. To Meg's
relief the Señora had not suffered in her absence, and
when Meg had suggested diffidently that maybe the

family would prefer her not to be there on this occasion the Señora had been horrified.

'But of course you *must* be there… You are a *heroine*, Meg. Christian's mother cannot praise you highly enough, and besides…' She stopped and said nothing. The very promising 'signs' the two old friends had spotted and discussed were, they had agreed by mutual consent, to remain their 'secret' for now.

And so, reluctantly, Meg was now dressing for the special celebration dinner. Juanita's husband Ramon and Sancho had returned from their business trip, arriving just as Meg was crossing the hallway. She had been slightly taken aback to be engulfed in a rather more amorous embrace by Sancho than she had either expected or wanted, but rather than appear rude she had suffered it unresponsively.

'I wish you could have come with us,' he had told Meg, his eyes studying her boldly. 'You would like Madrid…'

'I think my godmother is waiting for you, Meg.'

Christian's voice, cool and sharp, had cut across Sancho's conversation as he'd come down the stairs.

They had hardly spoken to one another since leaving Seville. A part of Meg was glad that he seemed unable to remember what had happened between them, but another part of her felt both furiously angry and desperately hurt that something that had been so precious to her meant so little to him. And the hardest thing of all for her to deal with was that for most of the time her pain far, far outweighed the strength of her anger.

Meg had dressed carefully for the family's New Year's Eve dinner, thankful that she had had the foresight to pack her favourite slinky but simple long black jersey evening dress which, worn with the diamond ear studs her parents had given her for her twenty-first birthday and the gold bangle which had been a present from her brother, looked impressively elegant. Her heart might be breaking but there was no way she was going to allow anyone else to see that.

'Oh, Meg, you look gorgeous.'

The Señora's admiring comment when Meg went to her room to help her downstairs brought a brief smile to Meg's lips.

The Señora too was dressed in black, with diamonds which Meg suspected must be family heirlooms flashing at her throat and ears.

As though she sensed what Meg was thinking, the Señora told her gently, 'My jewellery was a marriage gift from my husband. It had been passed down to him for his bride by his grandmother.' Her eyes became suspiciously over-bright and Meg guessed that she must be thinking of the husband she had lost.

She tried to imagine how she would feel in the Señora's shoes, alone, without the love and support of the husband she had plainly adored, and gave a fierce shudder as she tried and failed to imagine a world without Christian in it.

'There is a pair of matching bracelets, but unfortunately my wrists are so swollen now that I cannot wear them.'

They were the last to arrive in the salon which opened into the *castillo*'s formal dining room.

Immediately they entered the room Meg was conscious of both Christian and Sancho looking at her, and it was obvious that there was still a certain amount of hostility between the two men. An uncomfortable tension pervaded the room and Meg noticed the unhappy looks Juanita and her husband exchanged as Sancho finished his drink and immediately demanded a refill.

When he had finished that and started to pour himself a third, ignoring the concerned frown his brother was giving him, it was left to Christian to say quietly to him, 'I shouldn't, if I were you, Sancho.'

Sancho's reaction was shocking and immediate. Slamming his glass down, he turned on Christian, demanding loudly, 'And who are you to moralise to *me*?' He turned his head to look at Meg, his glance full of drink-fuelled anger that made her feel more alarmed than flattered.

'*You* took Meg to Seville and spent the night alone in your apartment there with her, after you refused to allow her to go to Seville with *me*. You are a man, Christian—and I cannot believe—'

'That is enough.'

It seemed to Meg as though the whole room echoed with the shocked gasp that Sancho's outburst and Christian's tense response aroused.

Juanita was casting her husband an imploring, anguished look, whilst Christian's mother and the Señora looked openly shocked. The young Spaniard who had been serving their drinks blushed to the tips of his ears and Meg knew there was no way she could bring herself to look at Christian. She knew, too, that her own feelings were making her face burn revealingly.

Above the heavy thud of her heartbeat, she could hear Juanita's husband saying his brother's name in a sternly disapproving voice, but it was Christian who cut through the miasma of shock that had choked everyone into silence, his voice cool, crisp, authoritative and totally unemotional as he said icily, 'Your remark is both ill-bred, Sancho, and ill-informed. I am sorry, Mama,' he continued, turning to his mother. 'I had intended to wait until after dinner to make our announcement, but I'm afraid Sancho has forced my hand.'

And then, before Meg could speak or move, he

was at her side, holding her hand in his, turning his body protectively towards hers in a pose that said spectacularly plainly just how possessive he felt about her.

'I am proud to tell you all that Meg has consented to become my wife.'

As though he felt her tremor of shock, his grip on her hand tightened warningly.

'As you all know, there is a tradition in this family that its men fall in love only once in a lifetime, and at first sight. To fall in love very quickly and very passionately—this has always been my fate. And now I can say too—' his voice had started to become lower and softer, like liquid honey, Meg thought dizzily, as her brain tried to cope with what was happening '—that it is also my pleasure…that Meg is my one true love…'

He didn't get any further. Juanita had run towards them and hugged them both, exclaiming tearfully, 'Oh, I am so happy. This is so wonderful…'

And then Ramon was shaking Christian's hand and kissing her formally.

'We can tell you now that we both sensed that this was going to happen,' the Señora exclaimed in delight as both she and Christian's mother kissed Meg warmly.

Meg tried to protest, to destroy the lie before it

snowballed totally out of control, but it was already too late.

Christian was holding her so tightly that she couldn't move, and then he bent his head and whispered into her ear in a gesture which was deliberately contrived to look tenderly lover-like to their onlookers, 'Don't argue. If you do I shall be forced to kiss you into silence.'

She dared not allow herself to question whether it was an urge to be honest or her longing to feel his lips against her own that motivated her to try to deny his announcement.

Either way, just the look in his eyes as he focused his gaze on her mouth was enough to make her tremble from head to food and remain silent.

'Very wise,' he murmured to her as he escorted her into the dining room several seconds later.

Very wise? No... What *she* had been and was continuing to be was very foolish, Meg admitted guiltily, as she recognised how easy and how pleasurable it would be to allow herself to believe in the fantasy Christian had so unexpectedly created.

His wife-to-be...the woman he loved... Unable to stop herself, she turned her head to give him a betraying look of misty emotion. For a small heartbeat of time he looked back at her, and Meg had the unnerving impression that not only was he going to sweep her into his arms and kiss her passionately, right there in front of everyone, but that he was also going to sweep her out of the room and—

'I'm so pleased for you both,' Christian's mother began to tell Meg happily as they all took their places at the table.

'You guessed that I had fallen in love with Meg?' Christian questioned his mother.

'We both did,' she replied, smiling at the Señora for corroboration.

In the tidal wave of happy comments and questions that followed Christian's announcement, in some obscure way Meg had actually felt relieved to have him seated next to her, fielding them for her.

'No, we have not set a date for the wedding yet,' he responded to his sister's excited question. 'Meg wanted to speak to her parents before they did that.'

'Yes', he had made arrangements to have his grandmother's engagement ring removed from the bank vault and cleaned for Meg to wear, he confirmed to his mother, whilst Meg's eyes widened at the confident way in which he uttered the blatant lie.

Now that her initial shock had begun to wear off, she felt sick inside, contemplating the problems his fiction of their betrothal and marriage plans would cause. And making her feel even worse than that was the searing sense of pain it gave her to know how cynically Christian was using what, in her opinion, was something that should be treated with tenderness and respect.

The long meal was drawing to a close. The staff had been dismissed to enjoy their own special celebration with their families and soon it would be midnight.

Champagne fizzed and sparkled in heavy priceless flutes, and suddenly Christian, who had been talking to his mother, got up and walked across to a side table on which stood a huge bowl of grapes. Carrying it, he solemnly walked round the table, meticulously cutting off small bunches of twelve grapes for everyone.

Everyone but *her*, Meg noticed in puzzlement as he placed a slightly larger bunch on his own dessert plate, before putting the bowl back on the serving table and coming to sit down again next to her.

'There is a tradition from Madrid that on each stroke of the plaza's clock one eats a grape, one for each stroke, twelve in all...'

'It is a custom I brought to the *castillo* on my marriage,' Christian's mother explained to Meg.

A little bemused, Meg wondered why she had not been given any grapes, but before she could say anything one of the boys cried out excitedly, 'It is midnight...' And, sure enough, they could all hear the first chime of the elegant antique clock on the mantel above the fire.

'Meg.' The soft sound of Christian's voice as he whispered rather than said her name drew Meg's attention to him. 'Open your mouth,' he demanded.

He was holding out a grape to her and, flushing, she did as he was demanding.

As the slight roughness of his fingertips brushed against the sensitive softness of her lips it was *that* sensation, *that* and his taste, that lingered on her lips, rather than the sharp sweet flavour of the grape she was eating as the first stroke of the final hour of the final day of the year started to fade.

'Again,' Christian was insisting and, dizzy with emotion, Meg realised that he intended to feed each and every one of the twelve grapes to her and that, with the eyes of his family on her, there was nothing she could do to stop him.

A sensual wave of reaction shivered over her body every time his fingers brushed against her mouth. What he was doing felt so erotic that she ached to be able to flick her tongue over his skin, to taste the delicious flavour of him, to lick and suck, to... Her eyes widened when—as though by some magical means he had read her most secret thoughts and yearnings—on the last stroke his fingers lingered, his thumb gently rubbing against her bottom lip whilst his index finger rimmed the sexually sensitive flesh her lips protected.

She couldn't help herself. Everything that she was

feeling blazed passionately from her eyes as her gaze locked on his.

His hand reached for hers and helplessly she allowed him to take it and hold it, his thumb scrolling delicate secret circles of bitter-sweet pleasure against her palm as he picked up his champagne glass with his free hand.

'A toast,' he announced, 'To Meg, my beautiful bride-to-be…'

'To Meg…'

'Aren't you going to kiss her?' Juanita was asking Christian mischievously.

'Yes,' Christian replied urbanely, giving Meg a long dark-eyed look of sensuality that turned her body liquid with longing. 'But not here!'

They were all laughing, happy for her, happy to accept her into their family, Meg recognised in distress—all of them, that was, apart from Sancho, who, after a few discreet but obviously sharp words from his brother, now left the room.

It was past two o'clock in the morning when the Señora and Christian's mother eventually decided they were ready to go to bed.

Juanita and Ramon had gone up earlier with the boys, and now, when Meg made to go with the Señora, her patient told her firmly,

'No. This is your night, yours and Christian's…'

She gave a small wistful sigh, her eyes bright with memories. 'I remember the night of *my* engagement. My parents were very strict, but they allowed us to have an hour alone together…and we made very good use of it!' she added with unexpected forthrightness.

Meg felt too agitated to do anything more than listen. The moment she was sure everyone was out of earshot, she stood up from the elegant brocade sofa where she had been sitting and started to pace the soft-hued Aubusson carpet, for once oblivious to the elegant beauty of her surroundings.

'How *could* you have told them that?' she demanded shakily of Christian. She was almost wringing her hands as her agitation increased.

'I had no option,' Christian informed her. 'I had to refute the slur Sancho was casting on both your reputation and my own…'

Meg tensed. A tight ball of tension was threatening to block her throat, but she had to say what had to be said, no matter how much it would hurt her.

'Surely it's no big thing these days for…for an unmarried couple to spend the night under the same roof? After all…' She paused and then took a deep breath, but Christian was already answering.

'Certain conclusions would naturally have been drawn by what Sancho had implied, and not just by my family. My family is a very old-fashioned one,

Meg… I have a position, a reputation to maintain—not just as its head but as a representative of my country as well. And, besides—'

The haughty arrogance of his profile might at any other time have angered her, but right now…

'—there is no way I want to be judged as the kind of man who indulges in casual, careless sex…'

Meg hated the thought of being anything less than completely truthful, but in *this* instance… After all, Christian seemed either to have genuinely forgotten or had chosen not to acknowledge what had happened between them.

Turning away from him, her voice muffled by her emotions, she said quietly, 'Couldn't we just have told them that nothing happened? After all…that is the truth…'

Her voice had become so low that she could barely hear it herself. 'The truth?'

There was a long pause whilst she held her breath, and then Christian was saying evenly, 'I hardly think *that* would have been a good idea…not given what the "truth" actually is.'

He knew! He had known all along! He *hadn't* forgotten; his memory had never been wiped clean by his fever.

Dismayed, Meg swung round. Her face was paper-white with shock and pain. She heard Christian's sharply indrawn breath, but had no idea what was causing it until he said starkly, 'Have you given *any* thought to the potential consequences of what happened?'

Meg could feel her face starting to burn. This was even worse than the worst possible scenario she could have imagined. Mortified, Meg was forced to tell him with stammering discomfort, 'I… There won't… My doctor prescribed the birth control pill for me for…for other reasons, so…'

She couldn't go on and bit furiously on her bottom lip to stop it from trembling. One of the side-effects on her body of being attacked had been the disruption of her normally regular monthly cycle, and her doctor had advocated she take the birth control pill in order to help re-regulate this.

However, instead of receiving her confidence with the relief she had expected, to her astonishment Christian was actually frowning.

'I wish you hadn't said that we are getting married,' she told him, unable to conceal her anguish.

'Meg…'

She made a small warning sound as he moved towards her and, forgetting his bandaged arm, accidentally knocked it against a heavy table lamp.

Immediately she could see from his expression that the blow had been a painful one, and without thinking she started hurrying towards him. To her chagrin, he immediately stepped back from her.

'For God's sake Meg, can't you see? It isn't you as a *nurse* I want, it's you as a woman—the woman you were in my arms, the woman you were for my body. Do you know what you have done to me?' he demanded thickly. 'Do you care that I lie awake at night longing for you, aching for you? You gave yourself to me with such passion, such emotion, but it meant nothing to you. I thought...I hoped... But...' He stopped and shook his head.

'Have you any idea what it's doing to me, knowing that my love for you, my lovemaking with you, is so repugnant to you that you prefer to pretend that it never happened?'

Speechless, Meg stared at him. What was happening? What was he *saying*?

'You don't love me,' she protested in a small croak. 'You can't!'

'Look at me,' Christian commanded softly.

Reluctantly she did so, sucking in her breath and then slowly releasing it in a series of tiny jolting breaths of disbelief as she saw what was blazing in his eyes.

Christian was looking at her as though—as though—instinctively, she took a small step towards him, and then another and then, 'Christian,' she protested as his arm fastened round her.

'Christian, my darling, my dearly beloved,' he insisted thickly, his mouth so close to hers that she could almost feel his words against her lips. 'Say it,' he urged her rawly. 'Tell me… You can't know how much I need to hear again those sweet words of love you whispered to me in the night, *querida*,' he told her emotionally.

'Why have you been so cold to me?' he demanded passionately. 'So determined to reject me, when every time I look into your eyes I can see there…?'

He stopped, his expression grave, haunted almost, causing Meg's heart to give a funny little bump.

'What? What can you see there…?' she asked him in a choky little voice.

Cupping her face with both hands, Christian looked down into her eyes.

'I can see the woman who lay in my arms and who gave to me the sweetest essence of herself and her love,' he told her rawly. 'And yet that same woman behaves towards me as though she loathes me…'

'Because I felt…because I was afraid that…that you didn't love me,' Meg admitted huskily. 'You've always treated me with such disdain, such *indifference*,' she told him defensively when he said nothing.

'I treated *you* that way?' Christian grimaced. 'Have you thought what it has done to me to have you all passionate intensity in my arms one minute, and all cold rejection the next? When we left my godmother's apartment to drive here—'

'I thought the boys were yours,' Meg defended herself. 'I thought you were married, and then when I discovered that you weren't... When my father ran the marina here in Spain, my parents would often talk about the way that some men regarded the girls who come to Spain on holiday, looking for sex, and I was afraid—'

'You thought I would think that of *you*!' Christian's outrage brought a rueful smile to her mouth. 'Now you *are* insulting me,' he told her. 'And for that you deserve to be punished.'

But his mouth was already slowly caressing hers, as though he was unable to resist its tempting sweetness.

Blissfully, Meg wrapped her arms around his neck and opened her mouth to the hungry insistent probe of his tongue.

A long time later, she opened her heavy-lidded eyes and told him emotionally, 'If *that* was meant to be punishment...'

'Don't look at me like that,' Christian groaned. 'If you do—right now, more than anything else in the world, I want to take you to bed and show you all the ways in which I love you...'

He could feel Meg starting to tremble as she leaned against him.

'Christian,' she whispered.

'No,' he told her regretfully. 'Not until we are married.'

Meg's eyes rounded as she accused, 'That's so old-fashioned.' But secretly a small part of her was pleased.

She suspected that both Christian's mother and the Señora were of the old school, and she knew *she* would not feel comfortable sharing a bed with Christian under the same roof as his family until they were married.

'What is your parents' telephone number?' Christian was asking her. 'There is a very important question I want to ask your father.'

EPILOGUE

'HAPPY?'

Smiling blissfully as she nestled closer to her new husband, Meg nodded her head.

'I don't think I *could* be happier,' she told him breathlessly.

They had just returned to Christian's Seville apartment, having said goodbye to the various members of their families and their wedding guests who were to spend the night at the *castillo* before going their separate ways. They had combined the celebration of their marriage with the excitement of the Seville Epiphany festival, when floats filled the streets and the children received their traditional presents.

Meg had been disbelieving at first, when Christian had announced how quickly he wanted them to be married.

'That's impossible,' she had squeaked but, as he had quickly proved to her, even the impossible could be accomplished by a man passionately in love.

Tomorrow evening they were flying to the Caribbean for their honeymoon, but tonight they were celebrating their marriage and exchanging those most personal of all marriage vows in the very same

place—the very same *bed* Christian had teased her—
as they had exchanged their bittersweet lovers' vows.

As she raised her head for Christian's kiss, the
glitter of the diamond bracelets she was wearing
caught Meg's eyes, shiny with emotional tears as she
recalled the moment the Señora had presented them
to her.

'Christian is my godson, Meg, and in the short
time I have known you have become very, very dear
to me. These bracelets were a gift of love for me
from my own dear husband and I want to pass that
gift of love on to you.'

Emotionally, Meg had hugged her as she thanked
her.

As he watched her now, Christian knew that the
moment he had turned to see her coming down the
aisle of Seville's cathedral towards him was something he would remember with intense emotion for
the rest of his life.

'And to think that none of this would have happened if I hadn't tried to steal your car,' Meg murmured provocatively.

'You may not have succeeded in stealing my *car*,'
Christian responded, 'but you certainly managed to
steal my heart.'

'And you mine,' Meg whispered as her eyes dark-
ened with loving passion, a sweet urgency entering

her voice as she begged him, 'Take me to bed, Christian. I want you so much...'

'No more than I want you,' Christian told her rawly as he reached for her, holding her tightly against him with his uninjured arm. The bedroom door was already open and through it Meg could see the bed.

'Christian...Christian...' As she whispered his name he turned his head to kiss her. This time *both* of them were burning with fever—the fever of loving one another, Meg acknowledged, as her body started to tremble.

CHRISTMAS IN VENICE

Lucy Gordon

Dear Reader,

Venice is the most romantic city in the world, and what could be more romantic than to be courted there? It happened to me. I met a handsome Venetian; we fell in love and got engaged in two days. So when I came to write about Sonia, who visited Venice and got engaged to Francesco, a Venetian she'd known only two days, it was inevitable that some of my own story should creep in.

We really did wander through the little dark alleys at night, I did get my feet soaked by a passing boat on the Grand Canal, and laughed so hard that my "Francesco" later said that was when he wanted to marry me. And we did become engaged on a bench in the Garibaldi Gardens. My friends dismissed it as a whirlwind romance, and said I'd really fallen in love with Venice. But years later we're still together.

For Sonia it was different. The beauty of the city crept into her heart, confusing her about her feelings. It was only when she thought her marriage over, and she saw Francesco once more at Christmas, that she understood she had discovered a love that was deep and true, and would never let her go.

Lucy Gordon

CHAPTER ONE

JUST a few more minutes—just ten—then five—then they would reach Venice, the city Sonia had sworn never to set foot in again. As the train rumbled across the lagoon she refused to look out of the window. She knew what she would see if she did. First, the blue water, sparkling under the winter sun, then the roofs and gilded cupolas, gradually emerging from the mist on the horizon. It was perfect, magical, a sight to lift the heart. And she didn't want to see it.

Venice, the loveliest place in Italy, in the world. She'd come here once before, and later fled, blaming it for her misfortunes. But for the summer beauty of the city she might never have been tempted into a disastrous marriage to Francesco Bartini. She knew better now. She'd fled Francesco and the heartbreakingly beautiful surroundings where they'd met, vowing never to be seduced by either of them again.

She tried not to think of him as he had seemed to her then, smiling, at ease with himself and everyone around him. He wasn't handsome—his features weren't regular enough for that, his nose too large, his mouth too wide. But his eyes were dark and full of delicious wickedness, his smile was brilliant, and when he laughed he was irresistible. She'd been enchanted by his charm and good nature, the speed with which he'd fallen in love with her, as though he'd been only waiting for her to appear to recognise the love of his life.

'But that's true,' he'd said once. 'Why delay when you've met "the one"?'

He'd been so sure she was 'the one' that he'd made her believe it too. But Venice had helped him, with its beauty, its glitter of romance that was there around every corner. Venice had helped to deceive her into thinking a holiday flirtation was a lasting love, and she would never forgive Venice for that.

So why was she coming back?

Because Tomaso, her father-in-law, had begged her, and she had always liked him. Even in the bad days of her marriage the hot-tempered little man had always made her feel how fond of her he was. On the day she left he had wept, 'Please, Sonia—don't go—I beg you—*ti prego*—'

Officially, she was only returning to England for a visit, to 'see how she felt'. But none of them were fooled, especially Tomaso. He knew she wasn't coming back.

He'd held onto her, weeping openly, and his wife, Giovanna, had regarded him with scorn, because who cared if the stupid English wife left? She'd been a mistake from the start and thank goodness Francesco had realised at last.

Tomaso had wept despite his wife, and Sonia had wept with him. But still she had left. She'd had to. But now she was back, because Tomaso had begged her.

'Giovanna is very ill,' he'd said, the day he turned up at her London apartment. 'She knows she treated you badly, and it weighs on her. Come home and let her make her peace with you.'

'Not home, *Poppa*. It was never a home to me.'

'But we all loved you.'

And that was true, she reflected. With one exception they had all loved, or at least liked her: Francesco's sisters in-law, his three brothers, his aunts, his uncle, his endless cousins, had all smiled and welcomed her. Only Giovanna, his mother, had frowned and been suspicious.

How could she return? It was nearly Christmas. Travelling would be a nightmare. Worse, she would have to see Francesco again, and what would they say to each other after the last dreadful meeting in London? He'd followed her there to make one final effort to save their marriage, and when it failed he'd been curt and bitter.

'I won't plead with you any more,' he'd raged. 'I thought I could convince you that our love was worth saving, but what do you know of love?'

'I know that ours was a mistake,' she'd cried, 'if it was love at all. Sometimes I think it wasn't—just a pretty illusion.'

He'd given a mirthless laugh directed at himself. 'How easily you talk love away when it suits you. The more fool me, for thinking you had a woman's heart. Well, you've convinced me. You want no more of me, and now I want no more of you. Go to hell in your own way, and I will go in mine.'

She'd never seen him like that before. In their short marriage he'd been angry many times, with the hot temper of the Latin, flaring now and forgotten a moment later. But this bitter, decided rejection was different. She should have been glad that he'd accepted her decision, but instead she was unaccountably desolate.

She'd tried to be sensible. She'd told herself that that was that, and she could draw a line under her marriage.

But the very next morning she'd woken up feeling queasy, and known that everything had changed. There had been tests but the result was never in doubt. She was carrying Francesco's child, and she'd learned it the day after he'd stormed out declaring he wanted no more of her.

She heard his voice many times repeating those words. She heard it every time she reached for the phone to tell him about their baby, and it always made her pull her hand back, until at last she no longer tried.

So when Tomaso had arrived in London his eyes had opened wide at the sight that met him.

'You're having his child and he doesn't know?' he demanded, shocked.

It had touched her heart the way he never doubted the baby was Francesco's. But Tomaso had always thought the best of her, she recalled. It made it hard to refuse him, although she'd tried.

'How can I go back now?' she'd said, indicating her pregnancy. 'When Francesco sees me like this it will revive things that are best forgotten.'

'Don't worry,' Tomaso had reassured her. 'Francesco is courting someone else.'

She'd suppressed the little inner shock, the voice that cried out, 'So soon?' After all, she had left him. He was a warm-hearted man who wouldn't stay alone for long. She had no right to complain.

She insisted that Francesco must be warned before she arrived, and Tomaso telephoned his son and gabbled something in the Venetian dialect which Sonia had never been able to follow. When the call was over he'd announced, 'No problem. Francesco says the baby is yours. He won't interfere.'

'That's fine,' she'd said, trying to sound pleased.

Well, it *was* fine. It was exactly what she wanted. If he wasn't interested in his own baby that suited her perfectly. And if she was being unreasonable, so what? She was eight months pregnant and entitled to be unreasonable.

Because she was so close to her time they couldn't fly, and had embarked on the twenty-four-hour train journey. That was how she'd made her first trip, because she'd booked at the last minute and couldn't get a flight. So she'd approached Venice by train over the lagoon and seen it rising from the sea in glory.

Tomaso glanced at her as she sat, refusing to go to the window. 'After all this time, don't you want to see Venice welcoming you back?'

'Oh, *Poppa*, that's just a pretty fantasy,' Sonia protested, smiling to take the sting out of the words. 'Venice deals in pretty fantasies, and I made the mistake of taking them seriously.'

'And now you make the mistake of blaming the city for being beautiful,' he replied.

'So beautiful that I fell in love with it, and thought that was the same as being in love with a man.'

He was silent, but regarded her sadly.

'All right, I'll take a look,' she said to please him.

But the sight that met her wasn't what she had expected. Where was the magic, the gradual appearance of gilded cupolas touched by the sun? How could she have forgotten that this was late December? A dank mist lay on the sea, shrouding the little city so that there was no sign of it. When at last it crept into view—reluctantly, it seemed to Sonia—it had a glum, heavy-hearted appearance that reflected her own feelings.

At the station she tried to carry her own bags but Tomaso flew into a temper until she let him take them. He commandeered one of the taxi boats, and gave the driver the name of her hotel. The Cornucopia.

Of course, he didn't know that this was where she'd stayed that first time. No matter. She would enter the Cornucopia again and banish her ghosts.

She'd had to brace herself for the sight of the Grand Canal on leaving the station. The railway station had a broad flight of steps leading down to the water and, on the far side, the magnificent Church of San Simeone. It had made her catch her breath when she first saw it three years ago, and again when she had arrived there in a gondola to be married, a few short weeks later. Now she tried not to look, but to concentrate as Tomaso handed her carefully down into one of the taxi boats in this city where the streets were water.

The chugging of the motor boat made her a little queasy, so she didn't have to look at the palaces and hotels gliding past. But she was aware of them anyway, she knew them so well, and every tiny *rio* as each little side canal was called: Rio della Pergola,

Rio della due Torri, Rio di Noale, taking her closer to the Cornucopia, until at last it came in sight.

The Cornucopia had once been the palace of a great Venetian nobleman, and the company that had turned it into an hotel had restored its glory. Beneath the mediaeval magnificence was a good deal of modern comfort, but discreet, so that the atmosphere might be undisturbed.

She was booked into a comfortable suite on the second floor.

'You look tired,' Tomaso told her. 'You need a rest after that journey. I'll leave you now, and call back in a few hours to take you to see Giovanna.'

He kissed her cheek and departed. It was a relief to be alone, to wash the journey off, and ease her heavy body onto the bed.

At least she wasn't in the same room as before. Then the city had been full for the Venice Glass Fair, with not a room to be had. Sonia, booking at the last minute, had been forced to accept a place nobody else wanted, at the top of the building.

It had been little more than an attic, she recalled, but she'd had her own bathroom, and she'd hurried into the shower to wash off the journey. When she'd finished she'd taken a whirl around the tiny room, thrilled by her first foreign trip for her employers, and her first visit to Venice. At this height there were only the birds to see her, and she finished by tossing

aside her towel and standing, arms ecstatically up-
stretched in a shaft of sunlight from the window.

The door opened and a young man came in.

She was totally naked, her position emphasising
her perfect body, long legs, tiny waist and full
breasts. And he was barely six feet away with a
grandstand view.

For what seemed like forever they stared at each
other, neither able to move.

Then he blushed. Even now it could make her
smile to think that he had been the one to blush.

'Scusi, signorina, scusi, scusi…' He backed out
hastily and shut the door.

She stared at the panels, but all she saw was his
face, mobile, vivid, fascinating, blotting out everything else in the world. Only then did she remember
to be indignant.

'Oi!' she yelled, snatching up her towel and dash-
ing for the door. In the corridor outside she found a
pile of large boxes, two hefty workmen and the
young man. 'What's the idea of barging into my
room like that?'

'But it's *my* room,' the young man protested. 'At
least, it was supposed to be—nobody told me you
were here. If they had—' his eyes flickered over her
and he seemed to be having difficulty breathing
'—if they had, I—I would have been here twice as
fast—'

Her lips twitched. Mad as she was, she wasn't immune to the flattery in those last words, or something in his look that went deeper than flattery.

The towel, inadequate at the best of times, was slipping badly. The two workmen watched her until the young man snapped something out and they vanished hurriedly.

'Let me put something on,' she said, retreating into her room, and grabbing a robe. The young man followed as if in a trance. She would have gone into the bathroom but she'd backed herself onto the wrong side of the bed.

'I don't look,' he said, understanding.

He turned away and covered his eyes in a theatrical fashion that made her laugh despite her agitation.

'No peeking,' he promised over his shoulder. 'I am a gentleman.'

'You shouldn't have followed me in here. That's not the act of a gentleman.'

'It's the act of a man,' he said with meaning.

She tied the belt firmly in place. 'OK, I'm decent now.'

He looked around. 'Yes, you are,' he agreed sadly.

'Will you please tell me what you're doing in my room?'

'Tomorrow the Venice Glass Fair starts, and one of the biggest exhibitions is in this hotel. The manager is a friend of mine. He said nobody ever wants this room, so I could use it to store some of my glass.'

'I booked at the last minute. I think it was the only room left in the city.'

'Forgive me, I should have checked.' He gave a rueful, winning smile. 'But then we would never have met. And that would have been a tragedy.'

There was a note in his voice that made her clutch the edges of the robe together lest he detect that her whole body was singing. Just a few words, and the glow in his eyes, and she felt as though he was touching her all over.

He had a slim, lithe figure and wonderful dark eyes, set in a lean, tanned face, still boyish as it probably always would be. Sonia was a tall woman but she had to look up to see his black hair with its touch of curl.

'You—you're exhibiting in the glass fair, then?' she said.

'That's right. I own a small factory, and I'm here to set up my stall.'

'I'm here for the fair. I'm a glass buyer for a store in England.'

His face lit up. 'Then you must let me take you on a tour of my factory. It's here.' He took a card from his pocket. 'Only a few tours for specially privileged visitors—'

'Would you mind if I got dressed first?'

'Of course. Forgive me. Besides I have to find somewhere for my glass.'

'But won't you have it downstairs on the stall?'

'Some yes, but some will be sold, or given away, or broken. So I must have spares nearby.'

'Doesn't the hotel provide you with storage space?'

'Of course, but—I've brought rather more than I should. I thought I could make it all right.'

Later she was to discover that this was his way: bend the rules and worry about the practical problems afterwards. And it usually did work out, because he had such charm and confidence. Even then, ten minutes after their meeting, Sonia found herself saying, 'Look, I don't mind—if there isn't too much.'

'There is nothing—almost nothing—you'll never notice it.'

In fact there were ten large boxes, but she didn't see the danger until they were all crowded into her room so that she could barely move. And then she lacked the heart to tell him to take them away. She'd even helped him carry them in. She'd actually *offered*. He was like that.

'Never mind,' she said brightly. 'There won't be so much when you've set up your stall.'

'It's up,' he explained. 'This is just the extras. You really are a bit cramped, aren't you?'

She gave him a baleful look.

'There's nothing for it,' he said with a sigh. 'I shall have to take you out to dinner.'

'That will be impossible,' she said crossly.

'Why?'

'Because all my clothes are in the wardrobe that is now completely blocked by your boxes.'

It took them ten minutes to get the wardrobe door clear, and then he wouldn't let her choose her dress in peace.

'Not that one,' he said, dismissing a deep blue silk that she'd bought specially for this trip. 'The simple white one. It's far more you.'

By this time she was beyond argument. In fact, beyond speech.

'I'll call for you in one hour,' he said. Halfway out of the door he looked back, 'By the way, what is your name, please?'

'Sonia,' she said, dazed. 'Sonia Crawford.'

'*Grazie*, Sonia. My name is Francesco Bartini.'

'How kind of you to tell me—finally.'

He grinned. 'Yes, perhaps we should have been formally introduced before you—that is, before I—'

'Get out,' she said, breathing fire. 'Get out while you're still safe.'

'Beautiful *signorina*, I haven't been safe since I

opened that door. And nor—I must confess—have you.'

'*Out!*'

'An hour.'

He vanished. At once a light seemed to have gone out of the room. Sonia stared at the door, torn between the impulse to hurl something and an even bigger impulse to yield to the smile that seemed to be taking possession of her whole body.

And the really annoying thing was that she discovered she actually did look best in the simple white dress.

Sonia came out of her reverie to find that she was smiling. However badly their love had ended, it had begun in sunshine and delight. Francesco had been thirty-three then, but so comical and light-hearted that he'd seemed little more than a boy, with a boy's impulsive enthusiasms. Better to remember him like that than as the domestic tyrant he became, or the embittered man of their last meeting.

Nor, however hard she tried, could she silence the voice that whispered the ending hadn't been inevitable, that something better could have grown from that first moment when he'd stared at her nakedness, smiling with admiration.

If she concentrated she could banish the lonely hotel room, and see again his expression, full of shock and the start of longing, feel again the happiness that just the sight of him had once brought her...

She forced herself back to reality. What was the use of thinking like that?

There was a knock on the door, and with a start she realised how much time had passed. This would be Tomaso to fetch her to the hospital. Slowly she went to the door, and opened it.

But it wasn't Tomaso. It was Francesco. And his eyes, as they gazed on her pregnancy, were once again full of shock.

CHAPTER TWO

'*MIO DIO!*' Francesco, murmured, sounding as though he could hardly breathe. '*Oh, mio dio!*'

He came in and shut the door behind him, while his eyes, full of accusation, flew to her face. 'How could you have kept such a thing from me?'

'But—you knew,' she protested. 'Tomaso told you on the phone when he—' The truth hit her like a blow. 'He didn't tell you, did he?'

'Not a word.'

'Oh, how like him! How like this whole family! He spoke Venetian, which he knows I can't follow unless it's very slow. And when he came off the phone he said he'd told you about the baby, and you weren't interested.'

'And you believed *that*?' he demanded.

'Yes, because he said you had someone else, and—oh, this can't be happening!'

'Maybe he thought I had the right to know,' Francesco said in a voice of iron.

She waited for him to say, 'Is it mine?' But he didn't. Like Tomaso, he never doubted the child was his, and she had a brief flicker of the old warmth.

These were good people, kind, eager to think the best. Why had she found it so hard to live with them?

'Don't expect me to blame *Poppa*,' Francesco said. 'It's obvious that he had to lie to get you here.'

'And I suppose Giovanna's illness was another invention?'

'No, that's true. My mother's heart is frail. She collapsed a few days ago. She wants me to take you to see her in the hospital.'

She thought of the big bustling woman who had always ruled her family, except for Sonia, who wouldn't let herself be ruled. To Giovanna, every detail of their lives was her domain. The others accepted it as natural and laughed, shrugging it off. But to Sonia, who'd lived alone since she was sixteen, and kept her own counsel even before that, it was intolerable.

Now Giovanna's inexhaustible heart was wearing out. It was like the end of the world.

'You don't mean she's dying?' she asked.

'I don't know. I've never seen her as tired as this before. It's as though all the fight's gone out of her.'

'Your mother—not fighting?'

'Yes,' he said heavily. 'I can't remember a time when she wasn't squaring up to somebody about something. Now she just lies there, and all she wants is to see you.'

'Why? She never liked me.'

'You never liked her.'

'She never wanted me to like her. Oh, look, we can't have this argument again.'

'No, we had it so many times before, didn't we?'

'And it never got us anywhere.'

The fight had carried them through the first few awkward minutes, but now, with round one over, they retired to their corners, and regarded each other warily.

The six months since their last meeting had made him a little heavier and there was a weary look in his eyes that was new, and which hurt her to see. His eyes had always danced—with mischief, with delight. And they had made her too feel like dancing. Now the dancing had stopped and the sun had gone in, and everywhere was cold.

'Where is she?' Sonia asked.

'In the hospital of San Domenico. It's not far.'

In any other city they would have gone by car, but there were no cars in this place where the streets were water, so when they left the hotel they strolled across the piazza before plunging into a maze of tiny alleys.

Sonia pulled her coat about her, shivering. A heavy mist had appeared and in the darkness of the narrow lanes it was hard to see far ahead. All she could make out clearly were the coloured lamps that had been hung up for Christmas, and the lights glowing from the windows of homes. People scurried up and down, carrying parcels, wearing smiles. It was Christmas, and despite the gloomy weather the Venetians were set on celebrating.

A turn brought them out beside a narrow canal, the water's surface pitted by raindrops. Here there were no lights, no people, just a dank chill.

Suddenly she became aware of their direction. 'Not this way,' she said sharply.

'This is the quickest route to the hospital.'

As he spoke they turned another corner and there was the place she hadn't wanted to see, the Ristorante Giminola, looking just the same as when she'd seen it for the first time. Francesco saw her face.

'So you're not as hard-hearted as you would like me to believe,' he said.

If only he knew, she thought, how far from hard-hearted she was. She should never have come back. It hurt too much. She drew a sharp breath. No weakening. She managed to shrug.

'As you say, it's the quickest route to the hospital. Let's go.'

But she walked past the restaurant without looking at it. She didn't want to remember the night when he'd taken her to it for the first time, and they'd fallen in love. That had been two and a half years ago, in another world, where the sun had shone and everything had been possible.

The simple white dress was as perfect on her as he had predicted. She tried on three sets of accessories before settling for a necklace of turquoises mounted in silver.

Then more decisions. Her hair. It was light brown and grew in wavy profusion halfway down her back. Up or down? Of course, he'd already seen it down, that afternoon. Not that he'd been looking at her hair, she recalled with a smile. Up, then.

She studied her face closely, wanting him to see it at its best. She'd been a professional woman ever since she'd first braved the world alone three days after her sixteenth birthday, with no family to help or hinder. She was used to applying make-up to emphasise the assets nature had given her, the lovely skin, regular features and large blue, expressive eyes. But, studying herself in this way, she missed the signs that warned of trouble ahead. Her mouth was curved and lovely, but a touch too resolute, the mouth of a woman who'd had to fight too much, too hard, too young. If she was unlucky it might become stubborn and unyielding, driving away the very thing for which she most yearned.

But right now the warnings were faint. She was in a city she'd dreamed of visiting, full of happy ex-

citement, and her mouth was ready for laughter
and—she considered thoughtfully—and whatever
else the evening might bring.

At five minutes to the hour there was a knock on
her door. Opening it, she found nobody there, just
one perfect red rose, lying at her feet. She managed
to fix it in her hair, just before the second knock.

This time it was him, and his eyes went straight
to the rose.

'Thank you,' he said simply.

She didn't ask where they were going. What did
it matter? When they were downstairs he took her
hand and led her out into the sunlight, and it was as
though she'd never known sunlight in her life before.
Across the piazza and into an alley so tiny that the
sun was blotted out, around corners, down more alleys, each one looking just like the last.

'How do you ever remember your way?' she asked
in wonder.

'I've known the *calles* all my life.'

'*Calles?*' She savoured the word.

'You would call them "alleys", the tiny streets
where we can walk and talk to our neighbours.'

Something in his voice made her ask, 'And you
love them, don't you?'

'Every brick and stone.'

When they burst out of the last *calle* she had to
stand and blink at the flashing of the sunshine on the

Grand Canal. Francesco grasped her hand more firmly and drew her to some sheltered tables beside the water. While he ordered coffee she gazed out on the bustle of the canal. Every boat in Venice seemed to be there, and arching over them a wide bridge, with buildings on both sides.

'That's the Rialto Bridge,' Francesco told her. 'Do you remember your Shakespeare? Shylock in *The Merchant of Venice*?'

'He asked, ''What news on the Rialto?'' ' Sonia recalled.

'Because in those days it was a great commercial centre, where all the money deals were done. Now it's mostly trinket shops and a food market.'

'All those boats!' she exclaimed. 'Gondolas, motor boats, all crowded together. You'd think they'd bump into each other. What's that long boat with a white roof?'

'That a *vaporetto*, a kind of bus. It plies the Grand Canal.'

He fell silent while she watched, entranced by the life and the vivid colours. There was so much she wanted to ask about, but not yet. For now it was enough to be here, entranced by the beauty and magic of her surroundings, feeling another, older kind of magic creep over her. She gave him a brief, sidelong glance, but she didn't need to do that to know he was watching her, smiling with delight.

'If you've finished your coffee, we might walk on,' he said at last. As they got to their feet he took her hand again, and led her over the Rialto Bridge.

As he'd said, there was a lively market, just beginning to wind down. He stopped at a stall, took two peaches and handed her one. The plump grocer watched him with a grin, which didn't fade even when Francesco said,

'Your peaches don't get any better. But I'll do you a favour and relieve you of a couple.' He strode on.

'Hey,' Sonia said, hurrying to catch up with him, 'shouldn't you have paid for those?'

'Pay?' he was shocked. 'Pay my own cousin?'

'That man was your cousin?'

'That's Giovanni. Every time his wife gets mad at him he comes to me and I give him a beautiful piece of glass for nothing, to placate her.'

'Does she get mad often?'

He considered. 'He's a good husband—in his way, but he has an eye for the ladies. I'm running out of glass and I haven't paid for my fruit for years.'

She chuckled. This was all mad, but it was like being on another planet, where the rules were different, and she could have a holiday from being her usual tense, cautious self.

Afterwards there were so many things to remember about that first night, but sometimes they all seemed to blur together, and sometimes each detail stood out sharply. All Venice seemed to be the same little street, one turning into another. Yet the Ristorante Giminola where he'd taken her to eat was clear in her mind.

It was a small cosy place where the owner greeted Francesco with a yell and showed them to a table by the window. The menu delighted Sonia. It was printed in three languages and the translations had been done by someone whose English was hit and miss.

'What on earth are "schambed eggs"?' she laughed.

'I think they're "scrambled eggs", but I wouldn't bet on it.'

'And "greem beans"?'

'Done by the same man, I should think. Also "roats potatoes".'

He ordered wine and *prosciutto* ham.

'Tell me about yourself,' he said. 'I want to know everything about you.'

An imp of mischief made her reply, 'I think you've already seen everything about me.'

'Please,' he begged, 'don't remind me of that.'

'Is it such an unpleasant memory?' she teased.

He gave her a speaking look. 'Do you really want me to answer? Well, I shall. But later. When we're alone together.'

She felt as if she was clinging onto a runaway

train. Two hours ago she hadn't even met him. Now they were rushing headlong into passion.

But the passion had been there from the moment he saw her nakedness and she saw his shock and admiration. The rest was talk.

'You wanted to know about me,' she said in a voice that wasn't quite steady. 'I'm English. I work for a chain of fancy goods stores—gifts, novelties, fine glass and china. It's just been bought by people who want to expand and they decided to try Venetian glass. They only took over this week, which is why my trip here was arranged at the last minute. It's my first big assignment and I'm going to make a success of it. And it's my first sight of Venice.'

'You put that the wrong way around,' he said gravely. 'It's your first sight of Venice that matters.'

'Well, you're a Venetian—'

'Yes, I'm a Venetian and I know that this is one of the wonders of the world. Now you have seen it, it will be with you all your life.' His merriment had faded, and she realised he was talking about something that mattered to him deeply. She hoped he would go on, but he smiled and said, 'Tell me some more. What about your family?'

'I have none. My parents are both dead. I studied Fine Arts in evening classes, specialising in glass. I want to have a shop with the best glass from all over the world.'

He gave a mock frown. 'But only Venetian glass matters. Why should you bother with any other?'

'Well—other countries do make good glass.'

'Not compared to Venice,' he said firmly.

It was impossible to tell if he was serious, but the gleam was always there in his eyes, and she decided it would be safer to take everything this charmer said with a pinch of salt.

'I think I'll keep my options open,' she said, refusing to be won over so easily.

'Of course you must,' he agreed readily. 'And then you will discover for yourself that Venetian is best.'

'If you say so. Now tell me about you.'

'I am Francesco Bartini. My parents are Tomaso and Giovanna Bartini—'

'And you're their only son,' she said impulsively.

'Of course I'm their only child—except for my brothers Ruggiero, Martino, and Giuseppe.'

'You made that up,' she laughed.

'No, truly. Why did you think I was their only child?'

'You've got so much self-confidence—as though—'

'Spoilt, you mean?' he challenged. 'You could be right. I may not be the only child, but I'm the youngest—and it's almost the same thing.'

'Are you spoilt?' she asked, laughing.

'Rotten. That's why I got out into the world at the

first chance and made my own name. I borrowed
some money from the bank and bought a disused
factory on Murano.'

'Murano?'

'It's one of the islands across the lagoon. They
each have their own speciality. With Torcello it's
fishing, Burano is lace-making and Murano is glass.
The factory had gone out of business but I told the
bank manager I could make it work. He didn't believe me—I was only twenty-two—but I talked and
talked until he got crazy and said yes to shut me up.'

'I don't believe this,' she laughed. But she did.

Under his gentle questioning she found herself
talking about things she'd never discussed before. To
say her parents were dead didn't begin to describe
the wilderness of pain that had engulfed her when
her father walked out on his wife and five-year-old
daughter. She'd been alone from that moment, for
her mother had collapsed back into herself, and never
been the same again. She'd struggled through the
next few years, sometimes managing to look after her
little daughter, often being looked after by her.

Sonia wasn't even certain that her father was dead.
She only knew that she hadn't heard from him for
nearly twenty years. Her mother had died when she
was twelve leaving a welfare system to take her,
more or less kindly, into its care.

'I pity anyone who had me as a foster child,' she

told Francesco ruefully. 'I was used to managing my own life and my mother's by that time, and I couldn't stop being bossy. I had three foster homes. They were all glad when I left.'

'I'm sure that's not true.'

It was true, but she didn't try to describe the chaos of her life. The child had developed a fierce independence that she found impossible to give up, and at sixteen she'd been left to confront the world alone, with only her excellent education to help. It had seemed like enough. Beautiful and talented, she'd attracted admiration easily, and if her relationships came and went too quickly, she could dismiss that as the result of her work. She hadn't yet understood that there might be another reason. And on this magic night, when her heart was melting as never before, it was easy to forget that she usually kept it safely guarded.

She talked on and on, rejoicing in the sense of freedom that was new and ecstatic. And suddenly she glanced up to find him watching her, and something caught in her throat. Their eyes held while the world seemed to stop.

After that she'd argued and rationalised, seeking to blind the truth by throwing words in its face. But in her heart she'd known there was no way back.

It was dark when they left the restaurant, and he did what no other man would have done, took her, quite naturally and without self-consciousness, to a tiny little church, tucked away in a back street.

'Come and meet my friend,' he said simply, and Sonia looked around for a priest. Instead he led her to a small niche near the altar where candles burned beneath a figure of a mother and baby.

'When I was a child I started to come here because I liked the Madonna so much,' he confided. 'She's different.'

Sonia saw what he meant. The figure had no trace of the wistful aloofness she'd seen on the faces of other Madonnas. She was plump and cheerful, like a robust little housewife, and she carried a chuckling infant that stretched out his arms to the world.

'I felt she was my special friend and I could talk to her,' Francesco said. 'She listened to my troubles and never disapproved, even when I was bad.'

'Were you very bad?'

'Oh, yes. I kept her working overtime.'

He added a lighted candle to the ones already there, smiled at the little group and gave them a cheeky wink before departing.

'You *winked* at the Madonna?' Sonia said as they left.

'She doesn't mind. She knows it's only me.' He suddenly took her hands. 'I never told anyone about this before. Do you think I'm crazy?'

'No,' she said softly. 'I think it's rather nice.'

Where had they walked after that? She never really knew. Away from the tourist centre, Venice lived in its narrow backstreets. She kept only the memory of their footsteps on the flagstones, the dark narrow *calles*, sparsely lit by lamps so far apart that there was always a pool of darkness halfway between, for lovers.

Somewhere in that darkness he had taken her into his arms and his lips had found hers. It was the culmination of something that had begun that afternoon and she rejoiced at it.

She had never before gone so easily into a man's arms on a first date, but time was rushing swiftly by with the flowing of the water, and magic had to be seized before it vanished. And besides, this was Francesco, who was different to every other man, because his lips were more thrilling and persuasive and made her long for him to hold her tighter.

When he raised his head to study her in the dim light she saw something in his face that made her heart beat faster. He was trembling and she waited for him to draw her closer. But instead he seemed to master himself with an effort.

'We should—go on,' he said.

They wandered on and found themselves by the Grand Canal, with a small flight of steps down to the water. She ventured down, followed by Francesco, determined to kiss her again because his virtuous resolution had already failed. And as they stood, locked in each other's arms, a large boat came up the canal, sending waves streaming to either side, making the water swell about her shoes.

They had cost her a fortune, those shoes, but in that enchanted night, it had all suddenly seemed terribly funny. Oblivious to Francesco's dismayed apologies, she leaned against him, shaking with laughter.

'That was when I fell in love with you,' he'd said on their honeymoon.

'Not until then,' she'd teased. 'What about when you first saw me?'

'No, when I saw you naked and beautiful I was determined to take you to bed. But when you saw the funny side of being soaked my heart became yours, and I decided to marry you.'

'Really? *You* decided?'

'Uh-huh! You never had any choice in the matter. Now, come here.'

Laughing, she'd gone into his arms. It had all been a delightful joke then that Francesco always got what he wanted. What did it matter? She wanted the same things as he, and of course she always would. That went without saying.

CHAPTER THREE

THE next day the Glass Fair began. After breakfast Sonia wandered into the great ballroom of the Cornucopia where last minute preparations were going on, and saw Francesco at once, talking into a mobile. He waved, beckoning her over, and she went, smiling. He wouldn't kiss her in front of this crowd of course, but he would give her a glowing look, meant for only her. Perhaps he would say something special and intimate.

But his first words were, 'If you're going out, can I have your room key so that I can collect what I need?'

'I—yes,' she said, pulling herself together. 'Here it is.'

'Bless you. Did you sleep well?'

'Not very. I was awoken in the night by a box falling on me.'

'That's terrible! Did anything get broken?'

'No, nothing was damaged,' she said with some asperity. 'Including me, thank you for asking!'

He grinned but the phone rang before he could answer. He mouthed, 'Later,' and turned away.

What had she expected? she thought. The lover of the night before was now all businessman. Her time would come—later.

The fair was spread out around five hotels, and Sonia conscientiously visited the other four, talking to salesmen, noting stock, putting in some orders. And all the time she was functioning on automatic. There was a presence in her mind that refused to go away. He just sat there, smiling wickedly at her, reminding her of the night before. Her lips seemed to tingle with the remembered pressure of his, and the anticipation of the evening to come.

By using every ounce of her self-control she managed to put off returning to the Cornucopia until the end of the day, but at last she was free to return. The great ballroom was still busy, for the fair had been a roaring success. Sonia made her way to the Bartini Fine Glass stall, eagerly looking for Francesco.

He wasn't there.

There was a young man in glasses, and two businesslike young women, deep in conversation with customers, but no sign of Francesco.

One of the young women finished with her customer. Sonia showed her business card and said coolly, 'I was hoping to speak to Signor Bartini himself.'

'I'm afraid he's gone for the day. He's taking some clients to dinner.'

It was like a blow in the stomach. He'd just vanished without waiting to see her. Suddenly she felt incredibly foolish. He'd wanted the use of her room and giving her the big romantic act was the simplest way to get it. After all, he was an Italian, wasn't he?

Moonlight, gondolas and magic. But the bottom line was—where else could he have stored all those boxes at a moment's notice?

She hurried up to her room and as she'd expected, every last box had gone. He'd taken what he wanted and left without even a thank you.

She flicked over her notes. She'd done a good day's work and there was no reason for her to stay any longer. The sooner she was out of here the better. She began packing furiously, arranging her clothes with deadly precision. The dress she'd meant to wear for him tonight was folded to within an inch of its life. Having vented her rising temper in this way, she went down to the desk.

'I'd like to check out. Please will you call me a motor boat?'

In a few minutes she was on her way to the station. She would catch the next train and put all this behind her, she decided sensibly.

But at the station she received a check. The last

suitable train had left five minutes ago, and the next one wasn't for three hours.

Oh, great! Oh, great!

There was nothing to do but sit on the platform muttering rude words about Francesco, which she did with enthusiasm. She was just starting again from the beginning when a frantic cry of, *'Sonia!'* made her look up to see Francesco tearing along the platform at full speed, arms waving, with the demeanour of a man watching his last hope disappear. She took a moment to enjoy the sight. She felt she'd earned that. Then she rose and faced him wryly.

He pulled up sharply and the words spilled out. 'Where are you going? I've been trying to find you, I've been expecting you all day, and then they told me you'd checked out and I've been going crazy.' It all came out almost in one breath.

'I've spent my day working,' she said indignantly. 'I've been around the whole fair. I called at your stall at the end and was told you'd left for the day. You should be entertaining clients to dinner. What are you doing here?'

'Trying to track down this awkward, prickly woman, who's so dim-witted she can't tell when a man's in love with her. I got through as much work as I could today so that we could spend tomorrow together, *and then you vanished.*'

'*I* vanished? *You* vanished—'

'I left a message at the stall for you to call me—'

'I never got it.'

'And I went up to your room, but it was empty. I thought I'd lost you, and I ran here…' He took hold of her hands. 'But now I've found you again and I won't let you go.'

He pulled her into his arms and she clung on tightly, overwhelmed with relief and happiness. He kissed her determinedly, just in case there was anything she hadn't understood, and she kissed him back, oblivious to their surroundings and the grins of passers-by.

'You're mad,' she choked. 'Quite mad.'

'I know, darling,' he said into her hair. 'I know.' He picked up her case. 'Let's get back quickly, so that you can change for dinner.'

'But aren't you—?'

'I'm going to take you to meet people, show you off.' He drew her firmly along the platform, never taking his arm from about her waist.

But at her hotel they found a snag. In the short time she'd been gone, her room had already been snapped up.

'That's it,' she said despondently. 'Now I can't stay here.'

'There is somewhere you can go,' he said, almost

shyly. 'There's a room in my apartment that no-body's using—'

'I don't think so—'

'You would be as safe as in church. I give you the key to the door and I take many cold showers.'

'Stop talking nonsense,' she said, trying not to laugh.

'You don't want me to take cold showers? That's wonderful! Then we can—'

'No, we *can't*,' she said firmly, yet not without a faint twinge of regret. 'This isn't really a good idea.'

At once he took firm hold of her. 'It's a wonderful idea because I won't let you leave me. Hurry now, we haven't much time.'

'Hey, where are we going?'

'I told you, to my home.' He'd seized up her case and was walking out of the hotel.

He lived in a second floor apartment overlooking a *rio*. It was tiny, kitchen, bathroom, one main room *and only one*—?

'Where's the second bedroom?' she demanded suspiciously.

He looked innocent. 'There isn't one.'

'You said you had a spare room.'

'No,' he said, with the air of a man thinking fast, 'I said I had a room nobody was using just now. And I'm not using it—look, it's quite empty—'

'That's not what—'

'And I'll sleep on the sofa. See, it's easy.'

I was like arguing with a cartload of monkeys. She ought to walk out now. But she didn't want to walk out. Nor did she want to have dinner with his clients. She wanted to stay here and—

'I'll get changed and then we can go out,' she said firmly. 'Can I have the key to the bedroom door, as you promised me?'

He looked guilty. 'Well, actually—'

'It doesn't lock, does it? Leave at once if you know what's good for you!'

'I take a cold shower,' he said, and vanished quickly.

She was left grinning at the door. She couldn't help it. He was mad. He was tricky. But he was full of life, and at the station he'd said something that had made her heart sing.

'...so dim-witted she can't tell when a man's in love with her.'

He was in love with her. But of course it was just another of his tricks and she must be even more on her guard than ever.

When she saw him half an hour later she had to bite back a murmur of admiration. He was in dinner jacket and black bow tie and looked more handsome than any man had the right to.

Tonight she was wearing the dark blue silk dress, the one he'd rejected, but he didn't seem to remember that.

'You are beautiful,' he told her. 'See, I've brought you a gift.'

It was a dainty pendant of silver, so perfect that she gasped. He draped it about her neck and she felt his fingers lightly touch her. But instead of moving away he stayed where he was, his hands on her shoulders, his warm breath whispering against her skin. She too remained quite still, willing him to draw her against him.

'We should leave now,' he said with an effort. 'We mustn't be late.'

'No,' she replied, hardly knowing what she said. Her head was swimming.

They took a motor boat back to the Cornucopia, where Francesco's party was waiting.

'Please forgive me for being late,' he begged, adding, with a grin towards Sonia, 'it's all her fault.'

Everybody laughed and when the introductions had been made they all moved out to the open air restaurant overlooking the Grand Canal, with a view of a floodlit church over the water. Darkness had fallen and the church seemed to be floating, holding Sonia's entranced gaze.

There were eight guests, mostly glass buyers from

abroad, plus a couple of Venetians involved in the trade. Sonia sat next to one of these, a man who spoke excellent English, and was soon deep in conversation with him. To her surprised pleasure she found that she could hold her own.

After the meal they left the table and strolled along the balcony. One of the other buyers, an Englishman, came up beside her.

'Heard you talking,' he said smoothly. 'You really know your stuff.'

'Thank you.' She wished he wasn't so close. His aftershave was nearly flattening her.

'I'm the head glass buyer at—' he named London's most luxurious department store. 'Just given Francesco the biggest order he's ever had.'

'I'm sure he deserves it.'

'Well, I believe in encouraging talent. Talking of which, the store is always looking for new blood. I could put a good word in for you.'

'Thank you, but I'm fine where I am.'

He considered a moment before indicating the floodlit church. 'Got nothing like this at home.'

But I'll bet you've got a wife at home, she thought crossly.

'That's true,' she agreed, moving away a little.

He moved closer. 'I get lonely when I'm away. I expect you do, too.'

He raised his hand to trail the fingers along her arm, but his wrist was seized in a hard grip. Francesco's eyes, friendly but implacable, looked directly into his.

'How is that lovely wife of yours, John?'

'She's—er—lovely.' The man flexed his wrist painfully.

'Good. Why don't you call her?'

John attempted a laugh. 'Hey, is that any way to treat your best customer?'

'I sell glass, I don't sell my fiancée.'

John threw up his hands. 'Say no more—misunderstanding—' he sidled away.

Sonia stared at Francesco. 'You said—'

'A figure of speech,' he replied hastily. 'Just to stop him arguing.'

'But he'll cancel his order after the way you treated him. He's your best customer, remember?'

'Yes, he is, and to the devil with him! If he'd touched you any more I'd have thrown him into the canal,' Francesco said deliberately.

'That's very nice of you, but I'm a big girl and I can deal with oafs like him.'

'Don't tell me that,' he complained. 'Tell me how thrilled you were to have me galloping to your rescue on my white charger.'

'No way,' she said stubbornly.

Before he could reply everyone was 'rounded up' by one of the guests who made a speech thanking Francesco for his hospitality, 'and for giving us the chance to meet his lovely bride.'

Sonia opened her mouth, then closed it again.

'I'm sorry,' he said as they were walking home. 'Someone must have overheard me.'

'And taken you seriously.'

'No, it was just an excuse for another drink. Nobody will give it another thought.'

He spoke with a touch of uneasiness that passed her by. She was busy watching the moon appear and disappear between the roofs.

On his doorstep he took her in his arms and kissed her long and lingeringly.

'Wouldn't we be better off doing this inside,' she murmured hazily.

'No, because once inside I cannot touch you again.'

'Why not?'

'Because,' he said in a shaking voice, 'I am a man of honour.'

He wouldn't budge from that. In the privacy of his apartment, with nobody to see what did or didn't happen, he ushered her into her room, bid her a chaste goodnight, and closed the door firmly on her. A few minutes later she heard the sound of the shower going, and smiled even as she thumped the pillow in frustration.

'John' left the next day, having first cancelled his order. Francesco shrugged, handed his exhibition stall over to his assistants, and announced to Sonia that he was taking her on a visit to his factory.

'Your employers will be most impressed that you've investigated real Venetian glass-making,' he promised her. 'What's the matter?'

'Nothing,' she said, looking about her. 'Except that I thought there was a woman over there, watching us.'

Francesco glanced up just in time to see the woman retreat into the shadows.

'Never mind,' he said, hurrying her along.

'There's someone else watching us on the other side.'

'I know. I saw.'

'But who are they?'

'The first one was my Aunt Celia, and the second was my niece Bettina. You've already met Giuseppe. Forget them. There'll be plenty more.'

'They're spying on us?'

'In Venice it's not called spying. It's called taking a family interest. The man leaning out of the window over there is my eldest brother Ruggiero.'

'You mean—last night—?'

'It's all over Venice by now,' he admitted. 'Baby brother has gotten himself engaged at last.'

'But we're not really—I mean it was only—'

'There's a boat,' he said hastily. 'Run.'

Seizing her hand he hurried to the jetty where a water taxi had just pulled in. The driver hailed him by name, and said, 'Murano, eh?' without waiting to be told. It was obvious Francesco was well known all over Venice.

The island of Murano lay across the lagoon. As the wind streamed through her hair Sonia had the feeling of travelling directly into the sunlight. It was all about her, glittering on the water, dancing in the distance, inviting her on to somewhere beautiful and exciting that she'd never dreamed of before. She laughed aloud, looking in Francesco's eyes, and reached out her hand to him.

The factory was like a furnace, a place where the traditional methods of glass-making were treasured. She watched, entranced, as a man created a vase by blowing, turning the pipe around and around. She didn't even notice another man, rapidly sketching her as she watched, but later there was a plaque with her own head etched on it. The perfect end to a perfect visit. Had she felt, even then, that it was too perfect, too romantic, too *much*? Or had she walked on, blinded by enchantment?

There had been so little enchantment in her life. Did she really blame herself for yielding in a weak moment, or regret those few days of blazing, heart stopping happiness?

They returned to the main part of Venice for lunch, wandering through the streets until they found a place to eat. And everywhere Sonia realised that she was being inspected. Once a beautiful dark-skinned young woman waved and vanished quickly.

'My sister-in-law, Wenda,' Francesco explained. 'She's Jamaican.'

'And I suppose you're also related to the oriental girl studying us from behind that stall,' Sonia retorted.

She'd spoken ironically but Francesco replied, 'That's Lin Soo. She's from Korea and she's married to my Uncle Benito.'

She burst out laughing. 'Have any of your family married Venetians?'

'One or two. But we tend to go travelling and bring brides home. When we all sit down together it's like the United Nations.'

They ate in a tiny *trattoria*, whose owner—as Sonia was growing used to—hailed him by name.

'It's as though you knew everyone in Venice,' she said in wonder.

'But I do,' he said in surprise. 'I've lived here all my life.'

'I've lived all my life in London, but I don't know everyone there.'

'That's because London's a huge city. Venice is called a city, because it's one of the great treasures of the world, but it's actually a small village. If you know the way you can walk from one end to the other in half an hour, and meet your friends around every corner.'

As they were drinking coffee his mobile rang. The subsequent conversation consisted mostly of Francesco saying, *'Si, Poppa—si, Poppa!'* When he had finished he said, 'I'm under orders to take you home to supper tonight.'

'Your father's orders?'

'Goodness no! My mother's. He was just acting as her messenger.'

She was amused. 'Suppose I have other ideas?'

'*I* had other ideas, but when Mamma speaks, we all jump.' He saw her regarding him with her head on one side, and he looked uneasy. 'It's better we do as my mother says.'

'All right, as long as you take me there in a gondola.'

'But a gondola isn't a method of transport,' he explained. 'They do round trips for the tourists.'

'You mean you don't have a gondolier friend who'll make an exception for you?' she teased.

And, of course, he did. Marco had been to school with Francesco, and gladly made a special trip for him.

'How can he row this thing with just one oar?' Sonia wanted to know. 'We ought to be going around in circles.'

'One side of the boat is longer than the other,' Francesco told her, straight-faced.

'Oh, really—'

'Honestly. It bulges more one side than the other, and that evens it out. It's like everything else in Venice, like the Venetians themselves. Cock-eyed!'

She began to laugh. He laughed with her, and somehow her head was on his shoulder as they floated onwards to the Rio di St. Barnaba, where his parents lived.

Marco helped them disembark, looking Sonia over with admiration, then watched them stroll out of sight before whipping out his mobile to spread the news that another good man had bitten the dust.

Now the gondolas were still. On the Grand Canal the *vaporetti* chugged noisily up and down. Christmas was nearly here, and last minute preparations were in full swing, yet the streets were strangely peaceful. No vehicles, only people, smiling, stopping to talk to each other, breaking off the shopping for a quick visit to a bar.

There was a bar on the corner, casting its glow over the dim light of the street, luring them with sounds of good cheer.

'I usually stop here for a coffee first,' Francesco said.

'Fine,' she said, glad to defer the coming meeting.

A light snow was beginning to fall as they slipped inside and she settled at a table while he brought them coffee. Italian bars were unlike American bars or British pubs. As well as wine and beer, they sold coffee, ice cream and cakes, and were places where the whole family enjoyed themselves together.

Today this one was busy with people crowded around little tables, toasting each other with cries of 'Buon natale' and 'Bon nadal.'

'How happy they look,' she murmured wistfully.

A burst of laughter from a table in the corner made her look more closely, frowning, for she was sure she recognised her sister-in-law, the Korean Lin Soo.

Soo, as the family called her, had with her two children of about ten, their faces a beautiful mixture of Italian and oriental, their eyes dark and excited.

They beamed when they saw her and hurried to throw their arms about her. 'Aunt Sonia!'

Then Soo came to embrace her, and behind her Teresa, Giuseppe's wife.

'We've just come from visiting Mamma,' they told her. 'We always stop here afterwards.'

The needless explanation told its own story. Sonia gave Francesco a wry look, which he met with bland innocence.

'What a coincidence,' she murmured. But she was really glad to see these two, whom she'd always liked. They settled down to talk about Mamma and the giddy spell—not a heart attack, they were quick to insist—that had taken her to hospital.

'We thought she'd be out after a few days' rest,' Soo mourned, 'but she just lies there, as though she's too tired to go on.'

With almost deafening tact they failed to mention her pregnancy, and Sonia guessed that Tomaso had warned them. Once more the mobile connections had been humming, spinning a web of anticipation about her, so that wherever she went there was a Bartini waiting. Once she had found it suffocating, but now she was grateful not to have to make explanations. There was, after all, something restful about people who knew and accepted you without question, and worried about you when you weren't there.

After a few minutes her sisters-in-law departed, despite Francesco's urging them to stay.

'Don't stop them,' Sonia said when they'd gone, adding, amused, 'They have to call *Poppa* and tell him that we're nearly here.'

'I already did that while you were talking,' he confessed.

After a moment she laughed. 'It's like being under surveillance by the CIA,' she said.

'But not spied on,' he said quickly. 'Watched over. They're all thrilled that you're here. Of course good news gets passed on.'

She preferred not to answer this directly. 'I remember the night you took me to meet them all. They were strange to me, but every one of them knew what I looked like. Everywhere we went in Venice there was a Bartini watching us and reporting back. I've never known a grapevine like it.'

'My father was especially anxious to meet you. Both Ruggiero and Giuseppe had told him how beautiful you were.'

'He was always nice to me,' she remembered with a smile.

When she remembered that meeting, Tomaso was the one she saw first, a little, bald-headed man, beaming all over his round face, advancing with arms outstretched, greeting her as a daughter, although she hadn't yet agreed to marry Francesco. She wasn't even thinking of it, she told herself.

And behind him, Giovanna, large, magisterial, her face set in an expression of welcome that didn't quite disguise its natural aloofness.

They were all there, and with the Bartinis *all* was a big word. As well as his brothers and their wives there were Tomaso's siblings, and Giovanna's. At various points in the evening miscellaneous nephews and nieces found excuses to drop in, greet Sonia, look her over, and smile a welcome. Once she reckoned there were as many as thirty people in the tiny place.

Tomaso spoke some English but Giovanna had none. Wenda acted as interpreter while Giovanna fired questions at her as though from a machine gun. Under such circumstances it just wasn't possible to explain that she and Francesco weren't really engaged. She did her best, stressing that they'd only met two days ago, but that only provoked Tomaso to recall that he'd fallen in love with Giovanna at first sight, too.

They ate in the pocket-sized garden, hung with coloured lamps. The meal was magnificent, course after course of perfectly prepared Venetian dishes, until she felt overwhelmed.

Perhaps that was the idea, she thought. Giovanna

CHRISTMAS IN VENICE

was watching her, but so were all the others. It seemed that everyone had contributed to the meal, and they all scurried back and forth to and from the kitchen. But their smiles were so genuine and their pleasure in her company so frank that she soon relaxed and forgot that she was 'on show'. When she left they each kissed her and murmured something about seeing her again soon, and she murmured something vague in return.

They were all crowded at the doors and windows to wave her farewell. At the corner of the street she turned and waved back, feeling as if all the world was there, smiling at her. At an upper window Giovanna stood alone.

CHAPTER FOUR

BY NOW Sonia was becoming used to the Venetian grapevine, so it didn't seem strange that when they turned the corner there was Marco and his gondola, waiting for them.

'Is he going to take us back to your apartment?' she asked with a smile.

'And a few other places first.'

It was late at night and most of Venice had gone to bed, so they had the little canals almost to themselves. Only one or two other gondolas were out, and for the first time Sonia heard the yodelling cries that gondoliers uttered when approaching a blind corner, to warn other traffic. In the warm night air those cries echoed back and forth across the water until they whispered away into the silence. She listened, entranced by the sound, by Venice, by her love.

'I have to go home tomorrow,' she said from within the crook of Francesco's arm.

'Why?'

'I've stretched this visit as long as I can. It began as a working trip and it turned into a holiday.'

He didn't reply, seeming sunk in thought. He knew now that this was the end of their time together.

Tonight they would set the seal on a beautiful holiday romance that she would remember all her life.

Because that was all it was, all it could ever be: a holiday romance. To think anything else was madness.

By now she thought she knew Francesco, a light-hearted charmer, full of tricks, able to turn any situation to his own account. But he was also, as he'd told her, a man of honour, and unexpectedly stubborn about it. When they reached home, tonight was the same as last night, the chaste kiss, the bedroom door safely closed on her.

It was up to her, then.

She waited until the night was quiet before slipping out of the bedroom and into the main room where he lay sleeping on the sofa, a blanket thrown over him. She could just see his face. In sleep it had an innocence at variance with his wicked charm. Dropping to one knee beside him she laid her mouth over his.

After a moment he opened his eyes and she felt his arms go about her. This was different from kisses they'd shared in shadowed alleyways. It was full of purpose as though he'd come to an inevitable conclusion. She stood up, taking his hand in hers, and led him into the bedroom.

Now he knew that she wanted him he threw off restraint as easily as he threw off the few clothes he was wearing, and eased her nightdress down from her shoulders so that it slipped to the floor, leaving her naked and lovely.

His first kisses on her neck and breasts were gentle, almost by way of introducing himself, then more urgent as he felt her flower under his touch. With a sense of blissful release she let go of caution. There would be another time to be cautious, but now was a time to love, even if only fleetingly.

Love should always be like this. Here was a poignancy of emotion and sensation that might never come to her again, so she would treasure it in her heart. She would remember too the way he touched her body as though she were the first and only woman in the world, and whispered strange, passionate words that she understood only through their intensity.

In the hot summer night they made love with the windows flung open so that the sound of softly flowing water streamed into her consciousness and seemed to carry her away. The moonlight limned his body, covering hers, but she was less aware of the sight of him than of the feel of pleasure and joy deep within. His caresses were skilled, but they touched her heart less than the near reverence with which he treated her, as though he was afraid she might vanish from his arms at any moment.

Afterwards, as they lay close, he murmured gently to her in words she didn't understand.

'What was that?'

'Te voja ben. Te voja ben.'

'What does it mean?' she whispered against his skin.

'It's how a Venetian says "I love you."'

Silence. He was waiting for her to say it too, but was she out of her mind? She barely knew him. She should flee this minute, back to her old, safe life.

'Te voja ben,' she whispered.

She hadn't meant to say it, and as soon as the words were out she knew she should take them back. But she couldn't. She had known perfection, and she wouldn't insult it with regrets.

'Te voja ben.' She framed the words again as she fell asleep.

She awoke to the sound of Francesco busy in the kitchen. She lay listening to him for a moment, smiling at her memories. But hard on their heels came the remembrance that this was the end.

'I'll get packing right away,' she said over breakfast.

'Of course,' he said readily.

Too readily, she thought, with a sinking heart. Surely after last night he had something else to say?

'It'll be enough if you catch the afternoon train,' he observed. 'This morning we can go for a walk.'

He took her along the waterfront with palaces on one side and the shining lagoon on the other until they reached the park known as the Garibaldi Gardens. Down the centre was a wide avenue of trees, lined with stone benches forty feet apart. He led her to one of these and they sat quietly together, while time passed, and still he said nothing.

At last he spoke. 'I'm sorry if Mamma overwhelmed you last night.'

'It was you, telling her that we were going to get married.'

'I didn't exactly tell her,' he protested. 'Just—'

'You just told everyone.'

'That's true. And Mamma picked up the idea because it's so much what she wants. Now she's set her heart on it.'

'Well, I'm sure you can explain after I've gone.'

He looked alarmed. 'But, darling, I always do what Mamma wants.'

It took a moment for this to sink in. 'What—are you saying?'

He looked pathetic. 'If I don't marry you, she'll beat me up. You wouldn't want that, would you?'

'Oh—*you*!' Laughing, she aimed a swing at him, but he imprisoned her arms.

'Oh, no,' he said firmly. 'If *you* want to beat me up, you have to marry me first. It's a family privilege.'

She was on the point of throwing herself into his arms when she was suddenly swamped by an attack of common sense. Normally common sense was her element, but it had been so much in abeyance recently that it returned now with the force of a gale.

'We can't do this,' she said hurriedly. 'We're crazy to be even thinking about marriage. We know nothing about each other.'

'We know that we love each other.'

'You don't know me. I'm not the person you've seen the last few days—laughing, relaxed, just letting things happen. I *never* just let things happen to me. I always plan, so that I've got some control. I feel safer that way. But here, with you, I'm different.'

'But that's good—'

'I'm different because I'm on holiday,' she cried. 'But when I'm me again I'm—someone else. Someone you might not even like.'

Why, oh, why hadn't he listened to her? she thought long afterwards. For she'd been right in every word, as though she'd had a ray of clairvoyance.

But instead of being sensible he'd looked at her and said gently, 'Are you saying you don't love me?'

'No—no, I *do* love you—'

'Then the rest can be sorted out.'

She hadn't the heart to protest further. She wanted

him too much, and in this lovely place it was easy to believe that all problems had an answer.

'*Te voja ben,*' he repeated. 'I love you.'

She wrinkled her brow. 'Which word means "love"?'

'None of them. Literally it is, "I wish you well."' He seized tight hold of her. 'I wish you well, Sonia.' Then, head thrown back, a triumphant shout up to heaven. '*I wish you well.*'

She began to laugh, not with amusement but with joy. He joined in and everything was laughter and happiness.

'Say yes,' he cried. 'Say it quickly before you have time to think. Say it, say it.'

'Yes,' she laughed. 'Yes, *yes, YES!*'

'Come!' he seized her hand and began to run.

'Where are we going?' she gasped, struggling to keep up.

'To tell my family. They'll be so pleased.'

'But—'

'Hurry, it'll take hours to visit them all.'

And it did, she thought later. *Even at that moment, he thought of the family first.*

But still, it was the happiest day I ever had.

Now here they were, little more than two years later, further apart than they had ever been as they walked side by side to the hospital to see his mother. The cold seemed to be in her heart, yet at the same time, it seeped into her from the outside: not crisp, bracing cold such as she'd known in England, but damp, depressing cold.

'This must be the most miserable city in the world in winter,' she said, shivering.

'No place is at its best in winter.'

'But the others don't have this much water. It's everywhere, all around you, and it makes everything so dank. I always disliked Venice in winter.'

'Yes, you were never a true Venetian,' he agreed. 'We love our home best now, because when the tourists have gone we have time for each other. But you never had time for any of us.'

'I was never given the choice. It was as though the whole family lived together. All fifty, or was it sixty? Your mother even chose where you and I should live.'

'My bachelor flat was too small for us. And you liked the new place until you realised *she'd* found it.'

'And it was only two streets away from her.'

'Venice is a tiny place. You're never more than a few streets away from anyone.' He added heavily, 'Well, you're far enough away now, aren't you?'

A few minutes more brought them to the hospital of San Domenico. It was a small place but finely equipped, and the white corridors looked pleasant and cheerful, especially now, hung with brilliant Christmas decorations. The way up to Giovanna's room lay past Maternity, and as they neared the door a plump little nun came briskly out, clutching a wad of files. Her face lit up as she saw Sonia's bulge.

'There, I knew I'd win!' she said, beaming. 'I'm Mother Lucia. I run the Maternity Ward. You're just in the nick of time.'

'For what?' Sonia asked, bewildered.

'Why, to have our Christmas baby of course. I bet Dr Antonio that we'd have one.'

'You took a *bet*?' she echoed, unable to keep her eyes from the little nun's habit.

Mother Lucia chuckled, understanding everything Sonia couldn't say. 'I bet him three chocolate bars, that we'd have a Christmas baby,' she said, 'but he insisted there was nobody due. He must have forgotten about you.'

'No, I'm not a patient here,' Sonia said hurriedly. 'I'm visiting from England.'

'Oh!' The little nun's face fell with almost comical disappointment.

'Besides, I'm only eight months gone.'

'Rather more, I should have thought,' Mother Lucia said, regarding her judiciously. 'I think I might win yet. I'll light a candle to our Madonna downstairs. She often solves problems.'

Sonia had grown used to the Italian way of regarding the Madonna less as a religious icon than as a friendly aunt, but even so she was left gaping by this practical speech. Mother Lucia gave a last speculative look at her pregnancy before bustling away.

Giovanna was in a room on the second floor, lying still, her hand in Tomaso's. He was sitting beside her, his eyes fixed on her face. Now and then he patted her hand gently and looked into her face for some sign of a reaction. But she seemed unaware of him, her eyes fixed on some distant world inside herself. Sonia thought she had never seen an expression more piteous than Tomaso's as he tried to recall her to him, perhaps before she slipped away forever.

He looked up and smiled briefly, coming towards them.

'I ought to be angry with you,' she told Tomaso. 'You told me you'd explained to Francesco about—' she indicated her bump.

Tomaso gave a shrug, very Venetian. 'Sometimes it's good to tell the truth,' he said wisely. 'Sometimes—better don't bother. She'll be so glad you came,' he hurried on before Sonia could speak. 'The others have all been in, but it's you she asks for.'

Sonia went to the bed, and was shocked to see how frail Giovanna looked. She had always been a big woman, tall and broad shouldered, with the air of someone who could cope with the whole world.

Now she seemed to have shrunk. She opened her eyes and looked at Sonia.

'You came,' she murmured, sounding surprised.

'Of course,' Sonia replied, not really knowing what to say.

'I thought you—refuse,' Giovanna said, speaking in her fractured English.

'No, I came as soon as I knew you wanted me,' Sonia said. It wasn't strictly true, but Tomaso was right. Sometimes it was better not to bother with the truth.

'Bad you go away,' Giovanna murmured. 'Better for me to go—I did harm, but—not mean to.'

'It wasn't you,' Sonia said. 'It was me. Our marriage was wrong from the start. Francesco can find someone who suits him better.'

'Better than wife he loves?' Giovanna asked. 'Better than his child's mother?' She hadn't previously reacted to the pregnancy, but she'd noticed it, Sonia now realised.

'You don't know—' Giovanna murmured.

'What don't I know?'

'A baby—changes everything. Nothing is the same—love is not the same. But *you* do not love *him*, eh?'

'No—maybe—I don't know.'

'My fault,' Giovanna said with a sigh of exhaustion. 'I tried to—but no good. Too late.'

'I don't understand you.'

'How can you? Long, long time ago.' She sighed, 'No matter now.'

'But it does matter,' Sonia said, alerted by something in the old woman's manner. Giovanna was trying to tell her something and she didn't understand. They had never understood each other. 'Try to tell me.'

Suddenly Giovanna's hand tightened on Sonia's, and a terrible urgency came over her. 'Not—like—me,' she said vehemently.

'I do like you,' Sonia lied. 'Or I could have done, if—'

'No!' Giovanna's face was contorted with effort. 'Not that—'

But it was too much for her. She released her grip and fell back against her pillows, her eyes closed.

'I'm sorry,' Sonia said to Tomaso and Francesco. 'I'm afraid I've tired her.'

'You did your best,' Tomaso said. 'You came here.'

Full of pity for the old woman, Sonia leaned over to kiss her, and was close enough to hear the soft murmur, *'No esser come mi.'*

She stared, but Giovanna lay still, and she couldn't be certain that she'd heard anything. She turned away, feeling despondently that her visit here had been a total failure.

As they walked away from the hospital, Francesco put his arm around her shoulder and said gently, 'Thank you, that was kind.'

'Will she die, do you think?'

'I don't know. I hope not. But if so, she will go more peacefully for having spoken to you.'

Sonia was silent, thinking things weren't that simple. Her failure to connect with Giovanna had given her a sense of floundering that was only too familiar. The old woman's last message had been spoken in Venetian, and she simply hadn't understood it.

'Perhaps you'll come and see her again before you go?' he said.

'I don't think so. I'm starting back tomorrow morning.'

'So soon? I thought—that is, I hoped—'

'I can't stay. I've done what I came to do, and I need to get back home.'

'But, in your state, should you take that long journey again?'

'I'll have a good night's sleep.'

He shrugged. 'Well then, you'd better clear out the last of your things.'

'What?'

'You left some stuff at the flat. I don't like to throw it out unless you tell me, but I need the space.'

For his new girlfriend, she thought. Well, that was all right.

'I didn't know I'd left anything behind. You never said.'

He shrugged. 'I suppose I got a bit sentimental about them. But it's water under the bridge, isn't it? You'd better come and see to it now.'

'Right,' she said cheerfully. 'Let's get it done.'

As he said, the time for sentiment was past. She would clear the last of her things out of the apartment, and they could both start the process of forgetting.

Her feet remembered the path to the little *rio*, then down this tiny street and into a turning that only those in the know realised was there. And there was the little canal and the short walk along its bank to the oak door.

Nothing had changed since she first entered this building, her arms full of things for the kitchen, her head full of plans for redecorating, only to find that the family had already worked out a colour scheme. It was a good scheme, she had to admit, and she would have liked it a lot if she and Francesco had worked it out together. But it had been Giovanna's idea, with Tomaso's help. Benito had obtained cheap materials from the shop where he worked, and Wenda was able to get a bargain on the perfect curtain fabric. There had been nothing for Sonia to do except host the party where they all looked around and congratulated themselves and each other. And even then Giovanna had baked the cakes.

The memories, with their burden of resentment, came back to her as she climbed the stairs to the upper floor where they had lived. Everything was the same, including the kitchen; modern cooking equipment, surrounded by beautiful blue and white tiles and hung with copper pans.

She looked around the flat, seeking signs of his new lover. But all she found was her own wedding picture, just where it had always stood on the sideboard, the bride and groom dazzlingly young and happy.

'Doesn't she mind you keeping that there?'

'Doesn't who mind?'

'Your new friend. *Poppa* said you were courting someone else.'

Some changed quality in the silence made her turn to find him regarding her more coldly than she'd ever seen.

'Don't be so stupid,' he said angrily.

She drew a sharp breath understanding what she should have realised before. Of course, it had been another of Tomaso's inventions to get her here.

'I should have thought—*Poppa*—'

'I suppose he knew you wouldn't come unless you felt safe from me,' Francesco said bitterly, and turned away to the kitchen. Sonia stayed where she was, trying to come to terms with the senseless happiness that had swamped her. He didn't love anyone else. Then she put a brake on her thoughts. What difference could it make to her now?

After a moment she followed him into the kitchen.

'I'm sorry,' he said at once. 'I shouldn't have gotten mad at you. Are you all right?' His eyes were on her pregnancy.

'Yes, I'm fine. I'm not going to collapse just because you were a bit cross. I've sailed through this pregnancy with less trouble than most women have.'

'Well, that's nice.' His smile was strained, reminding her that she was telling him something he should have been there to see for himself.

What could she say to him, she wondered, when every remark concealed a minefield?

'When did you know about the baby?' he asked her.

'Soon after you left England that last time. When I left here, I had no idea at all.'

'I wonder what you would have done if you had,' he murmured.

'I don't know. I never let myself think of "if only". What's the point?'

'There might be a point,' he mused. 'We might learn where we went wrong.'

'But we know that. We've always known. It was me. It's a wonderful life here, everyone so warm and

involved with each other. I just can't be that way. I
don't know how to be so close. I tried to warn you
once—or warn myself.' She gave a short laugh. 'I
didn't listen to myself, did I?'

'Perhaps you didn't want to.'

'That's right, I didn't. I wanted to believe your
pretty fantasy of everything being all right if we
loved each other enough. You once called me a cold
woman who prefers to live isolated—'

'I never said that,' he protested quickly.

'You did. In one of our last quarrels—how many
did we have in those final days?'

'It doesn't matter. I don't recall them. I only think
of you as I fell in love with you, sweet and generous,
and laughing.'

'That wasn't me, only my holiday self. She doesn't
exist any more. I never laugh now.'

'You need me to make you laugh,' he said gently.

She smiled. 'Yes, you could always do that.'

He returned to the stove where something was
simmering. 'What are you making?' she asked.

'How about "schambed eggs"?' he asked, with
an attempt at lightness.

'And "greem beans"' she capped it, also trying
to sound cheerful.

But it was no use. The pretence of cheerfulness
couldn't last. After a moment he went into another
room and emerged with a cardboard box.

'Better have a look through these,' he said shortly.

There was nothing valuable in the box, just silly little things. But somehow the story of their love was in those silly little things. Here was the cheap wooden brooch he'd bought her from a market stall on the day she returned to Venice for their marriage. It was worth about fourpence, but he'd presented it to her with great solemnity, announcing that this was her wedding present so she mustn't expect another. And they'd giggled like mad things, and been happy.

His real wedding gift had been a pearl necklace that she'd worn with her bridal gown, but the wooden brooch had been pinned beneath her dress, where only the two of them knew of it.

She had gone to her wedding in a gondola decked with flowers, like a traditional Venetian bride. Since she had no family Tomaso had given her away, beaming with pride as he handed her into the rocking boat and helped adjust her white satin dress and long veil. The gondolier had warbled a song of love as he ferried them along the Grand Canal to the Church of San Simeone. At the last moment they had glided under the Academia Bridge and a cascade of flowers had fallen from a crowd of children leaning eagerly over the railing above.

On the steps of the church Tomaso had helped her out, and the gondolier had kissed her cheek for luck. It had all been too lovely to be true.

Too lovely to be true.

Nobody should marry like that, she'd thought often since. *Sensible brides should pick a dreary civic office on a cold winter day, not let themselves be enchanted by flowers and music and beauty.*

And by a young man standing tall and upright, the laughter driven from his eyes by love. But Sonia quickly shut that thought off. How long could love last when it was built on illusion?

CHAPTER FIVE

THERE were more 'treasures' in the box, a stack of goodwill cards welcoming the newest Bartini; for that was how the family had seen it. She was becoming a Bartini, and abandoning anything else she might have been. They had never understood that she hadn't seen it that way.

Other women, with her lonely background, would have loved the welcome and melted happily into the family that was so eager to have her.

But I had to be awkward, she thought, despairingly. I felt suffocated.

'Why do we always have to have Sunday dinner with the family?' she'd demanded once, not too long after their marriage.

'But weekends are when we can all get together,' he'd said, baffled. 'They love having you.'

More cards congratulating her on being pregnant, and yet more, little funny teasers to cheer her up when it proved a false alarm.

'Why did you have to tell everyone?' she'd stormed. 'I was only a week late. There was no need for anyone to know.'

340

'I wanted them to share our happiness. Now they want to comfort you.'

She couldn't tell him that she didn't need comforting. The thought of a baby so soon had made her feel suffocated and she'd been secretly relieved at the chance to wait a little longer. But she couldn't say that to Francesco, the warm-hearted family man. And there were so many things she couldn't say to him, she came to realise.

She returned to the box and found a small booklet about Bartini Fine Glass, produced for tourists in several languages. The English version was like the menus, full of howlers. They had laughed over it together, and she'd enjoyed doing her first job for him, correcting the English so that it was perfect.

It was all going to be so easy. They had everything planned. She was a glass expert, he was a glass manufacturer. They would work wonderfully well together. But the blunt fact, as she realised in the first week, was that Francesco didn't need a glass expert. He already knew what he was doing, and that was producing fine Venetian glass in a centuries-old tradition. Sonia's ability to place his product in the context of the rest of the art world didn't help turn out more vases.

She was at her best when helping him to entertain customers. Then her knowledge was an asset. But even a successful manufacturer didn't entertain customers every night, and in between times there was little for her to do. She couldn't help with his paperwork because it was in Italian, which she didn't understand. Her one great talent which was useful in the factory, was as a packer. She packed very neatly. But she was the boss's wife, and it raised eyebrows.

'It'll be better, darling, when you've learned the language,' he said soothingly.

'What language?' she demanded crossly. She was smarting from the unaccustomed sense of inadequacy. All her life she'd been able to do whatever she set her mind to, and this new experience was hard to cope with.

'What use is Italian?' she demanded now. 'You all speak Venetian dialect.'

'Then learn Venetian,' he said, sounding exasperated with her for the first time.

But Venetian drove her crazy. In her ignorance she had assumed that a dialect was little more than a different accent on the odd word, but this 'dialect' was a whole new language, filled with the letter 'j', a letter Italian had never heard of.

It ended with her leaving the firm to acquire the language skills she needed. Italian, Venetian, German, and French, of which she already had a smattering.

For the first time since she was sixteen she had no job to go to. For Italian and Venetian she went out to lessons, but for French and German she studied at home.

'Trapped,' she said to herself once. 'Trapped at home like a housewife.'

She reassured herself that soon it would be over, when she acquired the necessary skills. But she had no aptitude for languages and the work came hard to her. Often she felt she was floundering in a quagmire, with no hope of escape. The walls of her home began to seem like a prison.

Worse was everyone's assumption that since she stayed at home she had infinite leisure. Everyone dropped in just when they felt like it, and expressed surprise that she didn't drop in on them. Wenda, Ruggiero's wife, confided to Sonia that she loved Venice because it was just like the village in Jamaica where she'd been born.

Seeing Sonia's look of surprise, she explained, 'It's small, you walk everywhere, and people are friendly.'

Giovanna came constantly, apparently to talk but actually, Sonia suspected, to cast her eagle eyes over the domestic arrangements and find fault with them. Not that she ever openly criticised, but it seemed to Sonia that her offers of help were an unspoken criticism.

She even learned to speak a sort of English, something she had never done for her other daughters-in-law. In Sonia's heightened state of sensitivity it seemed like the final insult.

'She's just trying to be kind,' Francesco argued. 'It can't be easy to learn a new language at her age, but she wants to communicate with you.'

'Does she? Or does she want to underline how useless I am? She can learn a new language at her age, but I can't learn one at mine. That's the message.'

'I'm sure it isn't. We all know English is easier to learn than anything else because of its simple grammar.'

'Then why didn't she learn it for Wenda instead of waiting for Wenda to learn Italian and Venetian? Because Wenda can manage languages and I can't.'

If Giovanna arrived when Sonia was studying she would ostentatiously look around for any housework that hadn't been done, and proceed to do it. Soon she knew enough English to tell Sonia to get back to her studying and leave everything to her. Which left Sonia feeling as though she'd been blamed for some unspecified crime.

'She even rearranges the china,' she complained to Francesco in frustration. 'She washes up, then puts things where *she* wants them.'

'She thinks of *you* as the one who rearranges the china,' Francesco said. 'She just puts it back the way I always had it.'

'And how did you decide how you wanted it?'

He gave a rueful grin. 'Mamma did it.'

'Exactly. Nobody's allowed to disagree with Mamma.'

A strange look came over his face. 'Don't let's quarrel about my mother,' he begged.

Only later did she realise that his words had contained a warning.

The one thing that she had never been able to discuss with him, and which baffled her to this day, was the truly subtle way Giovanna had undermined her by refusing to call her by her proper name.

She could trace it back to the day just before the wedding when Giovanna had chanced to see her passport, bearing the full name, Sonia Maria Crawford.

'Maria,' she said in a wondering tone. Then, as if she'd discovered something vital, 'Maria!'

'No, Sonia.' Sonia pointed to her first name. 'Sonia,' she repeated firmly.

But thereafter, whenever they were alone, Giovanna had addressed her as Maria. It was a small point, but it became more important as her feeling of being a fish out of water had increased. This society was so intent on swallowing her alive that she wasn't even to be allowed her own name.

Francesco was baffled by her objection.

'I've never heard her call you Maria,' he said truthfully.

'That's because she only does it when there's nobody else there. Why?'

His attempt to broach the subject with his mother had been a disaster. Giovanna had reddened, rapped out something in Venetian, and stormed out, slamming the door.

'She says she doesn't know what you're talking about,' Francesco explained. 'Are you sure you're not imagining this?'

'No, I'm not imagining this,' she said, glaring. 'But if you're just going to take her side there's no more to be said.'

'Why do I have to take sides?' he demanded angrily. 'Why are you always at odds with my family?'

'Because they won't let you go,' she cried. 'And you don't really want them to.'

'Nonsense. You just don't understand. It's called family closeness.'

'It's called being the youngest son and making the most of it!'

'I can't help being the youngest son.'

'You told me once you asserted your independence by getting out of the house and starting the business. But inside you you're still there.'

'I love my family. I can't help it. And I don't want to have to make choices.'

When had she decided to leave? The question was unanswerable because she never really had decided.

'I need a bit of time to myself,' she said to him one day. 'Just let me go to England for a little while and—we'll see.'

He'd made no objection. But when, after a month, he'd followed her and demanded point blank that she return, the result had been a fierce quarrel. Even that might have ended differently if he hadn't made the mistake of saying,

'I thought by now you'd have seen sense.'

She gasped. 'You haven't understood a word I've said, have you? To you it's just been one big sulk until I ''see sense''.'

'Well, hasn't it?'

It had gone of from there, spiralling from anger to more anger, until he'd stormed off. The next day she'd discovered that this time she really was pregnant. But from Francesco there was only silence.

As she grew bigger she'd known that soon she must come to a resolution, but she'd always put off the day. Now the resolution had been forced on her, and she tried to tell herself that she was glad.

'Ready?' Francesco asked, wielding plates.

His cooking was delicious, and perfectly judged.

'Something light because you don't want any dead weights on your stomach just now,' he said.

'How many expectant mothers have you cooked for?'

'Loads. All my sisters-in-law. Mamma trained me well.'

He'd always loved to cook, she remembered, especially if it was for herself. In fact, he'd always liked looking after her, being one of those rare men who was at his best if his wife was ill. The meal slipped down easily.

'What have you been doing since you went away?' he asked, pouring her a cup of tea. 'Did you return to the store?'

'Part time. I'm on maternity leave now, but they'll take me back later. While I wait I'm writing a book about the history of glass.'

'How are you managing with Venetian glass?' he asked wryly.

'Is there any other kind?' she riposted.

'You know my feelings about that. Can I help?'

'You could read my notes about Venetian glass and tell me what you think.'

'Fine, send them to me when—you get back.'

'I can do better,' she said, suddenly inspired. 'If I can use your computer I can break into mine.'

A few minutes' work brought her files up on Francesco's screen. He switched on his printer and the pages came flooding into the basket while she returned to her meal.

'All right?' he asked when she'd finished.

'Yes, it was delicious.'

'I think you should take a nap now. This is all a strain on you.'

His gentle tone was dangerous, she thought. It reminded her of how lovely he could be to live with, making her forget things she'd be better off remembering.

'I should go back to the hotel,' she murmured.

'Please, Sonia, let me care for you and our child just a little.'

'All right. Thanks.'

He gave her his arm into the bedroom, settled her on the bed and went to close the shutters.

'No, leave them,' she begged. 'I like to look at the sky.'

He'd been right to make her rest, she thought, closing her eyes and feeling drowsiness overtake her. She thought she felt his lips pressed against her forehead before she slept.

When she awoke the light was fading, although it was still day. Sonia slid carefully off the bed and went to look out at the little *rio* below. The water was quiet and the paths alongside it were empty. Windows glowed in the gloom. The Venetians had hurried home to get on with their Christmas preparations, and now their doors were shut against the cold and all the warmth was within.

Looking along the *rio* to the left she saw where it met the Grand Canal. A water bus was just passing, sending little ripples along the narrow strip of water, making a small boat tied opposite bounce noisily in the water.

There had been a boat that first night, she remembered, a gondola tied up right beneath her hotel window. And whenever a vessel passed along the Grand Canal the waves had slapped against the gondola. At home her bedroom window was over a main road, and she cheerfully slept through trucks rumbling past. But in the quiet of Venice those light sounds had kept her awake.

Or perhaps it wasn't the sounds but the young man she'd met that day and known all her life, whose kiss had lived in her after he'd said goodnight. Long after his footsteps had faded along the flagstones, her whole body had been alive with the consciousness of him.

She stood now, listening to the silence of the flat, wondering if Francesco had gone out. She went quietly to the door and opened it. The main room was in a half light from one tiny lamp, and she almost didn't notice Francesco in the arm chair. As she crept across she saw that his head had fallen forward. His eyes were closed, he was breathing deeply and regularly.

There was a stool near the chair. Quietly she drew

it forward and settled down beside him, looking up at his face.

With a pain she saw that the boyishness was gone for ever. There was a touch of hardness about the mobile mouth that had once been so merry. It had only been two and a half years since their marriage, but there were new lines on his face, and they weren't laughter lines. There was even a faint touch of grey at the sides.

But he's only thirty-six, she thought, dismayed. And hard on the heels of that thought came another, more painful.

I did this to him.

He had one arm on the side, the hand hanging free. Gently she took his hand between her own and studied it. Such a large, strong hand, such a gentle hand, that knew how to caress a woman for her delight. There was a small cut on one finger that looked as if it hadn't been attended to. He was always getting these little cuts, she remembered, because he involved himself so much in the process of glass-making. He loved to pick up half finished pieces and study them lovingly. And when he got home she would treat his cuts, and he would laugh and say, 'I'm indestructible. But don't stop. I love it when you look after me.'

Now she wondered how well or how often she'd looked after him.

She was struck by the bareness of the apartment, so close to Christmas. Where were the decorations? Francesco had put up tinsel and holly as soon as possible—'like a big kid,' she'd teased him, the first year. But the second year, their last Christmas together, the joke had sounded hollow as their marriage disintegrated, and the pretty lights shone down on emptiness.

And now this—this nothing at all.

The flat was spotless. He was good at housework, and doubtless Giovanna had enjoyed helping out. But 'looking after' was something else. Suddenly her heart ached as she thought of him returning to this lonely flat and that smiling picture, with nobody to make a fuss about a tiny cut. Instinctively she placed her cheek against the back of his hand and rubbed it gently. The remembered feel of it sent a pain through her. How often, how gently these hands had held her. And how empty life was without him.

A slight sound made her look up to find him watching her sadly.

'I've missed you,' he said.

'I've missed you too.'

'I thought I'd never see you here again.'

'Please, darling, it doesn't mean anything. I love you but I can't live with you. I can't fit into your world and you could never be happy away from here.

At the start it all looked so easy that we didn't look
at practical things, but we have to look at them now.'

He touched her bulge. 'Isn't this a practical thing?'

It would be so easy to say, 'I want to stay here
and never leave you again. I love you and we'll work
it out somehow.' So easy. And so impossible.

Like someone who'd suddenly found herself tot-
tering on the edge of a precipice, she drew back with
a sharp breath, looking for a distraction.

She found one in the printed sheets that had fallen
out of his hand onto the floor. They bore scribbled
marks as though he'd read them intently.

'What did you think of my writing?' she asked
hastily. 'I expect it read like nonsense to you.'

'No,' he rubbed his eyes as though forcing himself
back to reality. 'I've made a few notes that may help
you, but you've done an excellent job.' He added
wryly, 'You really do understand Venetian glass
now.'

Was there any conversation that didn't turn into a
minefield? He was saying that Venetian glass was all
she understood. The people were still a mystery to
her.

He read her thoughts and added quickly, 'No,
Sonia, please, I didn't mean—'

'It's all right. Whatever you meant to say, it's the
truth, and we both know it.' She rose to her feet.
'Take a walk with me.'

'A walk? Where?'

'To the Garibaldi Gardens. I want to see what they look like now.'

'Cold and damp, like everywhere else,' he said, also getting to his feet. 'Is that why you want to go?'

It was true she wanted to see the place at its worst, in the hope of dispelling other memories. She'd forgotten his flashes of insight, how unexpectedly shrewd he could be at reading her sometimes, and how dense at others.

They made their way along the grey waterfront, the lagoon hidden by the dense mist that shrouded it.

'Do you really remember that day?' Francesco asked.

'Oh yes,' she said sadly. 'I've never forgotten it.'

'You remember how I proposed to you?'

'You never did exactly propose to me,' she recalled wryly. 'You just informed the whole of Venice that we were engaged, then you promised me nobody would take it seriously, and left me to find out that everyone was planning the wedding. Your sisters-in-law had chosen our curtains before I even met them.'

'That's how it's done in Venice,' he reminded her.

'I know.'

Silence. It had been an unfortunate remark, reminding her of all she couldn't come to terms with.

'I was afraid to ask you direct,' Francesco said. 'It happened so fast for me and I couldn't believe it was

the same for you. So I sort of built a wall around
you first.' He made a face. 'But you can't build walls
around people. They always escape.'

In the quiet their footsteps echoed on the gleaming
flagstones, and their silhouettes approached in a
small puddle, then faded again.

'This place is full of ghosts,' she murmured. Then
she wished the words unsaid, for lost love was a kind
of ghost, whispering around corners, reminding them
of things best forgotten. But it was magical just the
same, not the glorious magic of summer, but the un-
earthly magic of soft lights and memories.

A few minutes walk brought them to the garden.
Sonia was picturing the stone benches that stood at
intervals against the railings, overhung with trees.
'Their' bench had been the second one down on the
left. It would be visible almost as soon as they entered, and suddenly she didn't want to look. There
had been so much joy here, and now it was all over.
As they went through the gates she found herself
averting her gaze. When she could do so no longer
she braced herself and looked at the bench.

It wasn't there.

'This isn't the place,' she said. 'It must be further
along.'

'No, it was the second one down,' Francesco said.
'That's where it was, where those two stones are
sticking out of the ground.'

'But it's *gone*,' she whispered, feeling the chill wind cut through her.

'I'm afraid so. I'm sorry, I didn't know. It was here a couple of weeks ago.'

'But it can't be gone,' she cried desperately. 'It was *ours*.'

The bench had gone, just like the sentimental illusions it represented. This should have been her moment of vindication. Instead she felt the anguish rise up to swamp her, and the next moment she was sobbing with heartbreak.

'Darling,' Francesco said, taking her in his arms. 'Please—it's only a bench.'

'It isn't,' she wept. 'It's everything—the end of everything—don't you see? It's all over—everything we had.'

'I thought that was over long ago,' he said gently.

'It was, but—now it really is,' she choked, grief stricken. Logic and common sense couldn't help her now. Everything had gone and now there was nothing but emptiness. All her defences seemed to collapse at the same moment, and she sobbed bitterly in Francesco's arms.

'We had so much,' she wept. 'Where did it go?'

'It hasn't gone,' he said urgently. 'It's still there. We don't have to let it go.'

She shook her head stubbornly. 'No more illusions,' she said.

'Illusions?' he said angrily. 'You thought if we came here in winter you'd prove that our love was no more than a summer illusion. Well? Have you proved it?'

Dumbly she looked at him, her face still wet. He relented, touching her cheek with gentle fingers. 'I didn't mean to shout at you. Come back home and we'll talk some more.'

But she shook her head. 'I'm going back to the hotel. I have to pack. I'm going tomorrow.'

'No, not yet. It's too soon.'

She took his face between her hands. 'Darling, darling Francesco, listen to me. It was my fault it went wrong. I've known that for ages. I'd never had a family, and then yours was so—so much.'

'I know about "so much",' he agreed. 'But there's "so much" and "so much". So much interference, so much nosiness, so much friendship, so much love.'

'I guess I just couldn't cope with the closeness. It suffocated me. I don't know what families do—I never did.'

'So what's your answer? Go and live like a hermit, and teach our child to be as isolated as yourself?'

'You're saying I don't know how to take love. And maybe you're right.'

'Then learn. There's still time. Take the love we've all tried to give you.'

'You make it sound so easy, but you know it isn't. It wouldn't work. I can't change. We'd soon be quarrelling again.'

'You're a stubborn woman,' he said bitterly. 'You're leaving me for no better reason than that you said you would. Can't you admit that you were wrong?'

'It seems that I can't,' she said sadly. 'I never could, could I? That's how I made you so unhappy.'

'You made me unhappy on the day you left,' he said. 'Never at any other time.'

'Oh, darling, that's not true. You know how often I made you angry—'

'Angry isn't unhappy. Anger doesn't destroy a marriage when people love each other. It doesn't have to destroy us. And how can you travel now? The baby—'

'The baby isn't due for another three weeks.'

'Do you know how close to Christmas it is?'

'That's why I must hurry. If I leave tomorrow I have just time to get home before Christmas Eve.'

'And you'll return alone to an empty flat, with nobody there if anything happens. And you prefer that to staying here with your family, with a man who loves you. *Thank you.*'

But his heart sank as he spoke. Looking into her face he saw sadness but no yielding.

'I'll take you to the hotel,' he said with a sigh.

At the hotel he insisted on coming as far as her room, and seeing her settled onto the bed.

'You're tired,' he said. 'I shouldn't have let you walk so far.'

'I'm all right, really. I'll go to bed as soon as I've eaten something. Would you call the station for me and see if there's a train about noon tomorrow?'

He did so, and made her a reservation.

'I'll call for you tomorrow and take you to the station,' he said.

'If you're sure you want to—'

He swore. 'No, I don't *want* to,' he said bitterly. 'You know what I want. But I'll be damned if let you drag your luggage there alone. I'll be here at ten thirty.'

As he strode away from the hotel the wet flag-stones gleamed under the lights, and his footsteps echoed mournfully. He found he was walking slower and slower, as though his feet knew that his heart didn't want to return to the empty apartment where there had once been so much love, and where now there was nothing.

He let his feet follow their own instincts, and they took him to the little chapel of St Michele, as he had known they would. There was nobody there, and when he had lit a candle he sat down wearily and looked up to the plump little Madonna with her friendly face and giggling baby. He thought of his own baby, whose laughter he wouldn't hear, and closed his eyes.

'If I still believed in miracles I'd ask for one more—just a little one—'

At last he opened his eyes. All was silence in the little chapel. Looking up he saw that the Madonna was looking a little shabby. After all, she was only wood. Suddenly he felt foolish.

Reluctantly he got to his feet, wondering what had come over him. He was a grown man now, and the age of miracles was past.

CHAPTER SIX

AT THE hotel Sonia called Room Service and had supper sent up. She had little appetite but knew she must keep her strength up for the journey to come. When she'd eaten as much as she could she sat by the window, trying to find the energy to undress and go to bed.

But it wasn't bodily weariness that troubled her, so much as a restlessness of spirit. There was something left undone, and she, a neat and orderly person, must tie up the ends before she left Venice forever. Resolutely she rose, put on her coat, and walked out of the hotel. Snow was beginning to fall, obscuring her vision, but by now she knew the streets of Venice like a Venetian, and she made her way easily to the Hospital of San Domenica.

'I'm Signora Bartini's daughter-in-law,' she explained to the nurse on duty. 'May I sit with her for a while?'

'She's asleep—' the nurse said cautiously.

'I won't disturb her.'

Giovanna was lying with her eyes closed and her face seemed more shrunken than ever. Sonia went to sit quietly beside the bed and took one of the old woman's thin hands in hers. At once Giovanna's fingers tightened on hers, and she stirred, but didn't awaken. Sonia grew still, and the two women stayed like that, motionless, for a long time.

After a while the nurse slipped in with a cup of tea.

'Excuse me, *signorina*,' she said, 'but may I ask your first name?'

'Sonia.'

'Oh,' she seemed disappointed. 'I thought perhaps you were Maria.'

Sonia was suddenly alert. 'Why do you ask that?'

'Sometimes she's confused and she talks a lot about Maria, but it's hard to tell which one she means.'

'Which one?'

'Sometimes it's clear she's talking about her daughter, the one who died as a baby. She showed me the picture once. After fifty years she still remembers her as though it was yesterday. But of course you know all about that. She also seems convinced that she has a daughter-in-law called Maria, who will come and visit her. But I think they've all come now, and none of them are called Maria.'

She bustled out, leaving Sonia feeling as though she'd been through a wringer. Doors had flown open in her mind at once, and behind them were a dozen pictures, never understood before, but so tragically clear now.

Fifty years ago Giovanna's first baby had died at birth. Afterwards she'd had so many children that it had occurred to nobody that her heart still grieved for her long-ago firstborn. And how could she have told anyone how she still suffered, that proud, unyielding woman who found it so hard to admit that she loved people and needed them?

Like me?

Sonia quickly pushed the thought away, but she knew that in her own awkward way her mother-in-law had tried to reach out to her. The words, 'But of course, you know all about that,' uttered in innocence, were like a reproach. Giovanna had managed to tell this stranger, but not the daughter-in-law she would have liked to tell.

If I'd been gentler she might have found a way to confide in me, Sonia thought sadly. I was the one she chose.

The nurse had mentioned a picture. Quietly Sonia pulled open the drawer and lifted out the picture she found there. It was black and white and a little faded, but she could still clearly see the young woman cradling her first baby, her face alight with pride and joy. Tears stung Sonia's eyes at how soon that joy was to be extinguished.

She sighed, seeing the pictures of her married life

float past, all changed under the differently coloured light that had suddenly been turned on them. Giovanna's visits that she interpreted as criticism— were they that, or a way of reaching out from a woman who didn't know how to use words? Her 'interference' with the housework could have been no more than her clumsy way of helping Sonia study; the name Maria from a woman who could still be hurt by it.

And when Francesco had asked her about it Giovanna had denied it, because she couldn't bear to explain. It was all so simple if you had the key.

The door opened quietly behind her and Tomaso slipped into the room.

'*Grazie,*' he said softly when he saw Sonia. 'I knew you would come back.'

'*Poppa*, I didn't know myself until half an hour ago.'

'But I knew,' he patted her hand, 'because I know your kind heart.'

His way of always thinking the best of her made her feel awkward. 'I wasn't very kind,' she murmured. 'Otherwise I'd have known about this.' She showed him the picture. 'Why did nobody ever tell me?'

'Because she would never have it mentioned,' Tomaso said sadly. 'On the day our daughter died she put all her baby clothes away and made me promise never to speak of it. I thought her heart would ease when our next child was born, but it never did. Our sons know nothing. It's as though it didn't happen.'

'Did you want to deal with it that way?' she asked curiously.

He gave a shrug that had something forlorn about it. 'In those days—men were not supposed to—I don't think it ever occurred to her that I was unhappy, too.'

'No,' she said softly. 'We do a lot of harm in our way.'

'We?'

'Women like Giovanna and me.'

'Ah, you see it. I wondered if you did.'

'Poppa, what does *"No esser come mi,"* mean?'

'It means "Don't be like me". Why?'

'It's what she said when I came here earlier. She was trying to warn me. Yes, I see it, but I can't change it, *Poppa*. It would take a miracle to do that, and I don't believe in them.'

'Not even at Christmas?' he asked sadly.

'Not even at Christmas.'

She looked kindly at her mother-in-law, her face still frowning in her sleep. Nowadays, she thought, there would be counselling and support groups. But fifty years ago, the young Giovanna Bartini had coped with her grief by denying it. And the denial had tortured her for years, until another Maria had arrived, offering a kind of hope, which, in turn had been destroyed. Sonia's heart ached for her, and ached even more because she knew it was too late to help her now.

She replaced the picture and kissed the sleeping woman.

'Goodbye, Mamma,' she whispered. 'I'm sorry I couldn't be what you wanted. I don't know how any more. But I did come to see you—as you always knew I would.'

On her way out she noticed the Madonna standing in her little niche by the door. This was the one Mother Lucia had said was good at solving problems. Unlike Francesco's jolly peasant Madonna, she was coolly beautiful and aloof, but her arm about her baby was secure and possessive.

'It's easy to talk,' Sonia told her silently. 'But, like I told him, I see it but I can't change it. I'm trapped inside myself and there's no way out. No miracles. Not for Giovanna, not for me.'

Then, in an unexpected flash of rebellion, she added, 'I'll bet *his* Madonna would find a miracle for him.'

Francesco was at her hotel promptly next morning. She was already down in reception, and he carried her bags out to the landing stage where the motor boat was waiting for them. He got in and reached up for her, putting his arms around her bulky body, feeling her cling to him against the boat's sway.

'Are you all right?' he asked softly, and saw her strained smile. He wondered why he'd asked. How could either of them ever be all right again?

For the short journey along the Grand Canal he sat with her hand in his, until at last the broad steps of the station came into view. The sight shocked him with its reminder of how little time was left.

He carried her bag onto the train, saw her to her seat and sat beside her.

'We're in good time,' she said, smiling.

'Yes,' he agreed in a forced tone. 'Another ten minutes.'

Sonia wished she could find something to say. In ten minutes the train would carry her away from him forever. She couldn't stop it happening. But would she if she could? She no longer knew that, or anything except that the pain over her heart was intolerable. To cover it she said something about Italian trains always being on time and he smiled and nodded.

Silence. The seconds ticked past. But words were easy. It was the living up to them was hard, and the sense of failure crushed her.

'Well, perhaps you'd better go,' she said. 'You don't want to be caught here when it moves.'

'*Sonia*—'

'No,' she cried desperately. 'I can't.'

'You can. All it takes is two words. "I'll stay."
Say them. *Say them.*'

'Words are easy. Remember those wonderful vows
we exchanged? But they were just words in the end.
If I stayed it would end the same way.'

He stroked her face. There was nothing more to
say.

Doors were slamming, people moving quickly. It
was time.

'Goodbye,' he said softly. 'Goodbye, my—' The
words ended in a choke and he pressed his lips
against her hands. 'Goodbye, goodbye.'

'Darling,' she whispered, '*please*—'

She didn't even know what she was asking for.
Please, let me go. Please let something happen to
stop me going. But the pain was getting worse.

'It's all right,' he said. 'I won't make it hard for
you. Goodbye.'

He rose to leave. She rose with him. And suddenly
the pain wasn't just in her heart but everywhere, stab-
bing her violently so that she gasped and clung to
him.

'What is it?' he demanded sharply.

'Nothing, I just—*ah! The baby*—' The pain came
again and she clutched her stomach.

'*Mio dio!* I have to get you to a hospital.'

'Yes—please,' she gasped. 'Quickly.'

With one arm firmly about Sonia he helped her off the train and guided her to a bench, leaving her sitting there while he dashed back for her bag. He just made it back onto the platform before the train began to move.

'Francesco—' She reached out a hand to him.

'I'm here,' he said, swiftly coming to her.

'Don't leave me.'

'Never. Hold onto me, *amor mia*, and we'll soon be at the hospital.'

Station staff had seen what was happening and were rushing to help them. A man ran up with a wheelchair and Francesco assisted her into it.

'Quickly,' she said.

'I'll have you at the hospital in no time,' he said tensely.

The word had gone around and people stepped aside to let them through. Someone hailed a motor boat, and by the time they were out of the station at the top of the steps it was waiting below. A crowd was gathering, understanding what was happening, and full of cheerful good nature. Some men rushed forward to help steady the wheelchair as Francesco eased it down the steps. Friendly arms stretched out to help her into the boat. The air was filled with shouts of encouragement.

'*Grazie, grazie!*' Francesco called back.

She'd forgotten about these people, Sonia thought: how kind they were, how they loved life and welcomed a birth. It was as though everyone in Venice was part of her family, welcoming, happy for her. As they chugged away a smiling woman called something.

'What did she say?' Sonia asked.

'She said it's nice to have a Christmas baby,' Francesco translated.

'Oh, yes,' she murmured. 'It's Christmas—isn't it? The day after tomorrow—or maybe the day after that—I forget?'

'Don't worry about anything,' Francesco said gently. 'Just think about the baby.'

She gasped against the pain and gripped him tightly. Suddenly there were no more words, no more misery or anger, just Francesco and the comfort of his arms about her, the sense of safety she found in burrowing against him. The boat bucked and she held him tighter.

'Is it much further?' she moaned.

'We're going to the same hospital Mamma's in. Not much further. Look at me, darling.'

His voice seemed to hypnotise her into doing what he said. Looking up, she found his eyes fixed on her, holding hers as though demanding that she forget everything but him. And suddenly the easiest thing was to follow his lead and let him take care of her.

'Trust me,' he whispered, 'everything's going to be all right.'

'Don't let go of me,' she begged.

She hardly knew what she said, but when he replied, 'Never in life,' it was just what she wanted to hear, and she relaxed.

The driver called ahead to alert the hospital and they arrived to find a team awaiting them. As they began to hurry her away Sonia gripped Francesco's hand. 'Come with me,' she insisted.

The nurse looked uncertain. 'Well—'

'I want him with me.'

'I'm staying,' Francesco said firmly.

Sonia drew a sharp breath of pain and after that there was no more argument. Francesco helped her onto the trolley and then they were on their way to the delivery room. The world became a ceiling sliding past overhead. Somewhere, walking close was Francesco, but she couldn't see him. She reached out a frantic hand and felt it gripped in his strong one.

'I'm here,' he promised.

'Darling—do something for me.'

'Anything.'

'Go and tell your mother about this.'

'Of course I will—in a while. I don't want to leave you now.'

'Yes, yes, she must know at once. And then call all the others.'

He frowned. 'Won't later do?'

'No, they'll want to share the excitement while it's happening, not find out when it's all over.'

He leaned close to her. 'Don't you want to keep this for just us?'

She smiled. 'It *is* just for us. We won't lose that because we share it. Hurry now and go to your mother. Tell her—tell her Maria came back. She'll understand.'

Something in her voice alerted him. After studying her face for a moment he nodded and said, 'I'm going.'

He slipped away, and for the next few minutes the medical staff worked to prepare her for her labour. Mother Lucia appeared, smiling broadly. 'Looks like you're going to win your bet,' Sonia murmured.

'Oh, I knew I would.'

Francesco returned, wearing a hospital gown. 'Mamma's thrilled,' he said. 'It's transformed her.'

'Did you give her my message?'

'Yes, and she sent you her love.'

Sonia's reply was lost in a gasp of pain. She reached for his hand again and gripped it tightly.

'Maybe it won't be too long,' he said, looking hopefully at Mother Lucia.

The little nun looked doubtful. 'First baby?'

'Yes,' Sonia said.

'They usually take a bit longer.'

As she'd said, it didn't happen fast, and even with the help of gas and air the birth wasn't easy. Sonia braced herself against the pain, telling herself that she was strong and had endured a good deal, on her own. But Francesco, the charming, spoilt child of the family, raised to be light-hearted and talk his way out of trouble: what had he ever endured?

Then she saw the wretchedness of the last few months in his eyes, and knew the answer.

'I have no right to give up on us so easily,' she murmured. 'You don't hate me?'

He leaned close, and whispered. 'I'll be honest, *amor mia*, I hated you at the start. No woman had ever left me before, and the one who did was the only one who mattered. I told myself that you would return. I believed it for months before I faced the fact that you were as stubborn as I.'

'Too stubborn,' she said. 'I should have come back long ago, but—'

'I know, I know. We'll learn together. We'll have help now.'

She winced as another pain came. He mopped her brow and they fell silent, content simply to be together with no more need for words. Everything in the world was concentrated here, her hand in her husband's as the two of them fought to bring this new life into the world, a life that their love had created.

She fixed her eyes on him, and saw that his own eyes were full of anguish for her suffering.

'Darling,' he said desperately.

'I'm—all right—' she gasped. 'This is normal.'

'*Amor di dio!*'

The pain tightened its grip but she pushed the thought aside. She must make him feel better. 'Don't worry,' she murmured. 'We're going to have a beautiful baby.'

'Any minute now,' Mother Lucia said triumphantly. 'One more push.'

And it was all over.

'It's a boy,' Francesco said in a voice she'd never heard him use before.

The cry grew louder, stronger, until it was a mighty bellow. Over the baby's head the parents' eyes met in mutual pride. This one was going to tell the world when he grew up.

At last her son was in her arms, unbelievably tiny, but vigorous and perfect. And the feeling sweeping over her was like nothing she'd ever known before. This was love, not the sweet romance that would fade, but an intense, primitive emotion that shook her until she was no longer the same person, but a new one, who'd discovered what was important and would do anything to protect it.

Francesco too was watching the child, transfixed, so that she was able to study his face, unnoticed. She saw again the change that she'd first noticed in the flat. He was older, a little weary with sad experience, but now full of a profound joy.

The fierce love that streamed from her to enfold her child seemed to have no end. It flowed on, encompassing the man also, and after him the whole world. But him above all.

'Francesco...' she whispered. 'Are you still there?'

'Si, amor mia,' he said, understanding her at once. 'I am still here. I always will be.'

'You were far away,' she murmured.

'So were you. I didn't know how to find you. But now that I have, I shall never let you go again. Either of you.'

'Mmm,' she murmured sleepily. The long hours of hard work were catching up with her. She felt the soft touch of his lips on her forehead, and the movement as he eased the baby out of her arms.

'Go to sleep now,' he told her. 'You can leave our son with me. He will be quite safe.'

Of course he would, because here was safety, life, love, all the things she'd missed since the day she'd left them for reasons she could no longer remember.

That was her last thought as she drifted into sleep.

When she awoke it was dark outside the windows, and she was full of blissful contentment. By her bed stood a cot, holding her sweetly sleeping child. For a moment she gazed on him in awe, but then her eyes searched the room anxiously until they found what she needed to see—Francesco, dozing in an armchair by the window. She relaxed. He was here. All was well.

An instinct seemed to alert him, and he awoke immediately, coming over to the bed, smiling. She opened her arms and he came into them, holding her tightly as never before.

'I love you,' he said. 'I love you more now than ever before.'

'How could I ever have gone away from you?' she asked, 'Loving you as I do.'

'Tell me that you love me,' he begged. 'Let me hear you say it.'

'I love you. I don't know how I could ever have thought I didn't—or that I could kill my feelings. How could I have tried to take your baby away from you? How could I leave you?'

'Swear that you'll never leave me again.'

'I'll never even think of it. I couldn't bear to be apart from you.' Something occurred to her. 'While I was asleep I understood the magic.'

'You understood?' he asked cautiously.

'Winter or summer, the magic was still there—because you were there. It wasn't a holiday romance at all.'

'I always knew that.'

'And tried to make me see it. Now I do.'

'I went to see Mamma after you went to sleep. She's longing to come and see you, and her new grandson.'

'Can she get out of bed?'

'She perked up wonderfully when she heard the news. Can I fetch her?'

'Yes, of course.'

When he'd gone she went to the cradle and lifted her child. She felt well and strong for the first time in months. There was an armchair by the window and she went to sit there, looking out at the darkness and the lights over the Grand Canal.

The feel of the baby against her was unutterably sweet. And now she knew how Giovanna had felt. To lose this precious scrap would break her heart, and it would stay broken, no matter how many other children were born afterwards.

'Such a family I've given you,' she murmured against the child's head. 'There's Ruggiero and Giuseppe, and Benito and Enrico, and Wenda and Soo, and all your cousins. You'll never come to any harm, because there'll always be one of them looking out for you at the corner of the street. And if you should ever wander away in the wrong direction, the whole ''United Nations'' will get together to bring you safely home again. That's what families are for.'

Francesco appeared with Giovanna in a wheelchair, Tomaso walking behind. The old woman's joy transformed her, and for the first time she turned to Sonia a truly heartfelt smile.

'Come and meet your newest grandchild,' Sonia said.

Francesco wheeled his mother across the floor until she was close to Sonia, who leaned forward to give her a good view of the child. Giovanna looked long into the baby's crumpled face, then raised her eyes to her daughter-in-law.

'Thank you—Maria,' she said softly.

And now she didn't mind the name, because she understood everything Giovanna had been too proud to tell her. Besides, to be called Mary at Christmas was a compliment.

'You were right,' she said to Giovanna, 'it changes everything.'

She spoke in a low voice, to include only the two of them. Francesco looked from one to the other, not having heard, but sensing somehow that all was well.

From beyond the window came the sounds of revelry.

'It's the Christmas Eve procession,' Francesco said.

Still holding the baby Sonia went to stand in the window to watch the torchlit gondolas gliding down the canal. Behind her, Francesco put his arms around her, enfolding her and their baby. She could see the three of them reflected in the dark window.

The reflection also showed her the moment when Ruggiero appeared in the doorway, with Wenda, Giuseppe and Lin Soo, their children, then another brother, another wife, a nephew, uncle, aunt, until the whole vast mob of the Bartini family was there, stretching out into the corridor, all eager to see the newest addition, but waiting for her signal.

'Invite them in,' she said to Francesco.

He beckoned to his family. Smiling, she watched them in the window's reflection, as they came in, one by one, until they filled the room as far as she could see, their faces beaming with joy at this birth, and rebirth. It had taken too long, but she had finally come home.

It was as though all the world was there. And at its heart, a man, a woman, and a newborn child.

These are the stories you've been waiting for!

Based on the Harlequin Books miniseries
The Carradignes: American Royalty comes

HEIR TO THE THRONE

Brand-new stories from

KASEY MICHAELS

CAROLYN DAVIDSON

Travel to the opulent world of royalty with these two stories that bring to readers the concluding chapters in the quest for a ruler for the fictional country of Korosol.

Available in December 2002 at your favorite retail outlet.

HARLEQUIN®
Makes any time special®